MISSILE MOUSE

RESCUE ON **TANKIUM3**

BY
JAKE PARKER

graphix

AN IMPRINT OF
SCHOLASTIC

New York   Toronto   London   Auckland   Sydney   Mexico City   New Delhi   Hong Kong

ACKNOWLEDGMENTS

Planetary praise and galactic gratitude are in order for Anthony Wu, Jason Caffoe, Kohl Glass, Katie Smith, and Phil Falco. This book was fueled by their time and talents. Also, interstellar salutations to Judy Hansen, Adam Rau, and David Saylor for their support and guidance. Above all, the shining star of this project is my wife, Alison — thank you for everything.

OFFICIAL
GSA
DOCUMENT

FOR
EYES
ONLY

ISBN 978-0-545-11716-6 (hardcover)
ISBN 978-0-545-11717-3 (paperback)

Library of Congress Cataloging-in-Publication Data Available

10 9 8 7 6 5 4 3 2 1   11 12 13 14 15

First edition, January 2011
Edited by Adam Rau
Creative Director: David Saylor
Book design by Phil Falco
Printed in Singapore   46

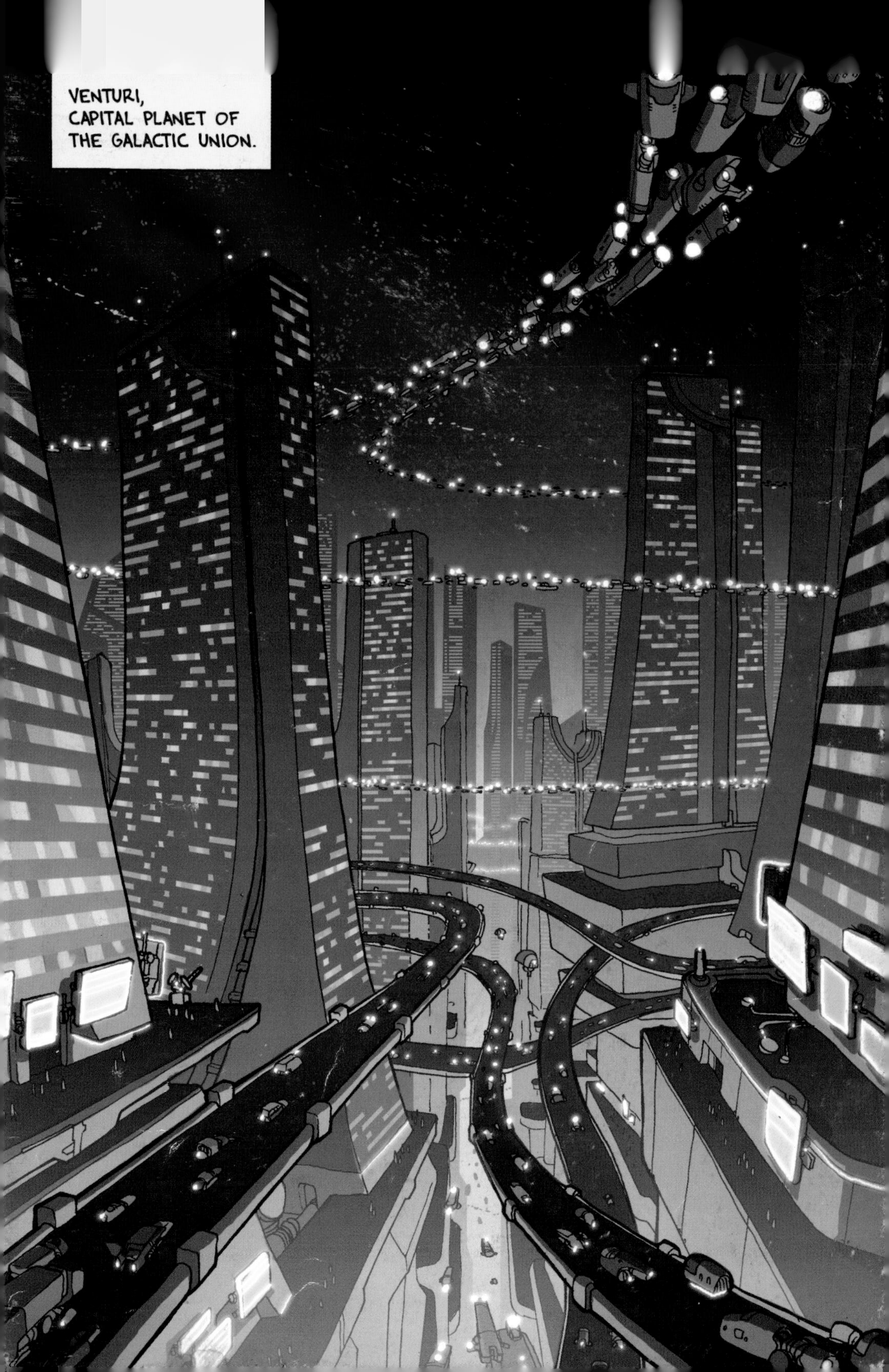
VENTURI,
CAPITAL PLANET OF
THE GALACTIC UNION.

FREEZE, OR I BLAST YOU!

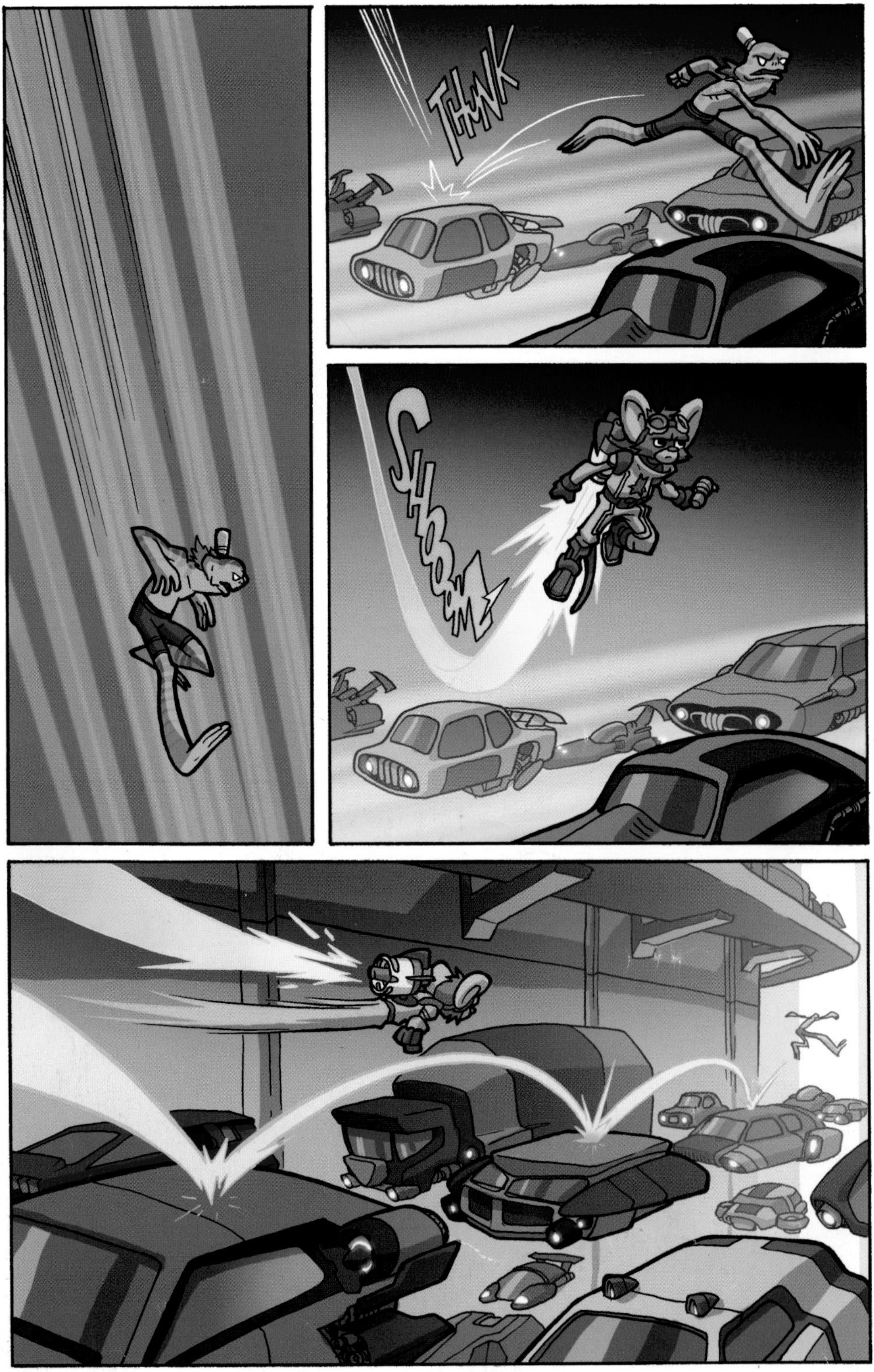
THUNK
SHHOOOM

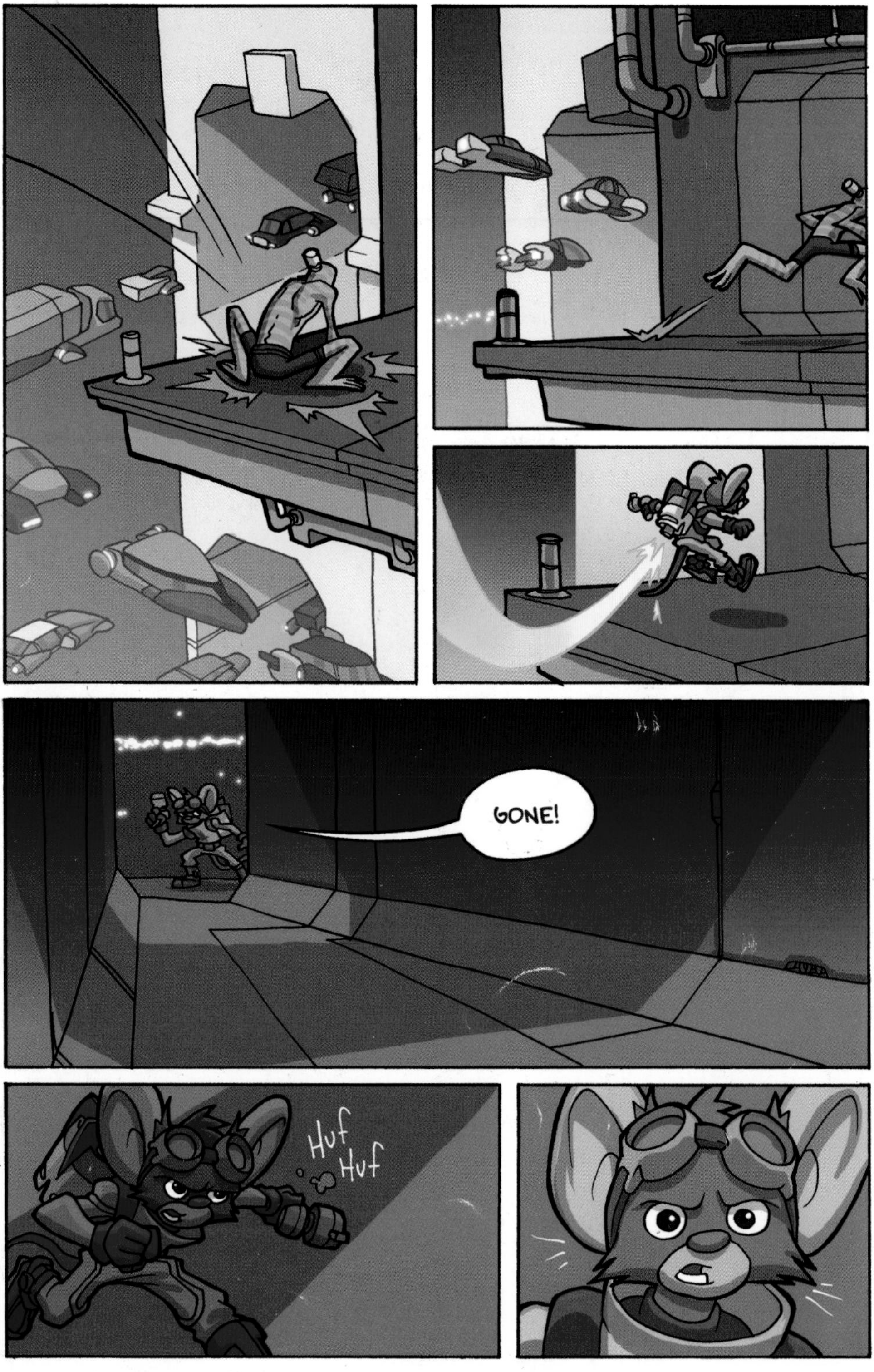
GONE!
Huf
Huf

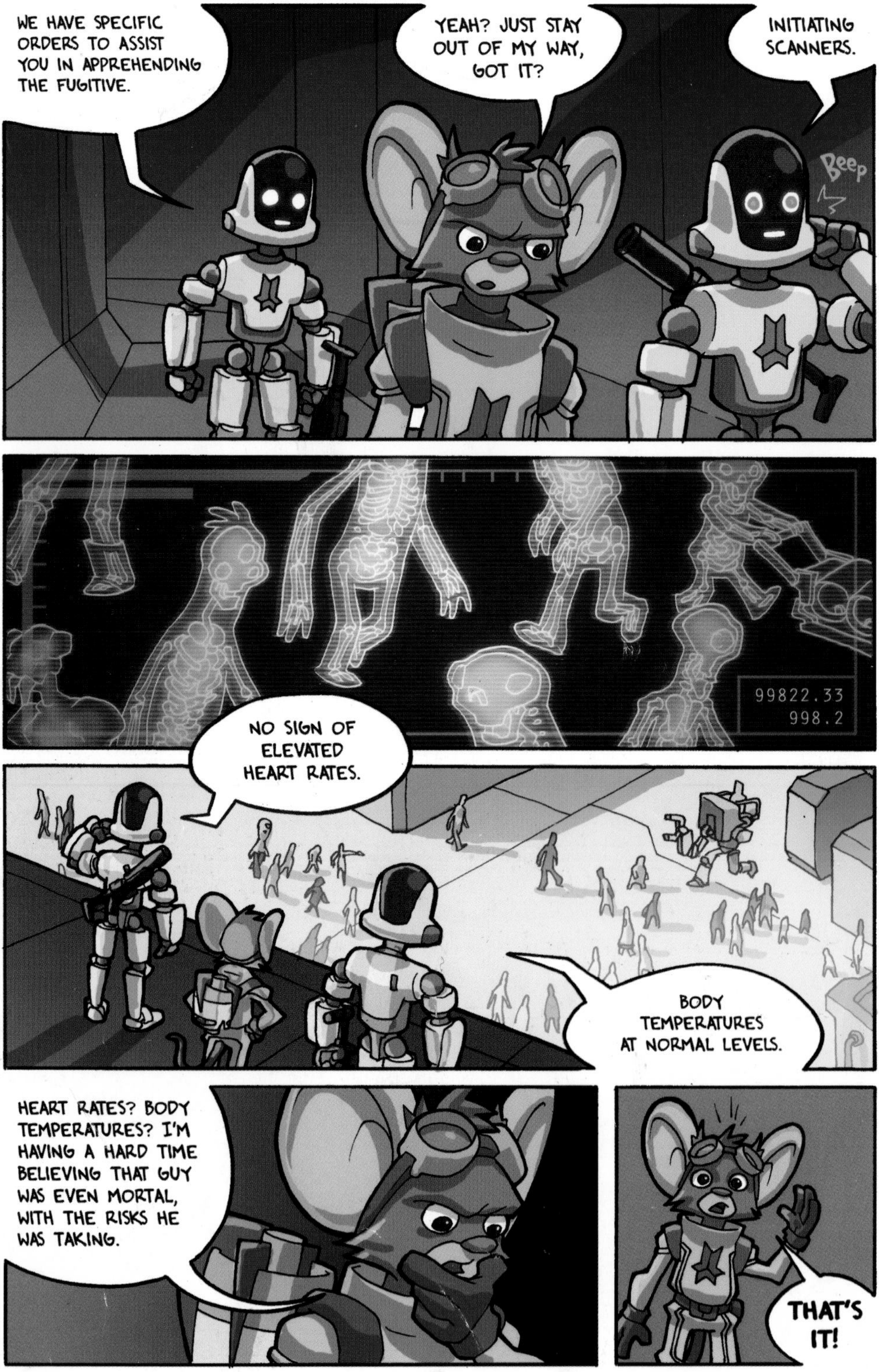
WE HAVE SPECIFIC ORDERS TO ASSIST YOU IN APPREHENDING THE FUGITIVE.
YEAH? JUST STAY OUT OF MY WAY, GOT IT?
INITIATING SCANNERS.
Beep
99822.33
998.2
NO SIGN OF ELEVATED HEART RATES.
BODY TEMPERATURES AT NORMAL LEVELS.
HEART RATES? BODY TEMPERATURES? I'M HAVING A HARD TIME BELIEVING THAT GUY WAS EVEN MORTAL, WITH THE RISKS HE WAS TAKING.
THAT'S IT!

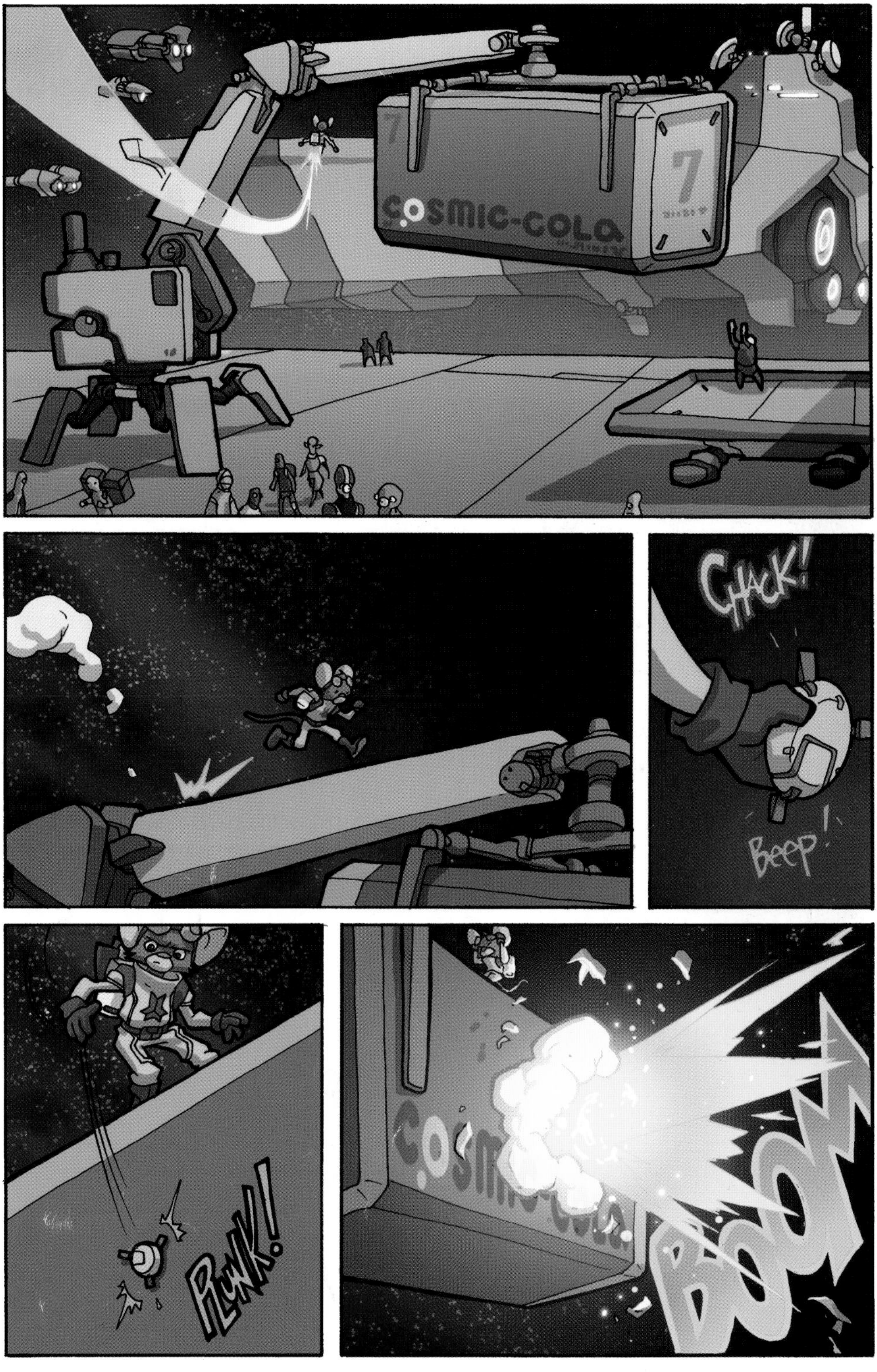
COSMIC-COLA
CHACK!
Beep!
PLUNK!
BOOM

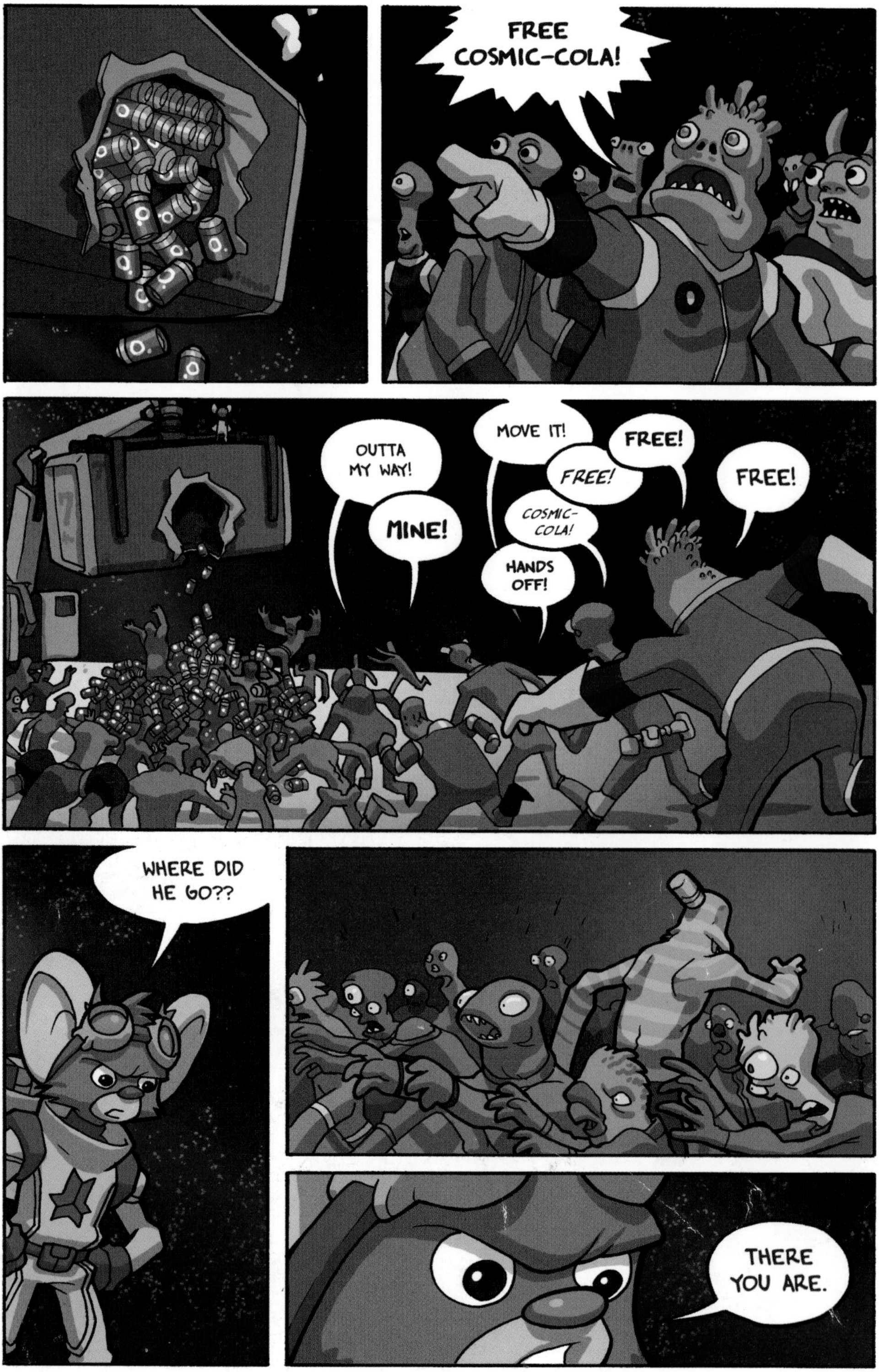
FREE COSMIC-COLA!
OUTTA MY WAY!
MINE!
MOVE IT!
FREE!
FREE!
COSMIC-COLA!
HANDS OFF!
FREE!
WHERE DID HE GO??
THERE YOU ARE.

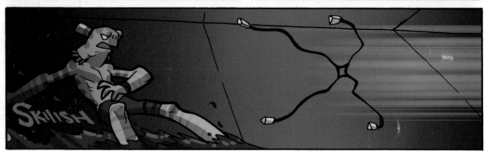

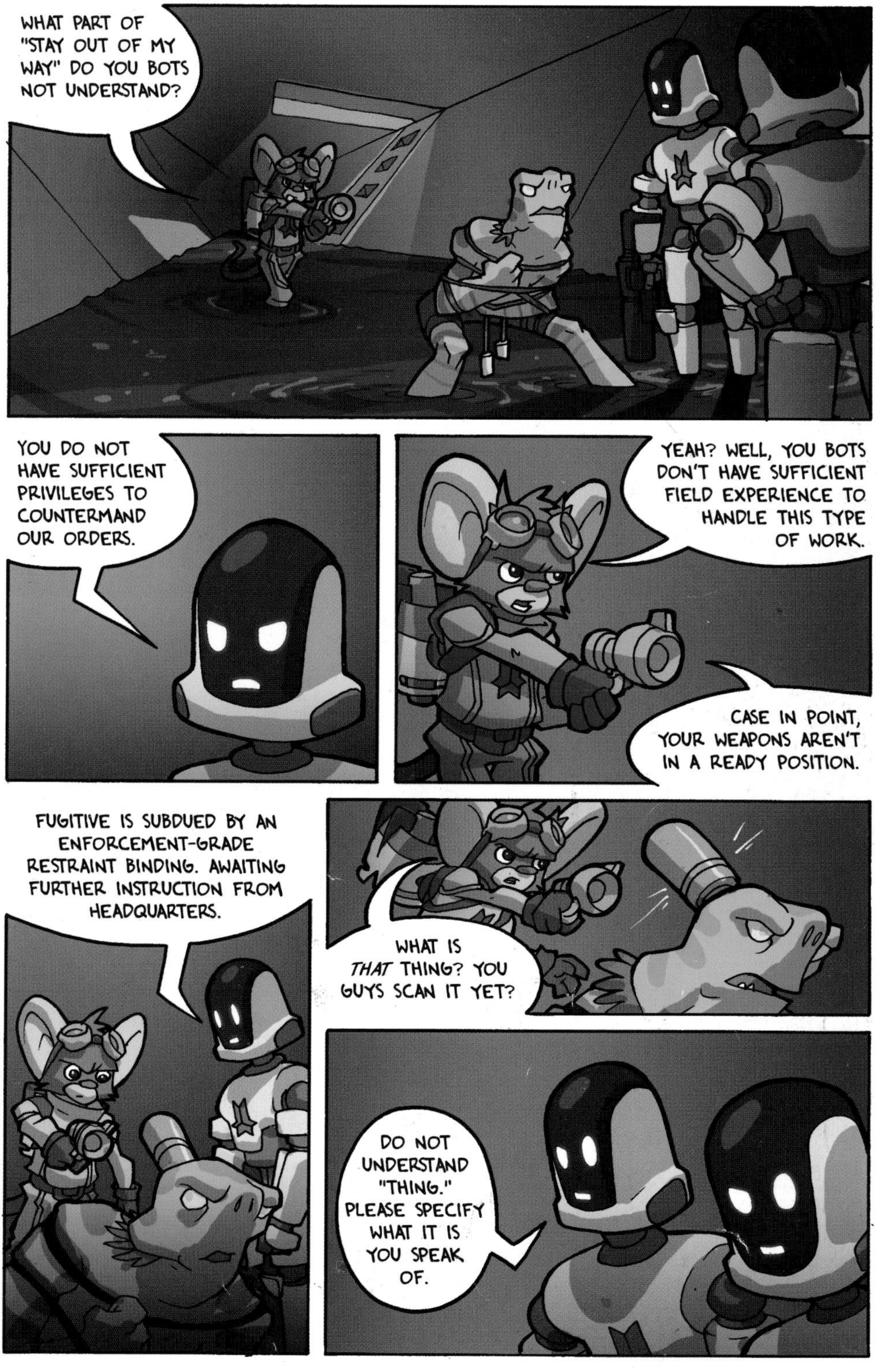
WHAT PART OF "STAY OUT OF MY WAY" DO YOU BOTS NOT UNDERSTAND?
YOU DO NOT HAVE SUFFICIENT PRIVILEGES TO COUNTERMAND OUR ORDERS.
YEAH? WELL, YOU BOTS DON'T HAVE SUFFICIENT FIELD EXPERIENCE TO HANDLE THIS TYPE OF WORK.
CASE IN POINT, YOUR WEAPONS AREN'T IN A READY POSITION.
FUGITIVE IS SUBDUED BY AN ENFORCEMENT-GRADE RESTRAINT BINDING. AWAITING FURTHER INSTRUCTION FROM HEADQUARTERS.
WHAT IS *THAT* THING? YOU GUYS SCAN IT YET?
DO NOT UNDERSTAND "THING." PLEASE SPECIFY WHAT IT IS YOU SPEAK OF.

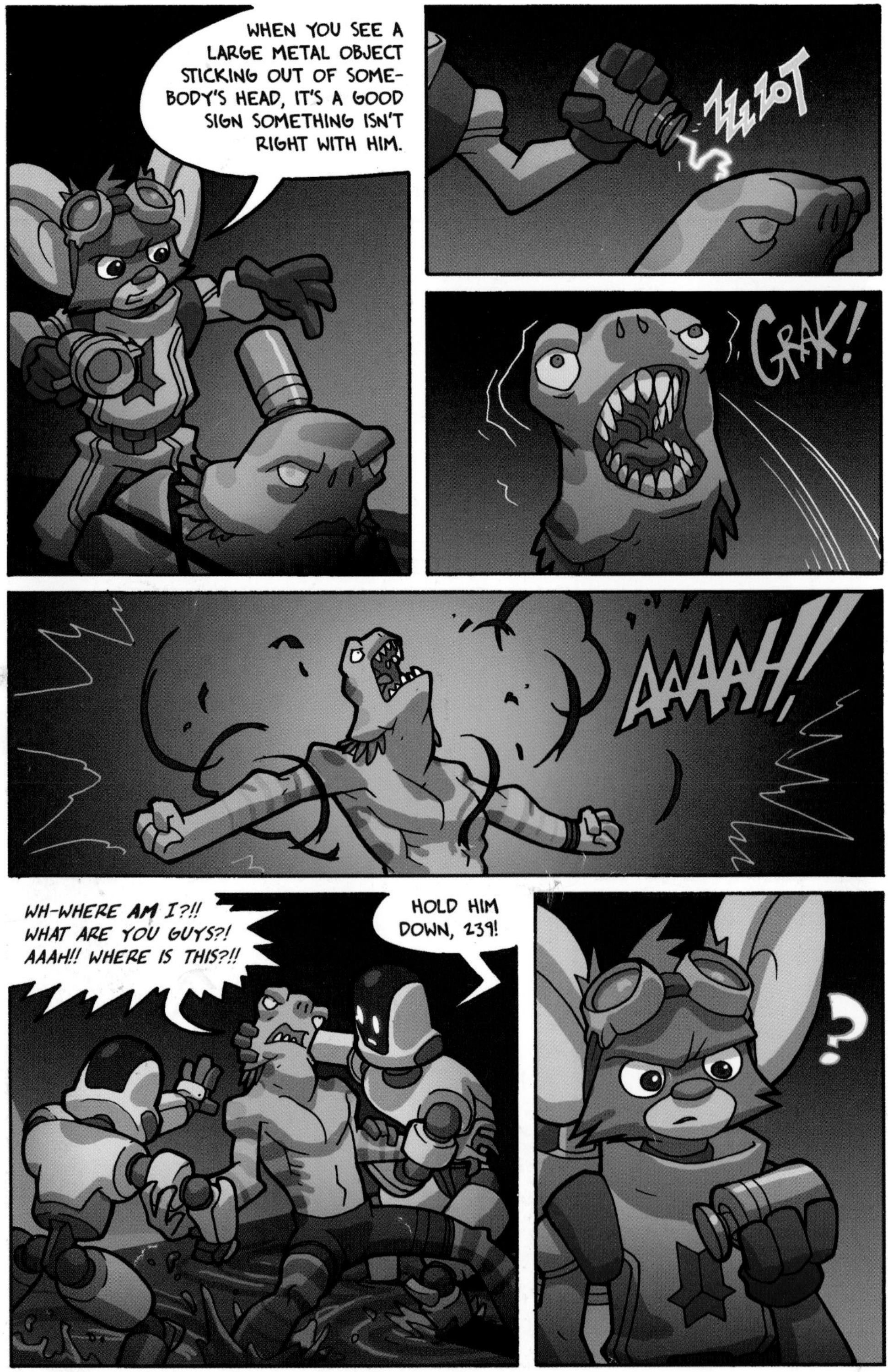
WHEN YOU SEE A LARGE METAL OBJECT STICKING OUT OF SOME-BODY'S HEAD, IT'S A GOOD SIGN SOMETHING ISN'T RIGHT WITH HIM.
ZZZZOT
GRAK!
AAAAH!!
WH-WHERE AM I?!! WHAT ARE YOU GUYS?! AAAH!! WHERE IS THIS?!!
HOLD HIM DOWN, 239!
?

HUF HUF HUF

S-S-TTAND...
D-D-DOWN,
FUGITI-I-IVE!

Grrr

EASY, EASY. I'M
NOT GOING TO
HURT YOU.

SPLOOSH

SPLOOSH

SPLOOSH

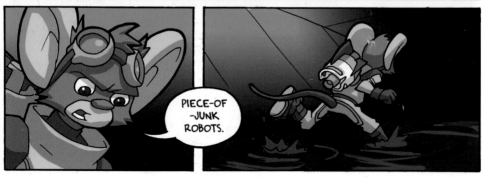

PIECE-OF
-JUNK
ROBOTS.

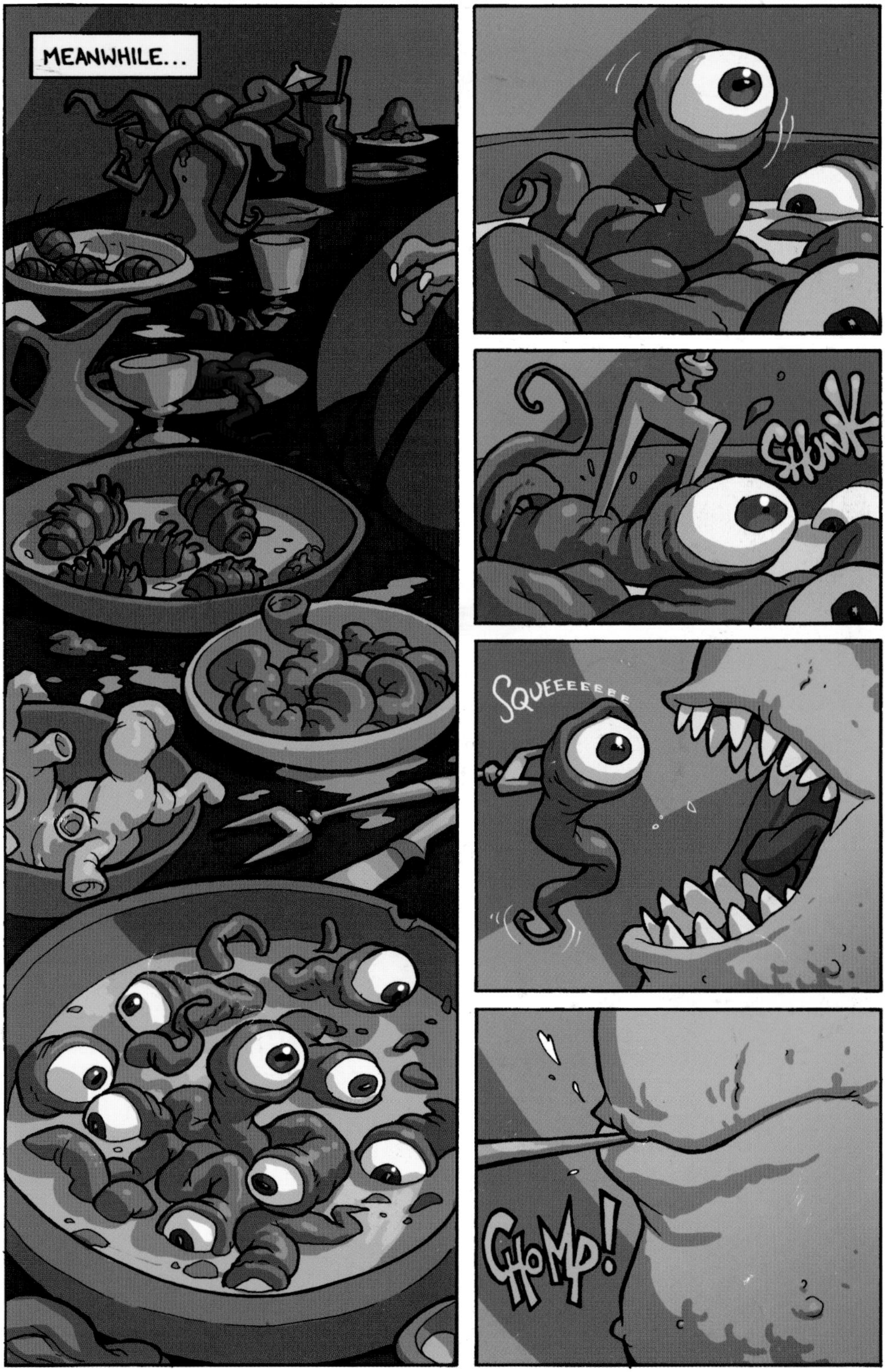
MEANWHILE...
SHONK
SQUEEEEEEE
CHOMP!

EX-EXCUSE ME...
KING BOGNARSH?
I HAVE AN-AN
URGENT M-MATTER.

THE GAGWARTS
ARE DELICIOUS
TONIGHT!

TELL THE CHEF I'LL
HALT HIS TORTURE FOR
THE NEXT THREE DAYS.

VERY M-MERCIFUL
OF YOU. BUT, S-SIR...IF
I MAY, WE HAVE A
P-PROBLEM.

GO ON!
WHAT IS IT?!

ONE OF THE SLAVES
HAS GONE OFF-LINE AND
THE DELIVERY ON VENTURI
WAS A FAILURE.

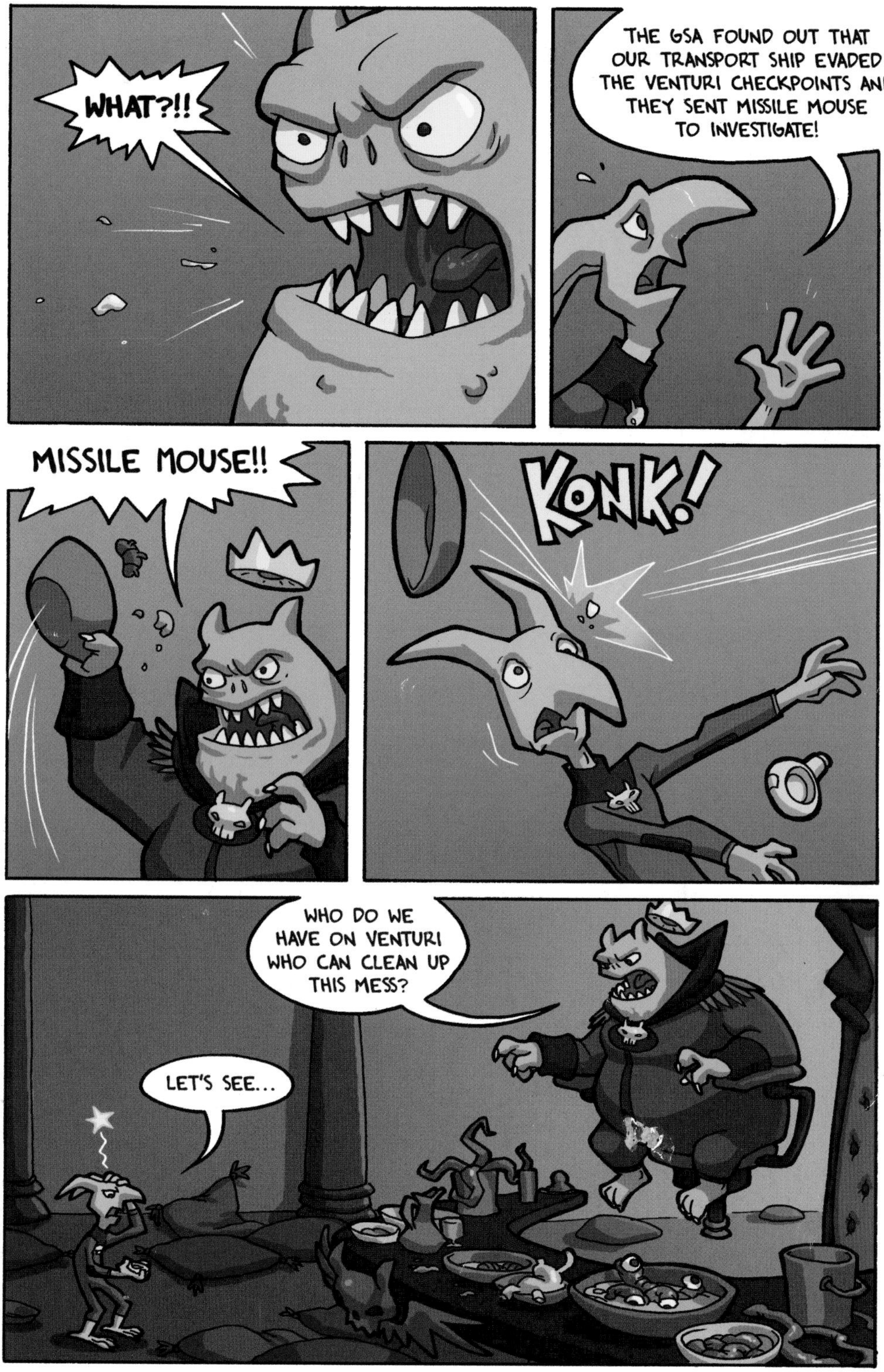
WHAT?!!
THE GSA FOUND OUT THAT OUR TRANSPORT SHIP EVADED THE VENTURI CHECKPOINTS AND THEY SENT MISSILE MOUSE TO INVESTIGATE!
MISSILE MOUSE!!
KONK!
WHO DO WE HAVE ON VENTURI WHO CAN CLEAN UP THIS MESS?
LET'S SEE...

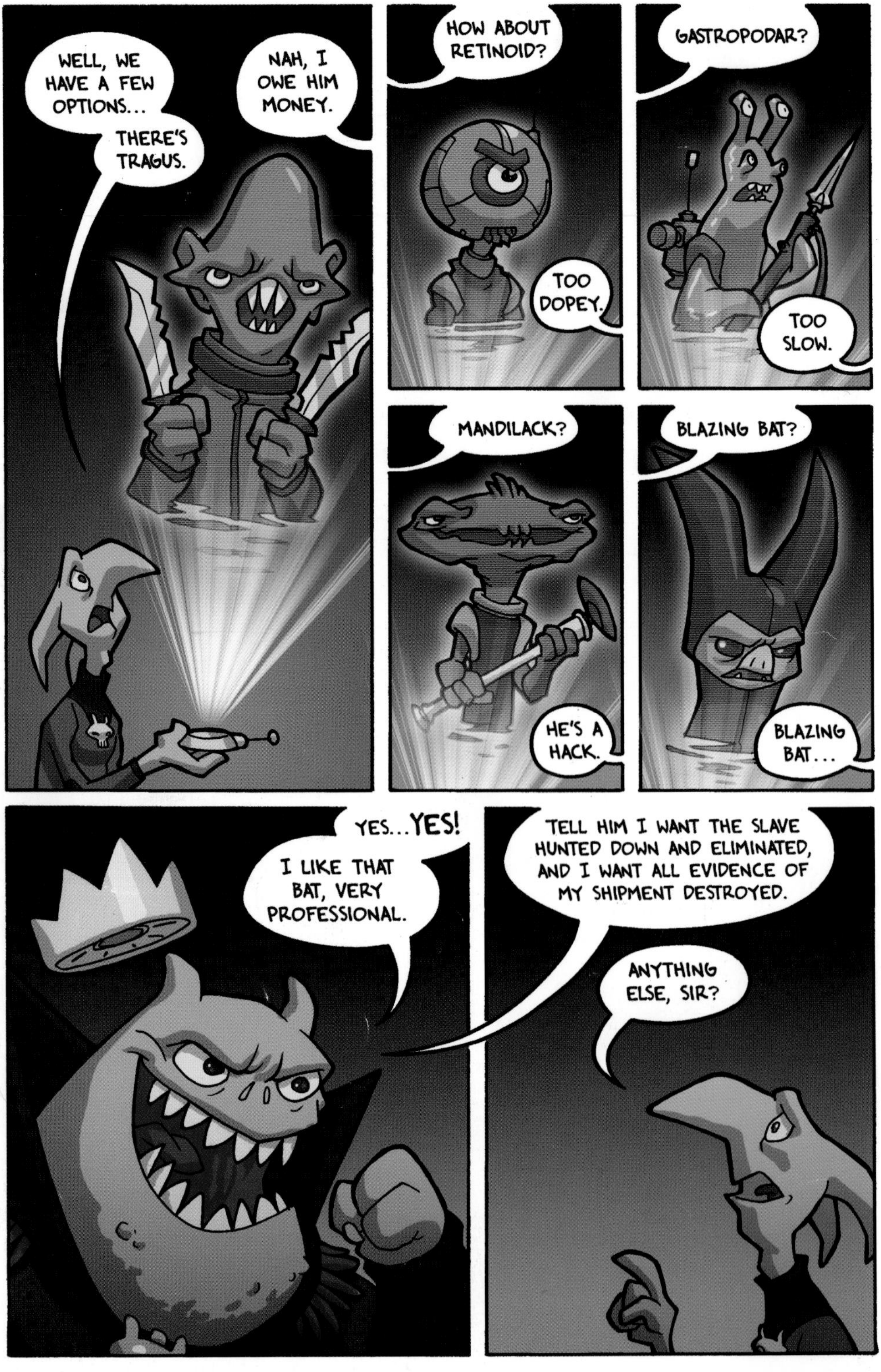
WELL, WE HAVE A FEW OPTIONS...
THERE'S TRAGUS.
NAH, I OWE HIM MONEY.
HOW ABOUT RETINOID?
TOO DOPEY.
GASTROPODAR?
TOO SLOW.
MANDILACK?
HE'S A HACK.
BLAZING BAT?
BLAZING BAT...
YES...YES!
I LIKE THAT BAT, VERY PROFESSIONAL.
TELL HIM I WANT THE SLAVE HUNTED DOWN AND ELIMINATED, AND I WANT ALL EVIDENCE OF MY SHIPMENT DESTROYED.
ANYTHING ELSE, SIR?

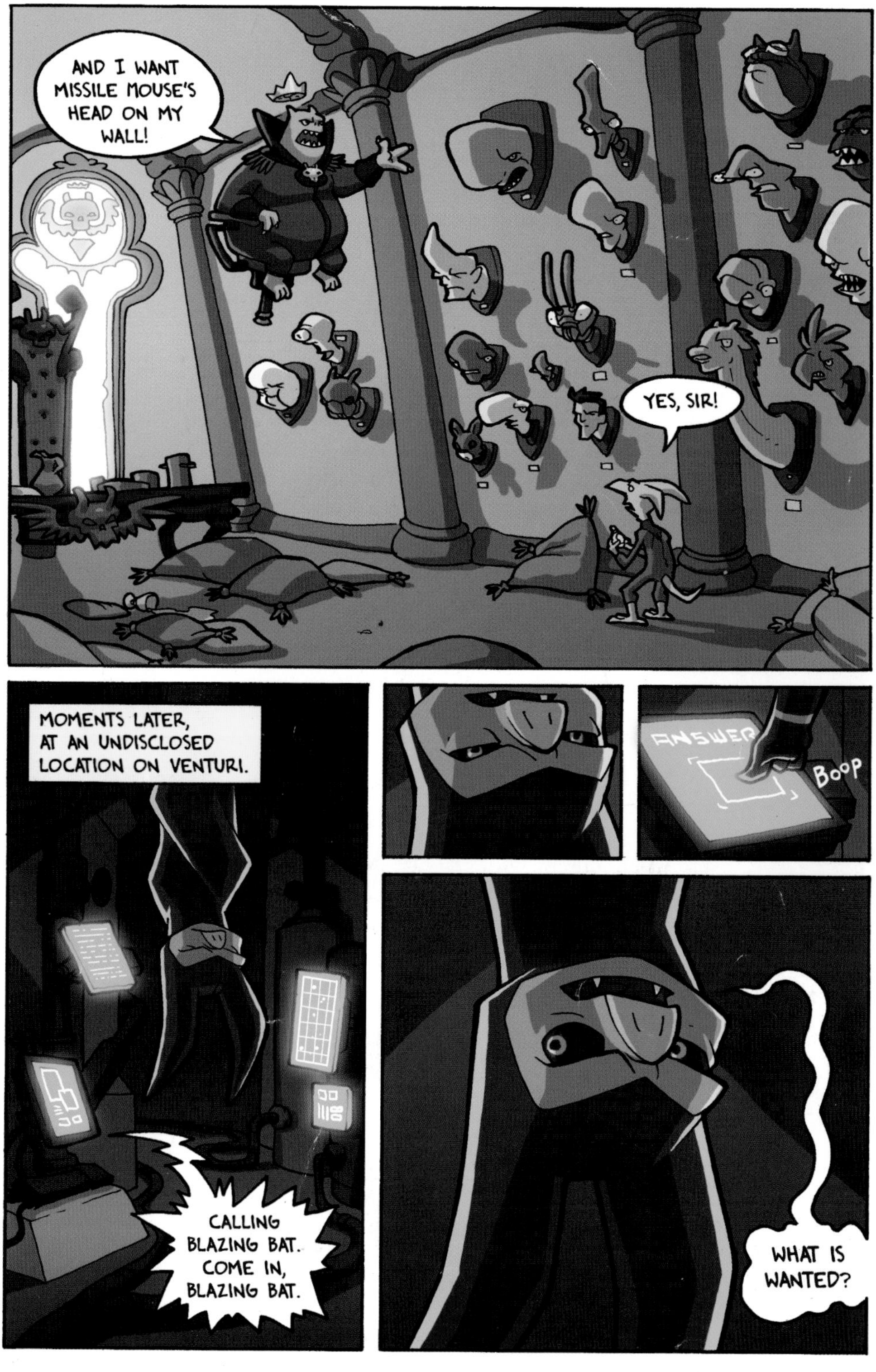
AND I WANT MISSILE MOUSE'S HEAD ON MY WALL!
YES, SIR!
MOMENTS LATER, AT AN UNDISCLOSED LOCATION ON VENTURI.
CALLING BLAZING BAT. COME IN, BLAZING BAT.
ANSWER
BOOP
WHAT IS WANTED?

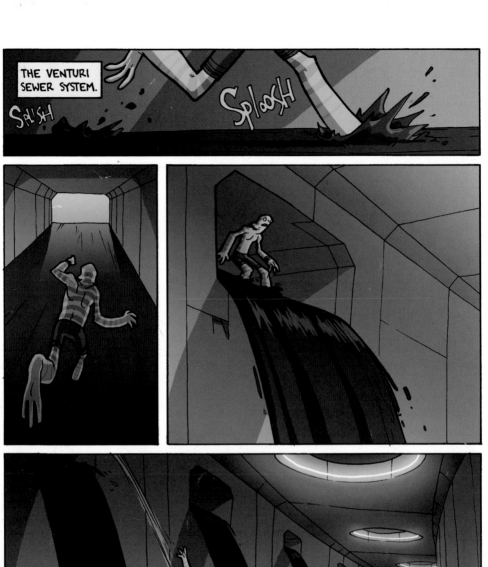

THE VENTURI
SEWER SYSTEM.

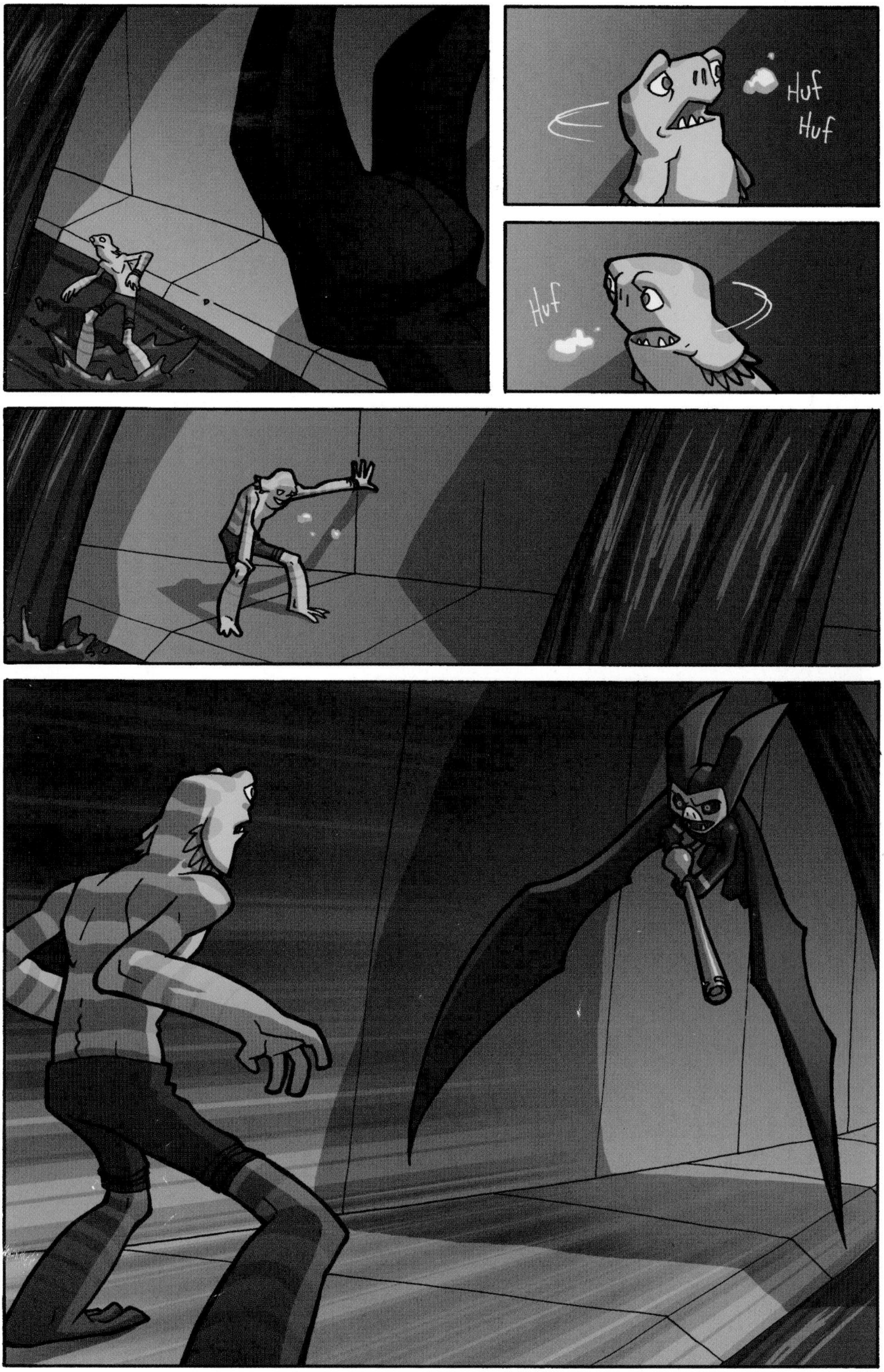
Huf
Huf
Huf

FWASHHH!

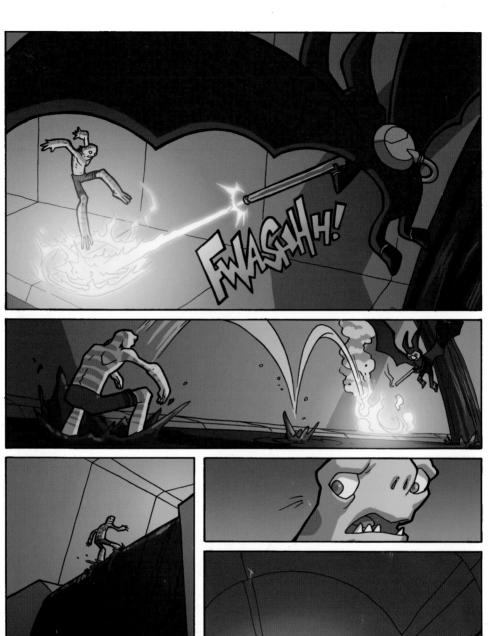

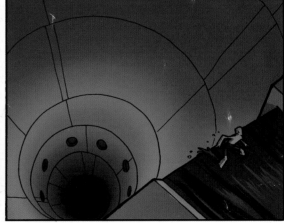

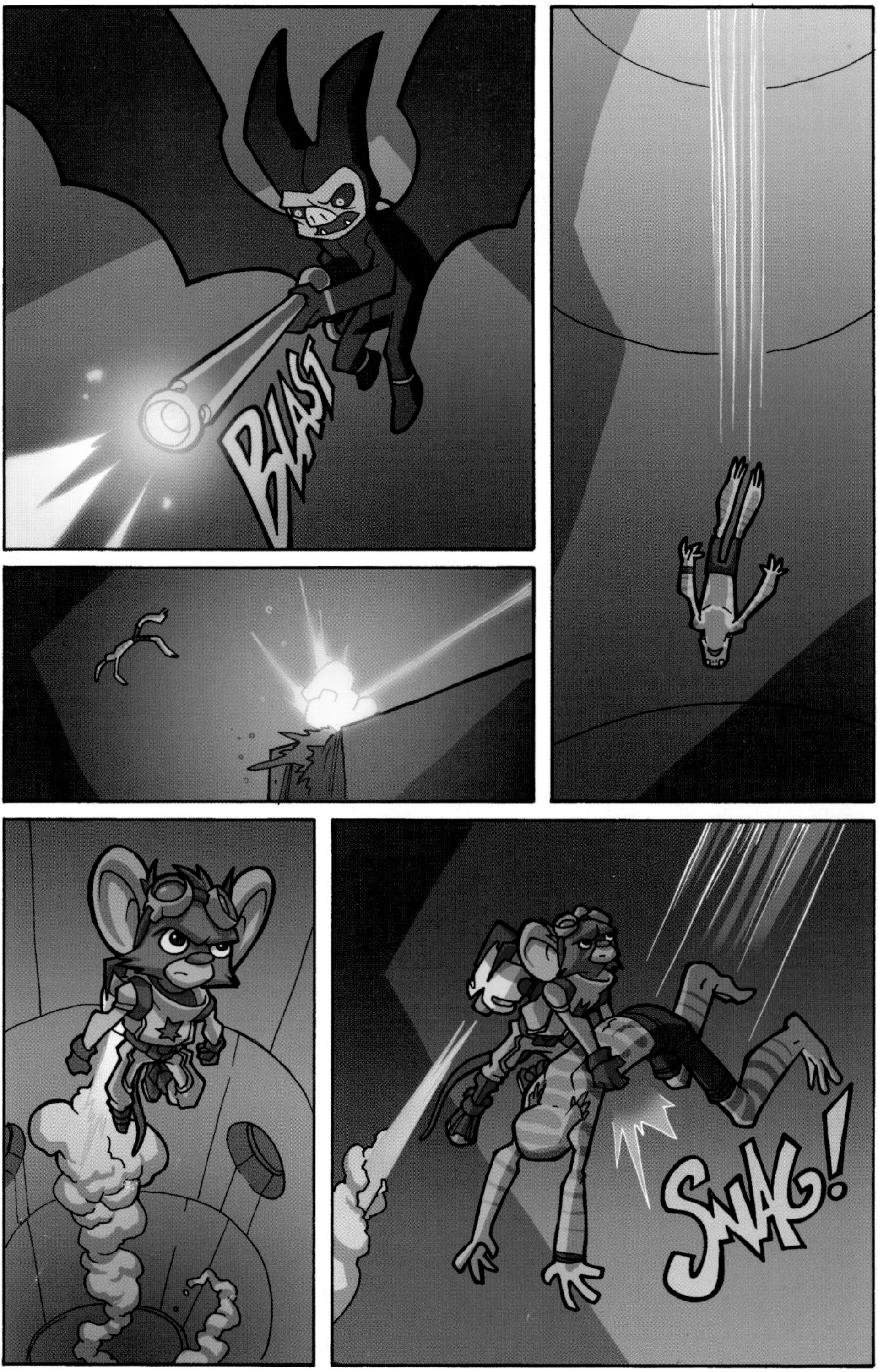
BLAST
SNAG!

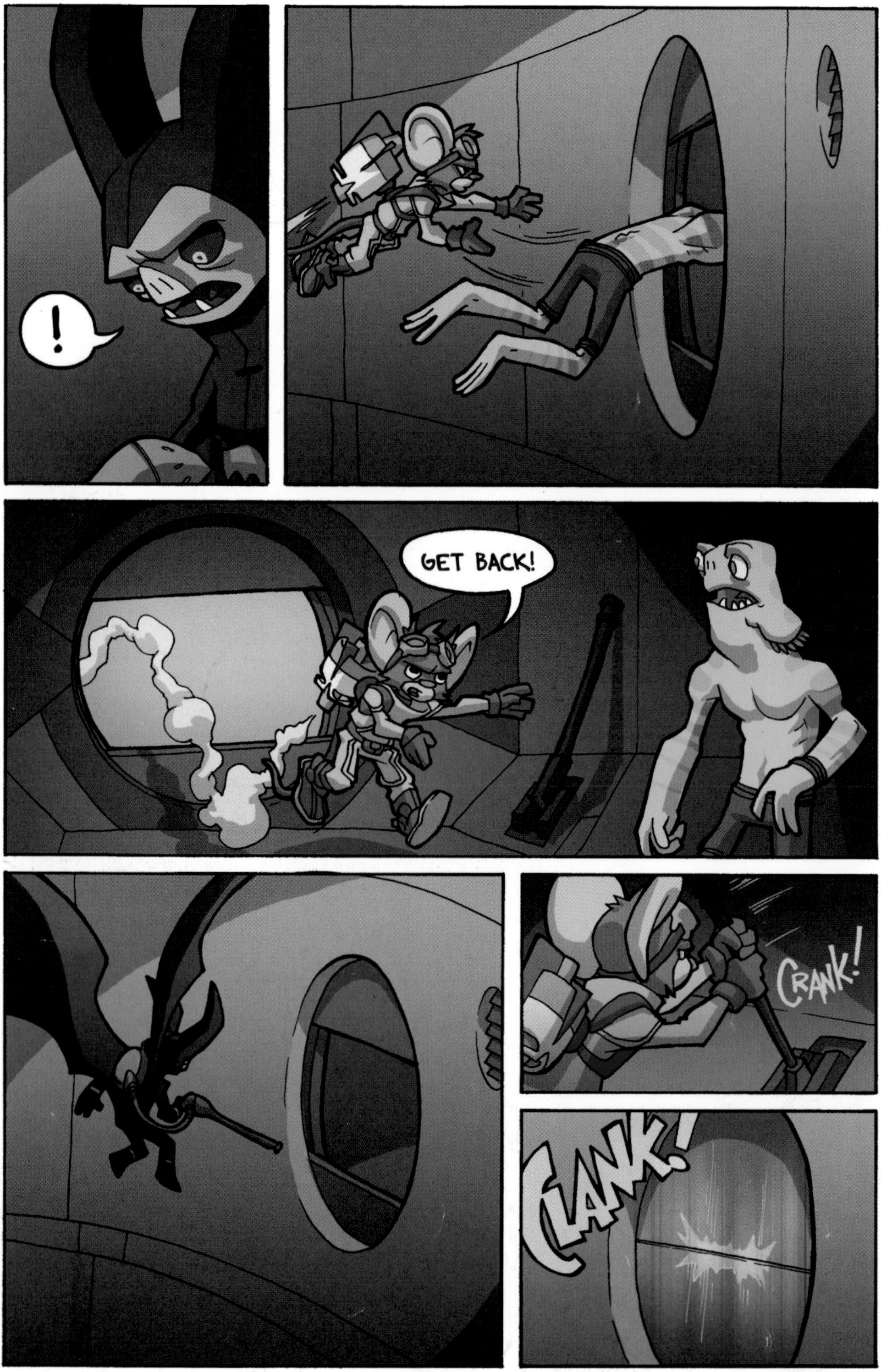
!
GET BACK!
CRANK!
CLANK!

RUN! **RUN!**

THIS IS MISSILE MOUSE. I NEED A TRANSPORT AT EXTRACTION POINT 33-B **RIGHT NOW!**

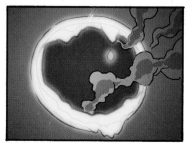

ARE YOU ALL RIGHT?

I'M FINE. THANK YOU.

LOOKS CLEAR.

I'M AGENT MISSILE MOUSE. I'M HERE TO HELP YOU.

YOU SAVED MY LIFE. THANK YOU.

MY NAME IS LASUKUS, AND I WANT TO GO HOME.

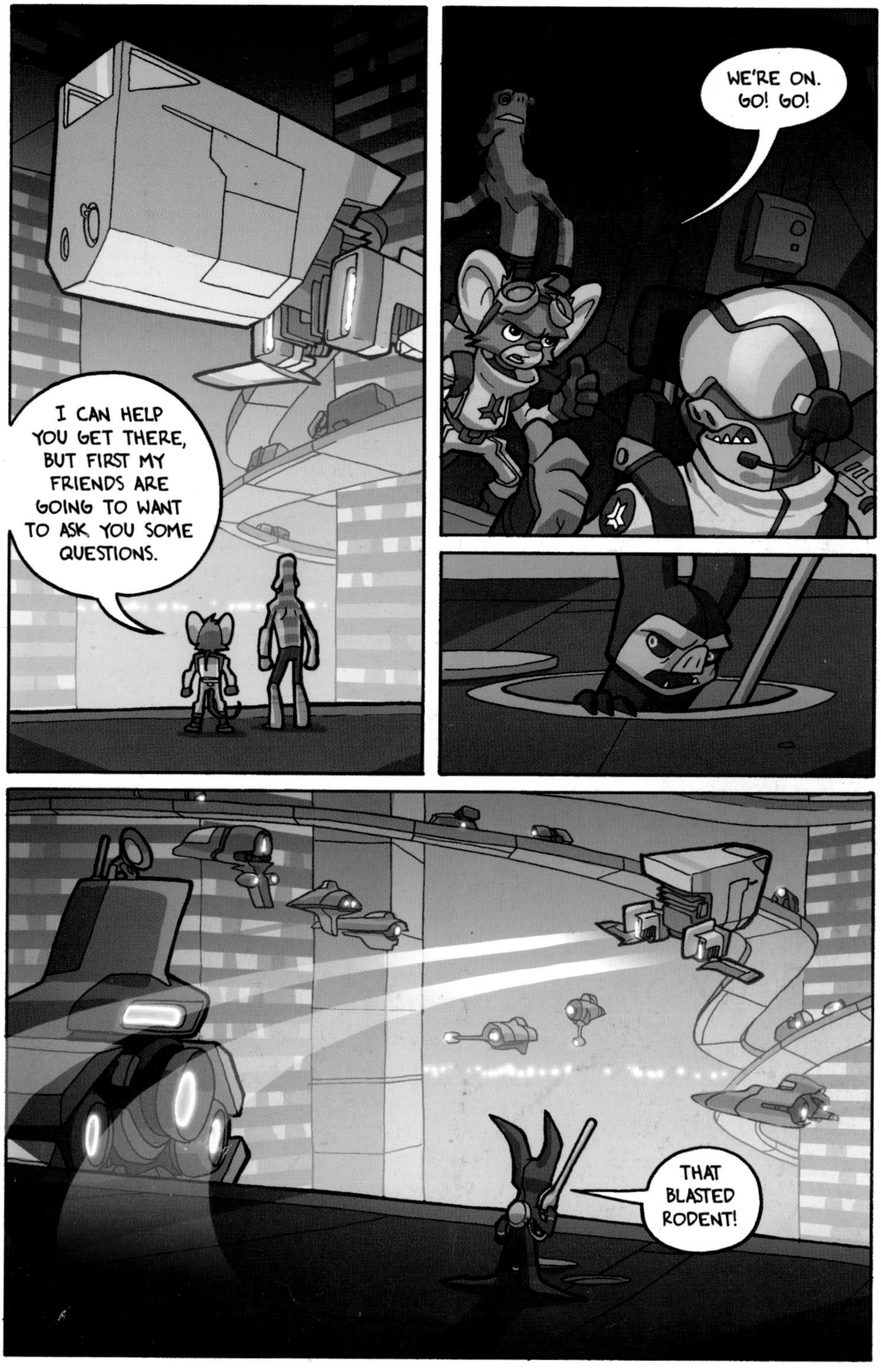
I CAN HELP YOU GET THERE, BUT FIRST MY FRIENDS ARE GOING TO WANT TO ASK YOU SOME QUESTIONS.
WE'RE ON. GO! GO!
THAT BLASTED RODENT!

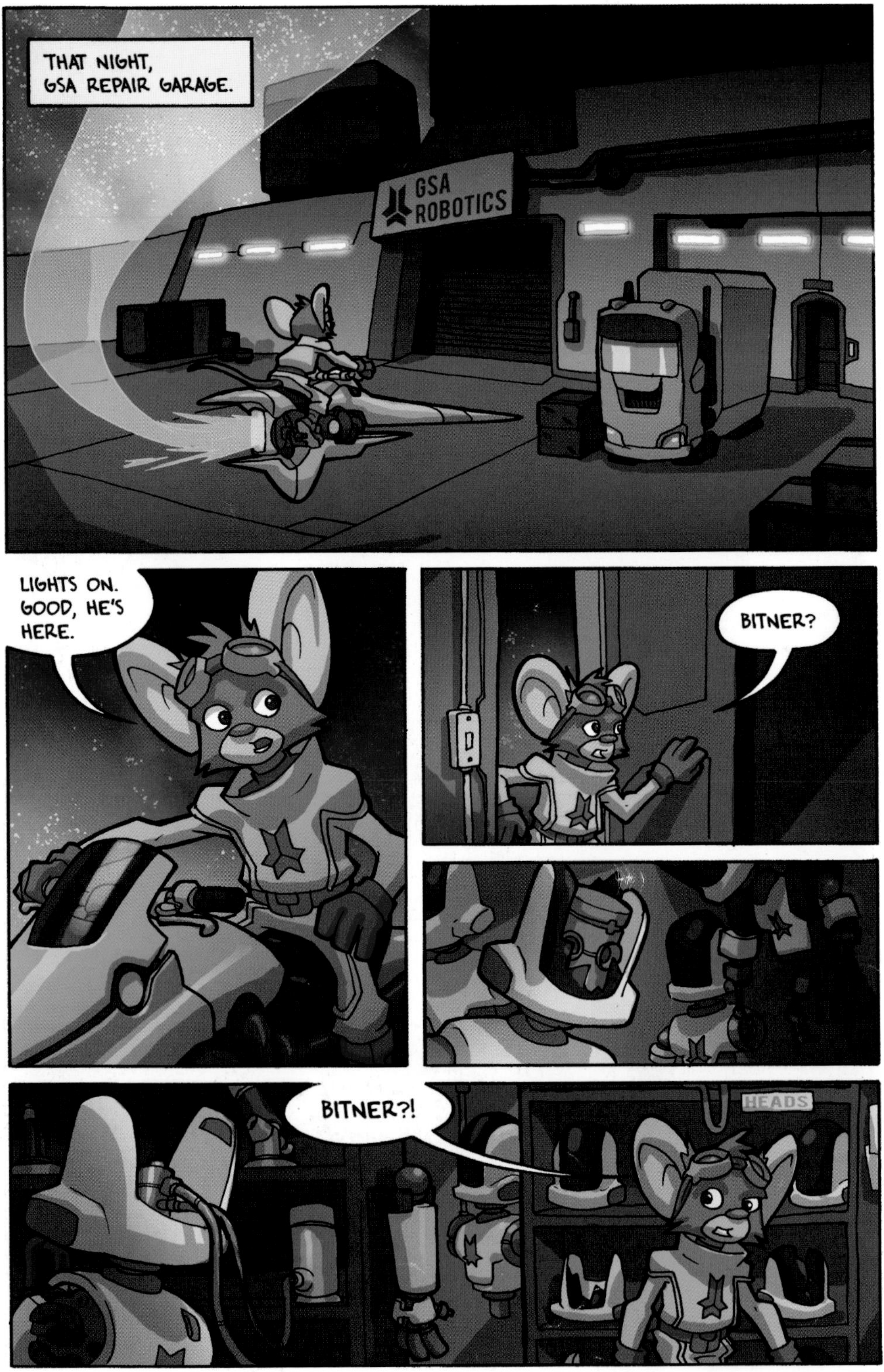
THAT NIGHT,
GSA REPAIR GARAGE.
GSA
ROBOTICS
LIGHTS ON.
GOOD, HE'S
HERE.
BITNER?
BITNER?!
HEADS

THERE YOU ARE.

HEY, BITNER, YOU HEAR ME?!

DO BE DOO DO BA DAAA!

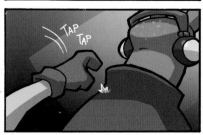

TAP TAP

GAH!

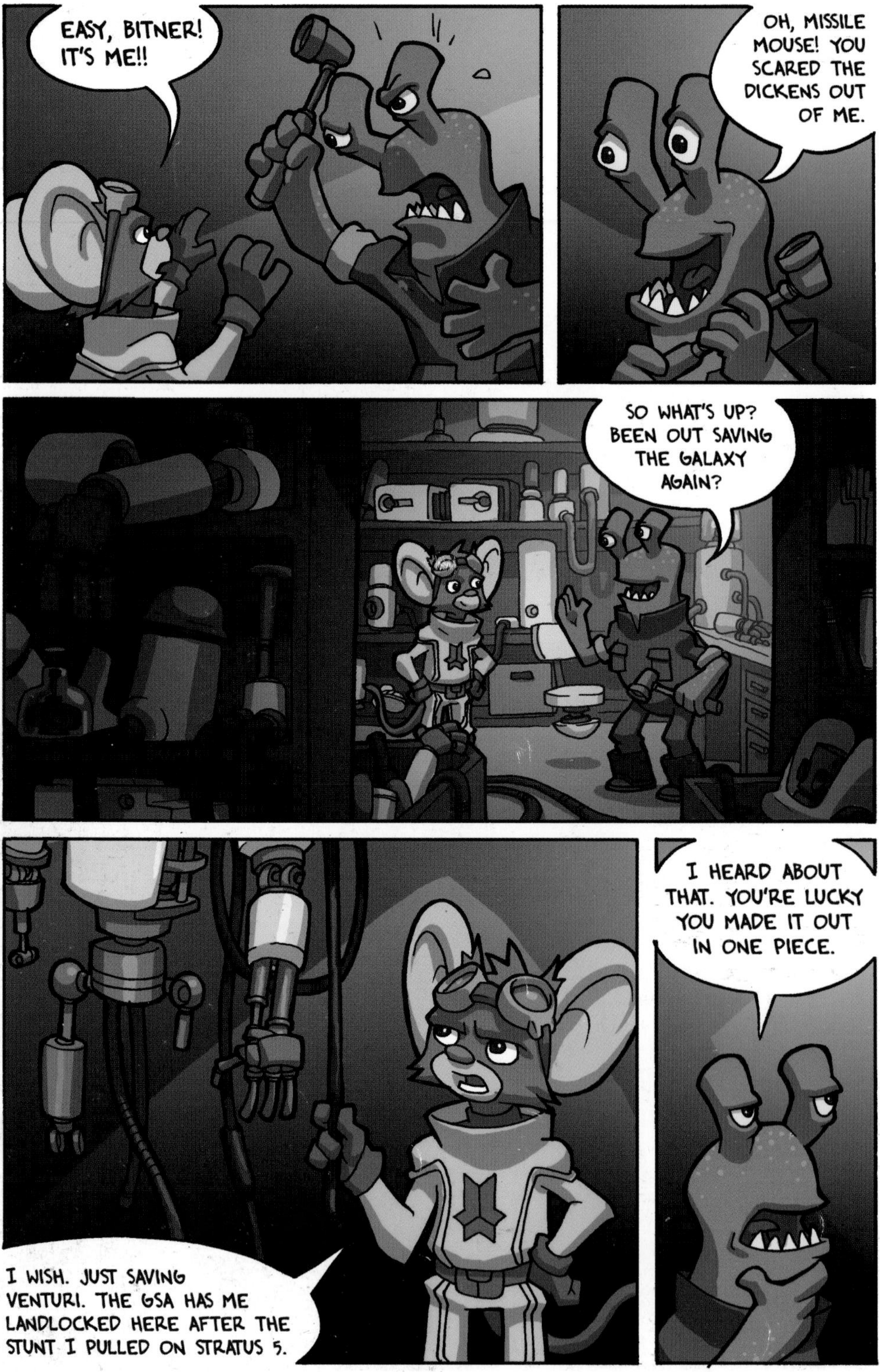
EASY, BITNER! IT'S ME!!
OH, MISSILE MOUSE! YOU SCARED THE DICKENS OUT OF ME.
SO WHAT'S UP? BEEN OUT SAVING THE GALAXY AGAIN?
I WISH. JUST SAVING VENTURI. THE GSA HAS ME LANDLOCKED HERE AFTER THE STUNT I PULLED ON STRATUS 5.
I HEARD ABOUT THAT. YOU'RE LUCKY YOU MADE IT OUT IN ONE PIECE.

YEAH, WELL, IT LOOKS LIKE THESE GUYS AREN'T AS LUCKY.

VENTURI IS TOUGH ON THESE GUYS, BUT THEY DO GOOD WORK.

I'D STILL RATHER HAVE SOMETHING WITH A CONSCIENCE OUT THERE ON THE STREETS.

THESE BOTS MAY DO A GOOD JOB, BUT IN A TIGHT SITUATION THERE'S NO SUBSTITUTE FOR QUALITY GRAY MATTER AND A BEATING HEART.

TRUE, BUT YOU KNOW THE GSA IS STRAPPED FOR GOOD AGENTS...FOR PLUTO'S SAKE, THEY HIRED YOU!

VERY FUNNY, BITNER.

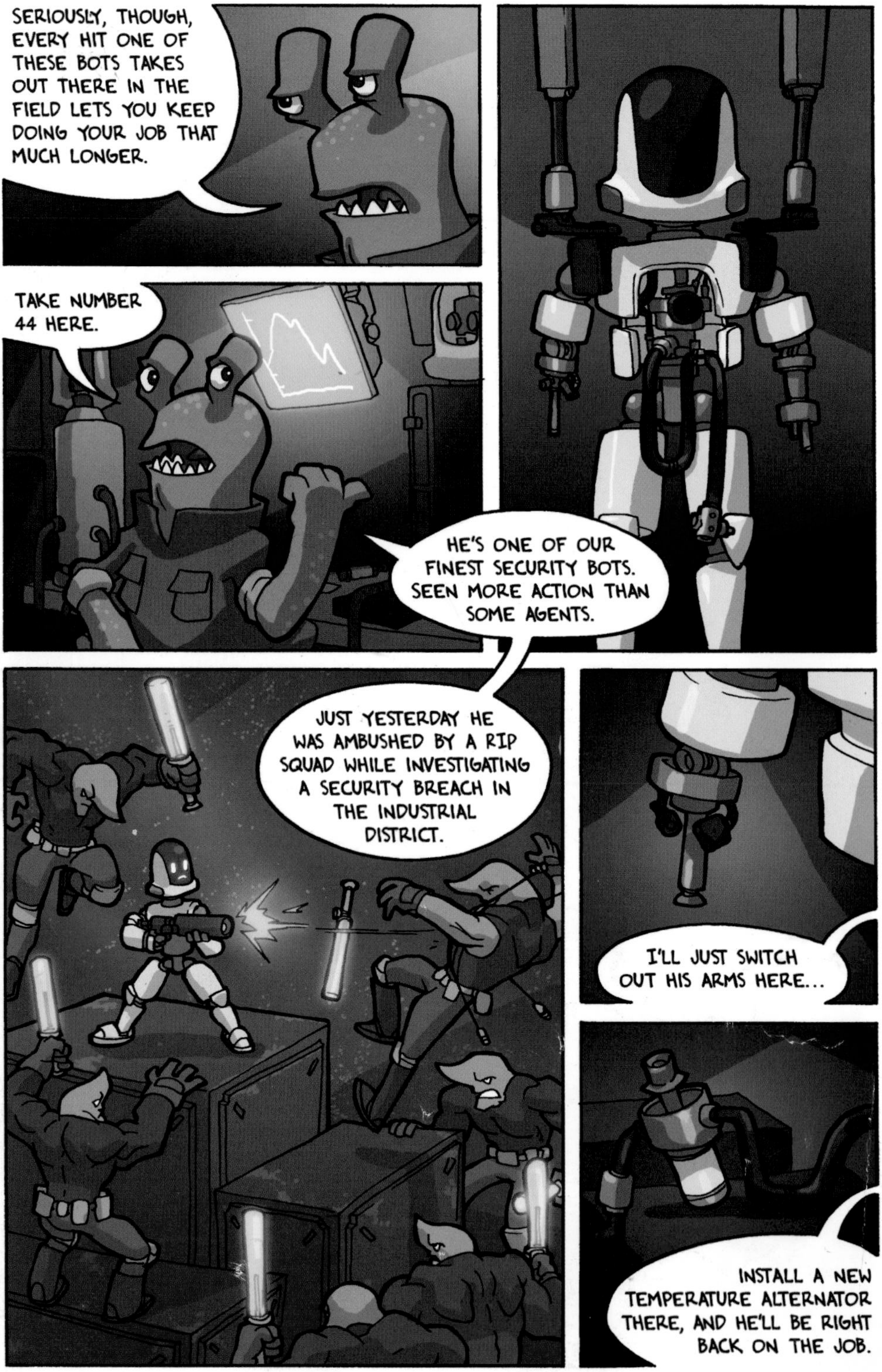
SERIOUSLY, THOUGH, EVERY HIT ONE OF THESE BOTS TAKES OUT THERE IN THE FIELD LETS YOU KEEP DOING YOUR JOB THAT MUCH LONGER.
TAKE NUMBER 44 HERE.
HE'S ONE OF OUR FINEST SECURITY BOTS. SEEN MORE ACTION THAN SOME AGENTS.
JUST YESTERDAY HE WAS AMBUSHED BY A RIP SQUAD WHILE INVESTIGATING A SECURITY BREACH IN THE INDUSTRIAL DISTRICT.
I'LL JUST SWITCH OUT HIS ARMS HERE...
INSTALL A NEW TEMPERATURE ALTERNATOR THERE, AND HE'LL BE RIGHT BACK ON THE JOB.

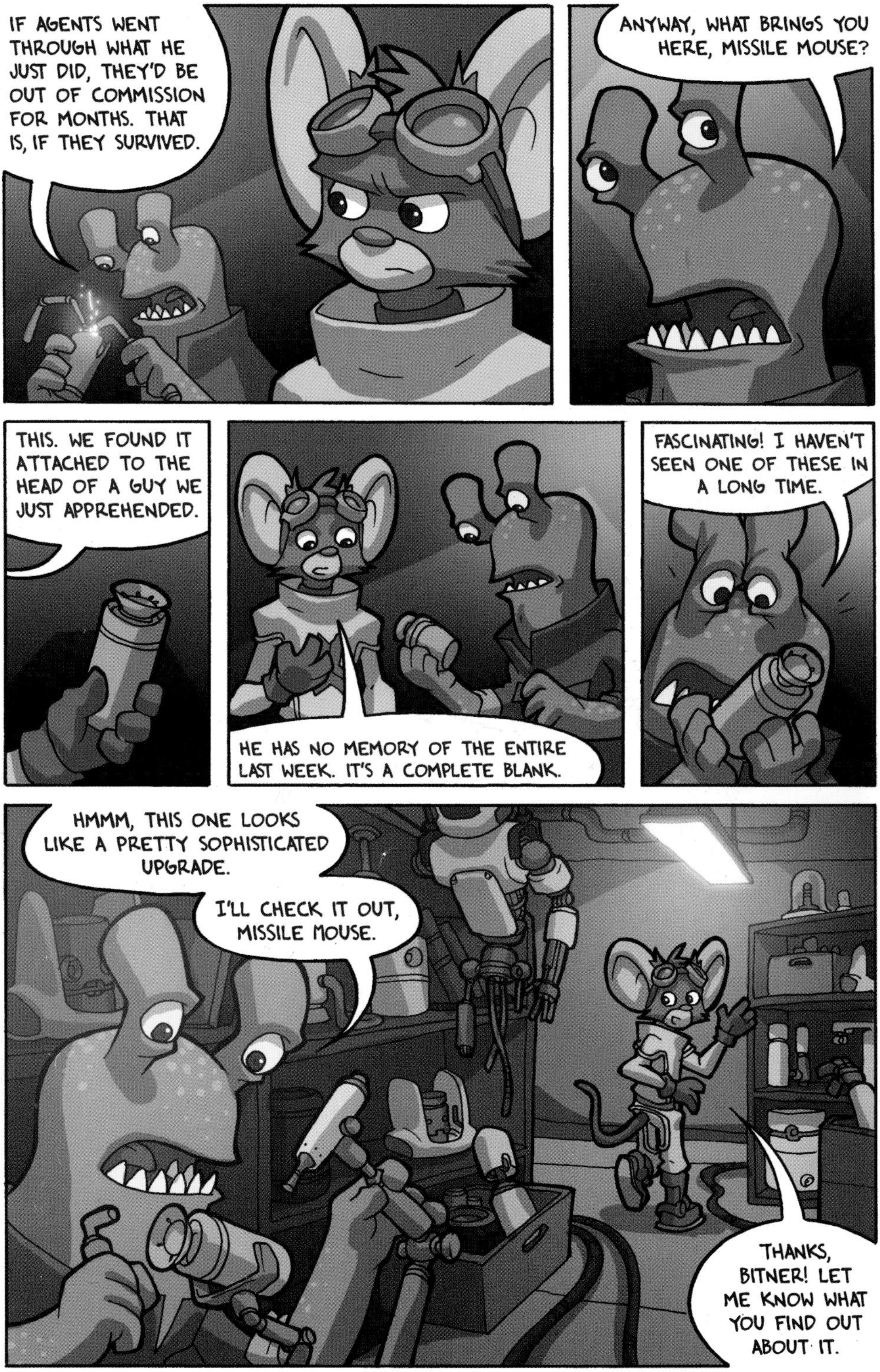
IF AGENTS WENT THROUGH WHAT HE JUST DID, THEY'D BE OUT OF COMMISSION FOR MONTHS. THAT IS, IF THEY SURVIVED.
ANYWAY, WHAT BRINGS YOU HERE, MISSILE MOUSE?
THIS. WE FOUND IT ATTACHED TO THE HEAD OF A GUY WE JUST APPREHENDED.
HE HAS NO MEMORY OF THE ENTIRE LAST WEEK. IT'S A COMPLETE BLANK.
FASCINATING! I HAVEN'T SEEN ONE OF THESE IN A LONG TIME.
HMMM, THIS ONE LOOKS LIKE A PRETTY SOPHISTICATED UPGRADE.
I'LL CHECK IT OUT, MISSILE MOUSE.
THANKS, BITNER! LET ME KNOW WHAT YOU FIND OUT ABOUT IT.

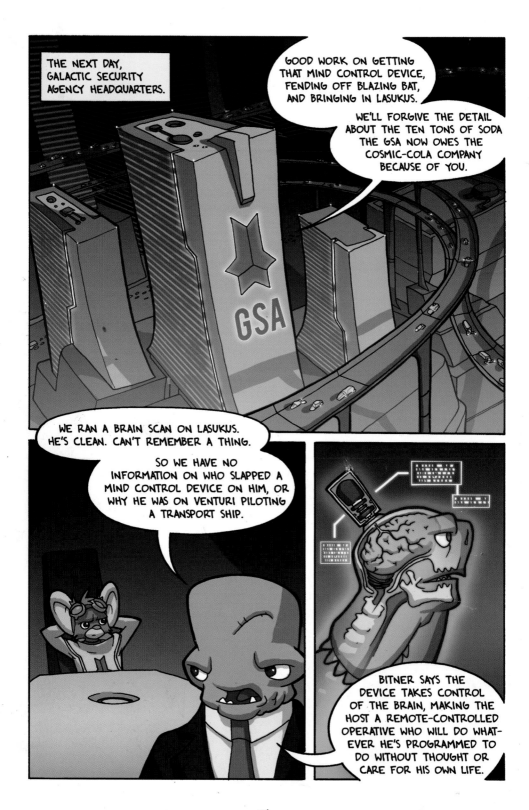

THE NEXT DAY, GALACTIC SECURITY AGENCY HEADQUARTERS.

GOOD WORK ON GETTING THAT MIND CONTROL DEVICE, FENDING OFF BLAZING BAT, AND BRINGING IN LASUKUS.

WE'LL FORGIVE THE DETAIL ABOUT THE TEN TONS OF SODA THE GSA NOW OWES THE COSMIC-COLA COMPANY BECAUSE OF YOU.

WE RAN A BRAIN SCAN ON LASUKUS. HE'S CLEAN. CAN'T REMEMBER A THING.

SO WE HAVE NO INFORMATION ON WHO SLAPPED A MIND CONTROL DEVICE ON HIM, OR WHY HE WAS ON VENTURI PILOTING A TRANSPORT SHIP.

BITNER SAYS THE DEVICE TAKES CONTROL OF THE BRAIN, MAKING THE HOST A REMOTE-CONTROLLED OPERATIVE WHO WILL DO WHAT- EVER HE'S PROGRAMMED TO DO WITHOUT THOUGHT OR CARE FOR HIS OWN LIFE.

WHICH WOULD MAKE HIM THE PERFECT TOOL FOR TRANSPORTING SOMETHING YOU DIDN'T WANT ANYONE TO KNOW ABOUT.

WE WEREN'T ABLE TO RETRIEVE THE SHIPMENT OF WHATEVER LASUKUS WAS TRANS- PORTING. IT WAS BLOWN UP, DESTROYING ALL THE EVIDENCE OF WHERE IT WAS FROM. THE BLAST SUGGESTS IT WAS DONE BY BLAZING BAT HIMSELF.

THERE'S SOMEBODY WHO DOESN'T WANT THE GSA TO FIND OUT WHAT'S GOING ON.

EXACTLY. THE ONLY LEAD WE HAVE IS FROM LASUKUS. HE SAYS HE'S FROM THE OUTER COLONY WORLD OF TANKIUM3.

WE WANT YOU TO GO THERE.

RETURN LASUKUS, AND SEE IF YOU CAN GET TO THE BOTTOM OF WHO'S BEHIND THIS WHOLE ORDEAL AND WHAT THEY ARE SHIPPING TO VENTURI.

TANKIUM3

TANKIUM 3

THAT'S A BIG JOB. I'LL NEED A GOOD TEAM OF AT LEAST FIVE AGENTS.

YOU'LL BE HEADING UP A TEAM OF SECURITY BOTS.

SECURITY BOTS?!! NO WAY, MAXWELL, I'M NOT WORKING WITH THOSE GUYS.

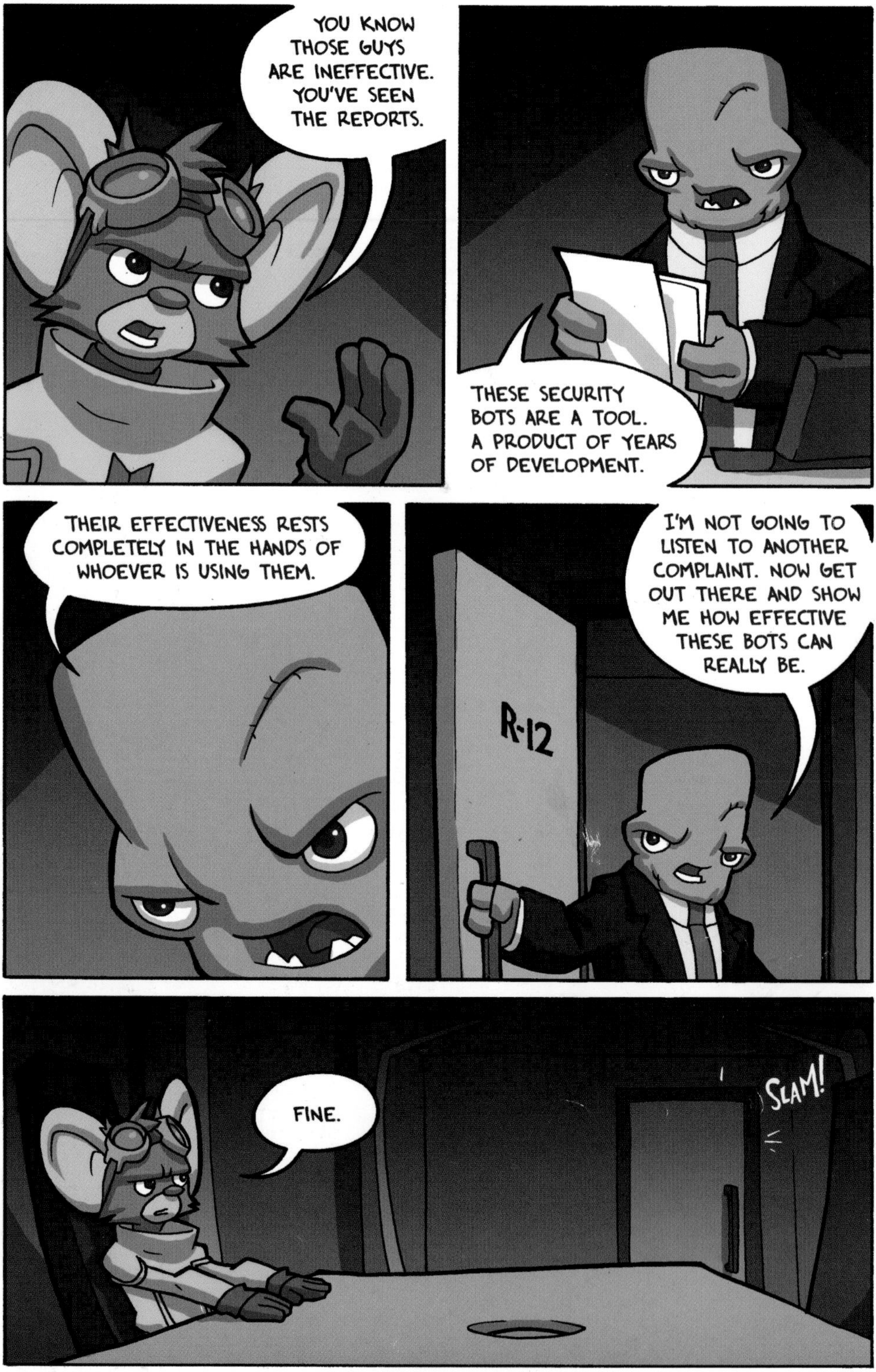
YOU KNOW THOSE GUYS ARE INEFFECTIVE. YOU'VE SEEN THE REPORTS.
THESE SECURITY BOTS ARE A TOOL. A PRODUCT OF YEARS OF DEVELOPMENT.
THEIR EFFECTIVENESS RESTS COMPLETELY IN THE HANDS OF WHOEVER IS USING THEM.
R-12
I'M NOT GOING TO LISTEN TO ANOTHER COMPLAINT. NOW GET OUT THERE AND SHOW ME HOW EFFECTIVE THESE BOTS CAN REALLY BE.
FINE.
SLAM!

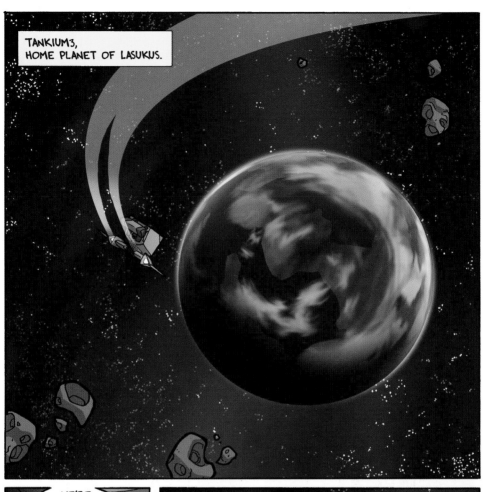

TANKIUM3,
HOME PLANET OF LASUKUS.

WE'RE ENTERING THE ATMOSPHERE.

HOLD ON TIGHT!

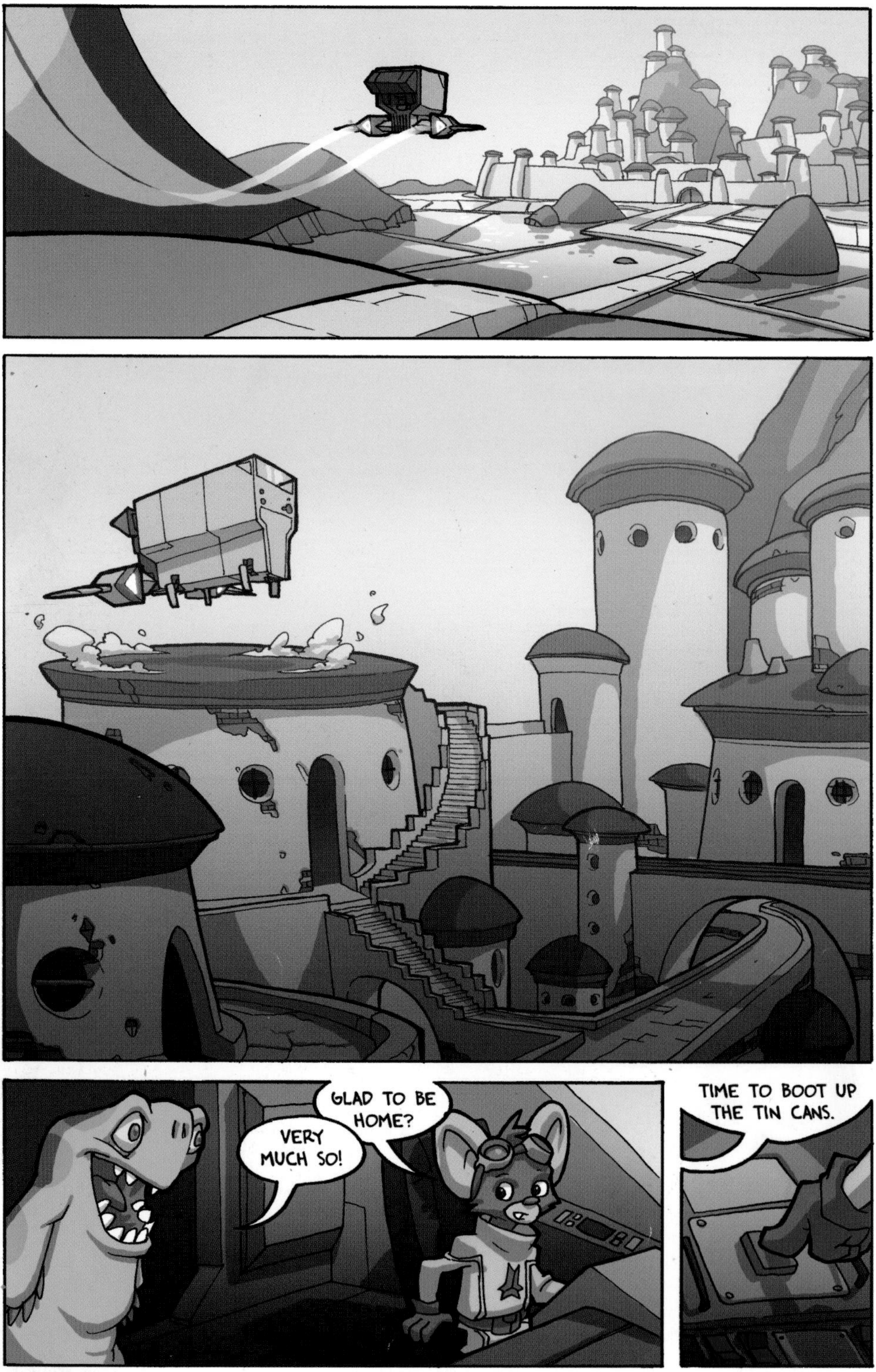
GLAD TO BE HOME?
VERY MUCH SO!
TIME TO BOOT UP THE TIN CANS.

WRRRRRRRRRRRRRRRR

CLICK CLICK CLICK CLICK

ALL RIGHT, GUYS, LET'S GET DOWN TO BUSINESS.

I WANT YOU ALL ON HIGH ALERT. FAN OUT AND FORM A PERIMETER AROUND THE CITY.

ROBOT 44, YOU COME WITH ME AS MY PERSONAL BACKUP.

THAT MEANS NO MATTER WHAT, YOU'VE GOT MY BACK.

GOT IT?

AFFIRMATIVE.

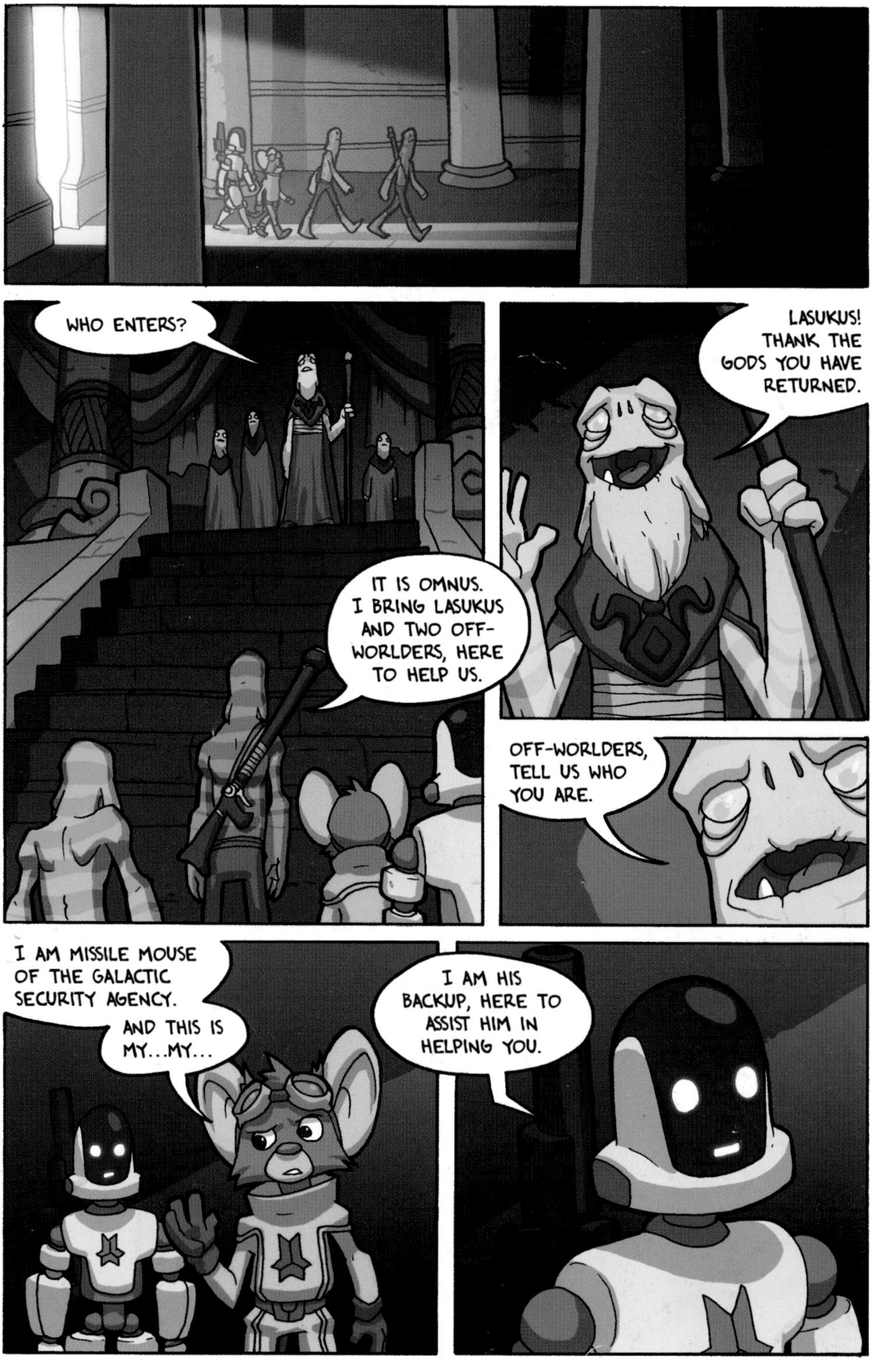
WHO ENTERS?
IT IS OMNUS. I BRING LASUKUS AND TWO OFF-WORLDERS, HERE TO HELP US.
LASUKUS! THANK THE GODS YOU HAVE RETURNED.
OFF-WORLDERS, TELL US WHO YOU ARE.
I AM MISSILE MOUSE OF THE GALACTIC SECURITY AGENCY.
AND THIS IS MY...MY...
I AM HIS BACKUP, HERE TO ASSIST HIM IN HELPING YOU.

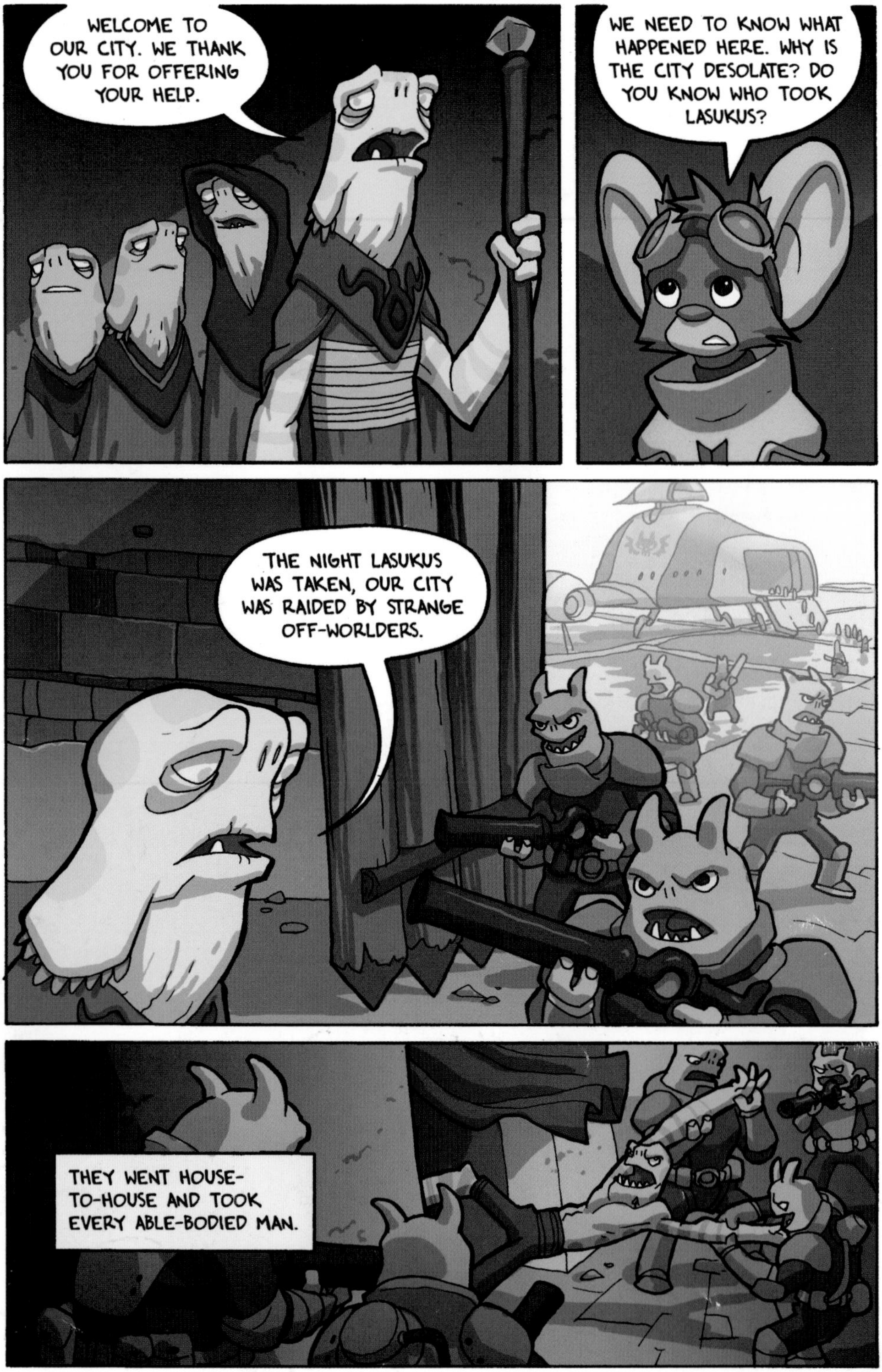
WELCOME TO OUR CITY. WE THANK YOU FOR OFFERING YOUR HELP.
WE NEED TO KNOW WHAT HAPPENED HERE. WHY IS THE CITY DESOLATE? DO YOU KNOW WHO TOOK LASUKUS?
THE NIGHT LASUKUS WAS TAKEN, OUR CITY WAS RAIDED BY STRANGE OFF-WORLDERS.
THEY WENT HOUSE-TO-HOUSE AND TOOK EVERY ABLE-BODIED MAN.

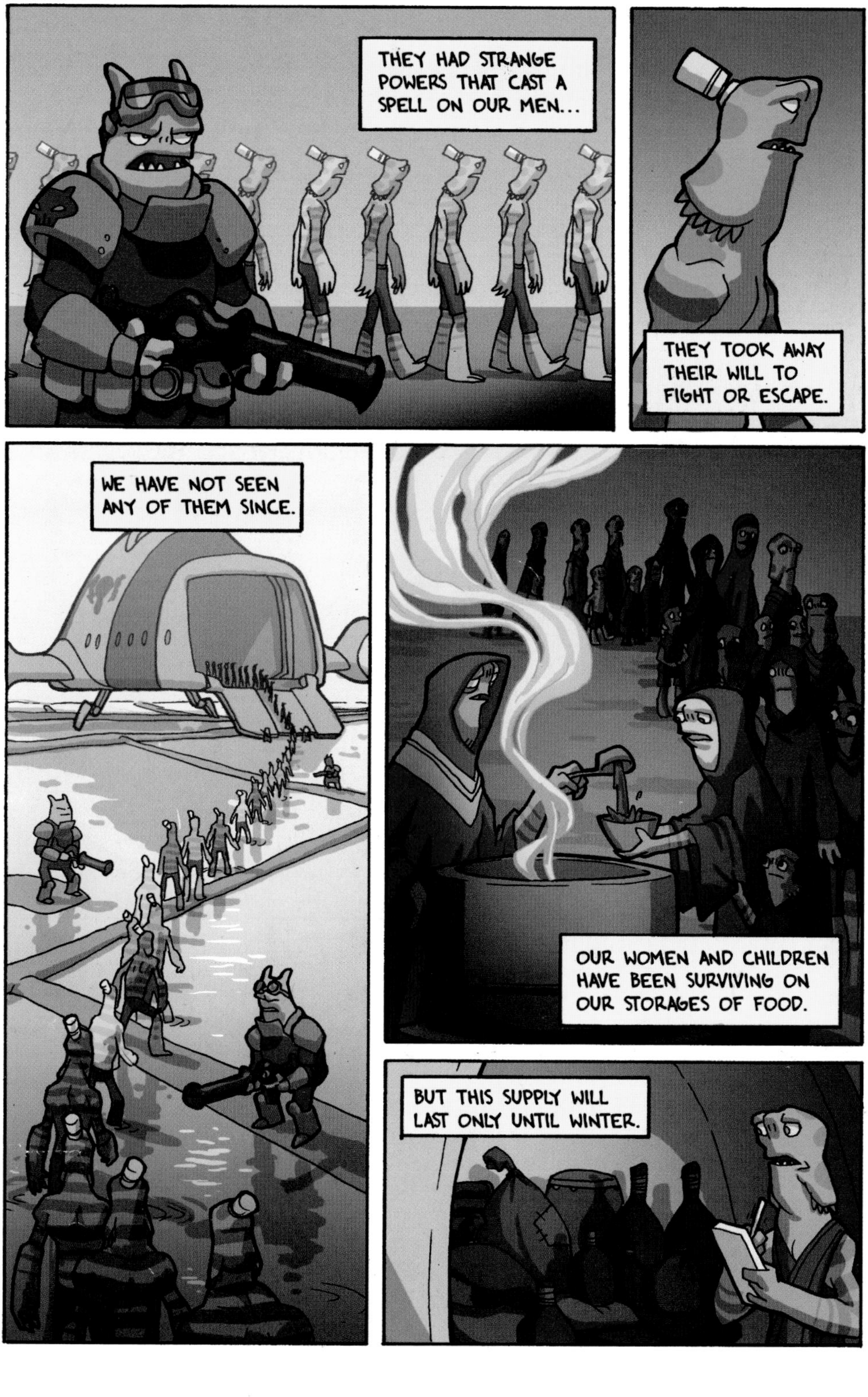
THEY HAD STRANGE POWERS THAT CAST A SPELL ON OUR MEN...
THEY TOOK AWAY THEIR WILL TO FIGHT OR ESCAPE.
WE HAVE NOT SEEN ANY OF THEM SINCE.
OUR WOMEN AND CHILDREN HAVE BEEN SURVIVING ON OUR STORAGES OF FOOD.
BUT THIS SUPPLY WILL LAST ONLY UNTIL WINTER.

MISSILE MOUSE, YOU ARE OUR LAST HOPE.

THE FEW MEN WHO WERE SPARED HAVE GONE SEARCHING FOR THE LOST MEN BUT HAVE FOUND NOTHING.

ELDERS, I GIVE MY PROMISE THAT I WILL FIND AND RETURN YOUR MEN.

AS DO I!

THEN IT IS WITH GREAT HONOR THAT THE COUNCIL PETITIONS THE GODS OF PROTECTION ON YOUR BEHALF.

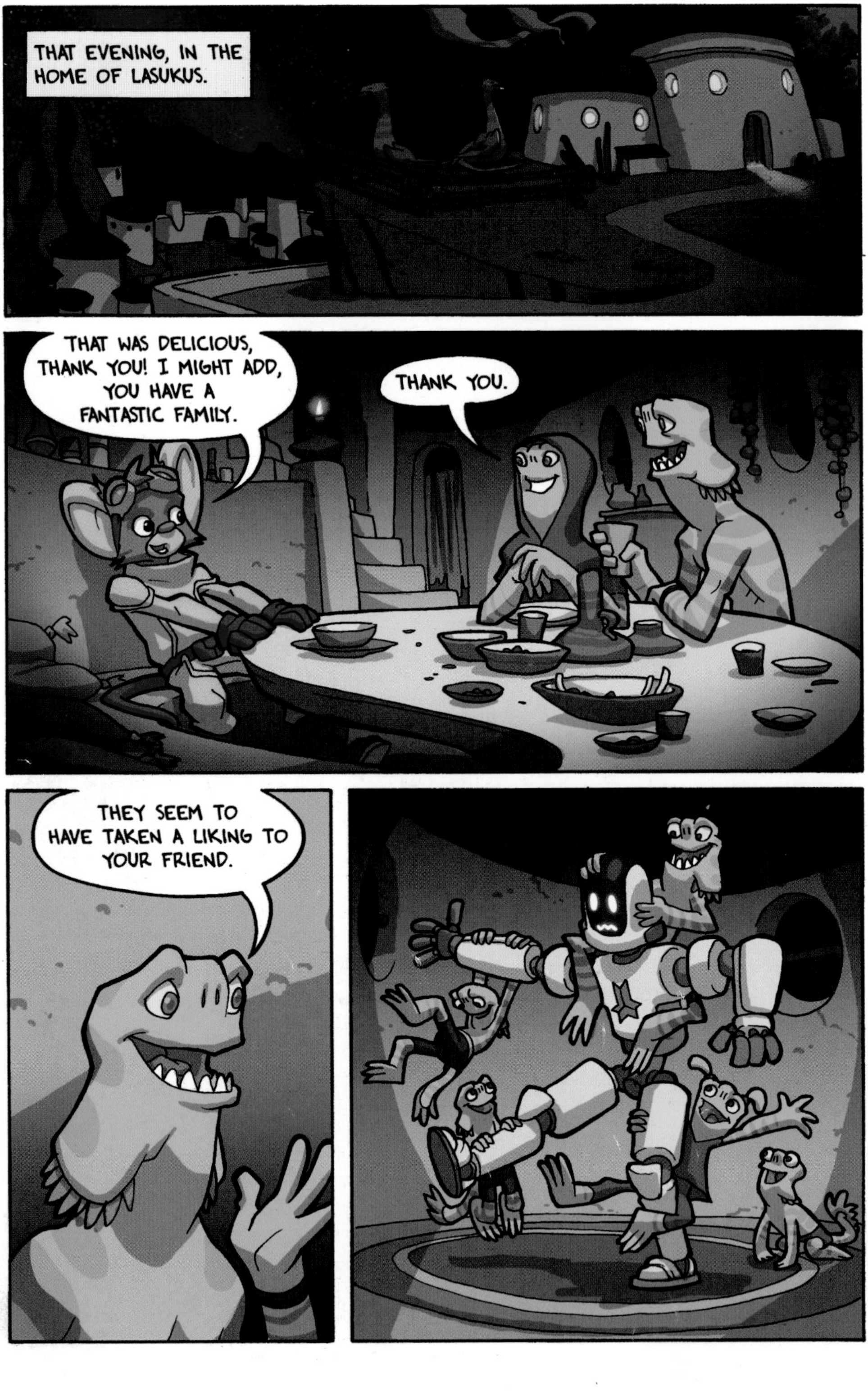

THAT EVENING, IN THE HOME OF LASUKUS.
THAT WAS DELICIOUS, THANK YOU! I MIGHT ADD, YOU HAVE A FANTASTIC FAMILY.
THANK YOU.
THEY SEEM TO HAVE TAKEN A LIKING TO YOUR FRIEND.

HA HA HA HA HA HA HA

MISSILE MOUSE, COME QUICK! YOUR ROBOTS ARE UNDER ATTACK AND THE TRANSPORT IS DESTROYED!

44, LET'S GO!

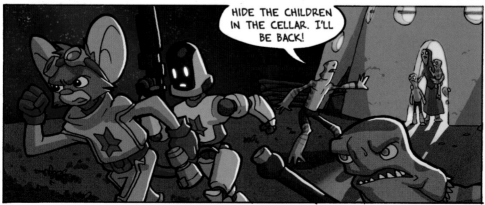

HIDE THE CHILDREN IN THE CELLAR. I'LL BE BACK!

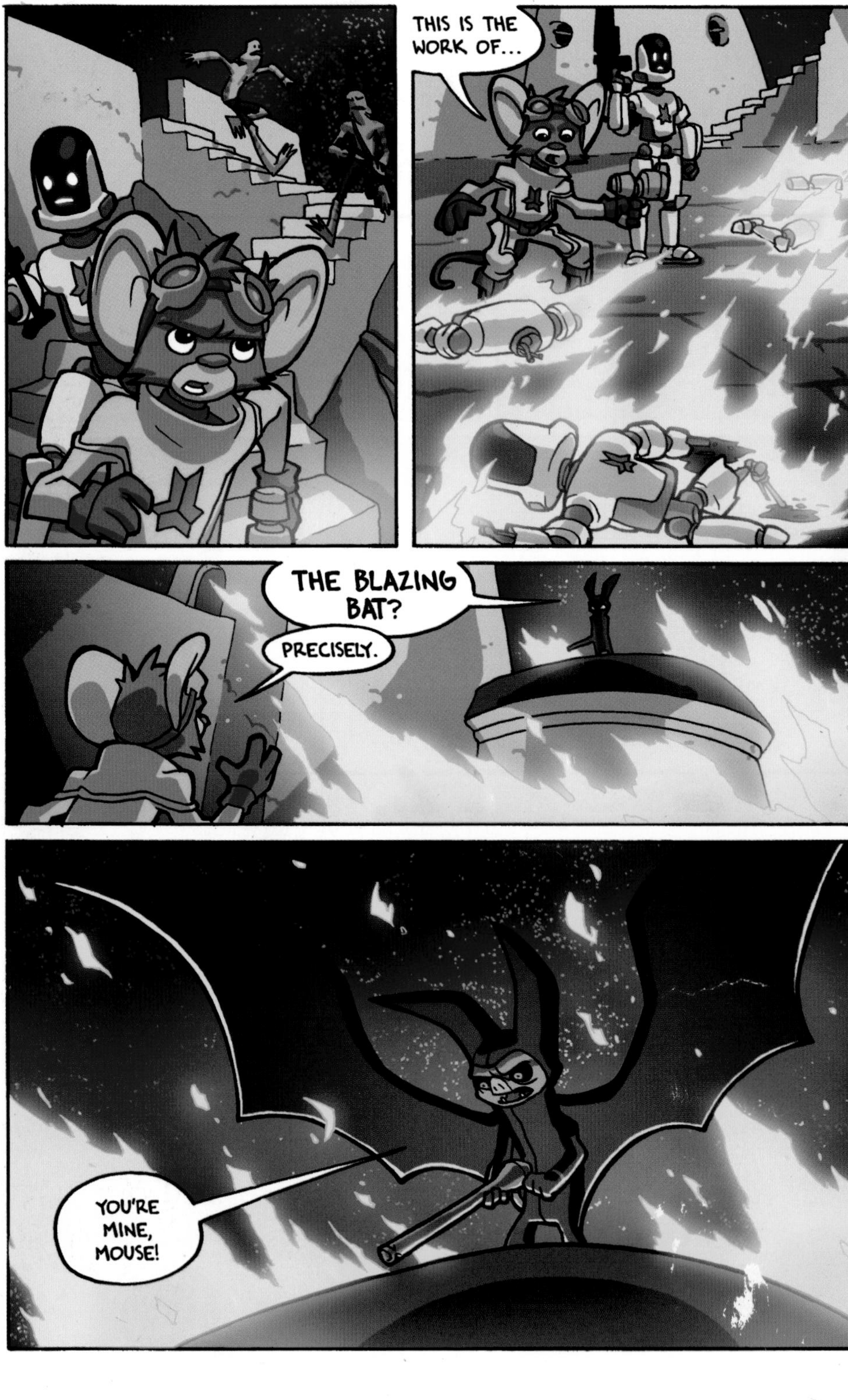
THIS IS THE WORK OF...
THE BLAZING BAT?
PRECISELY.
YOU'RE MINE, MOUSE!

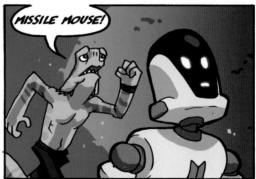

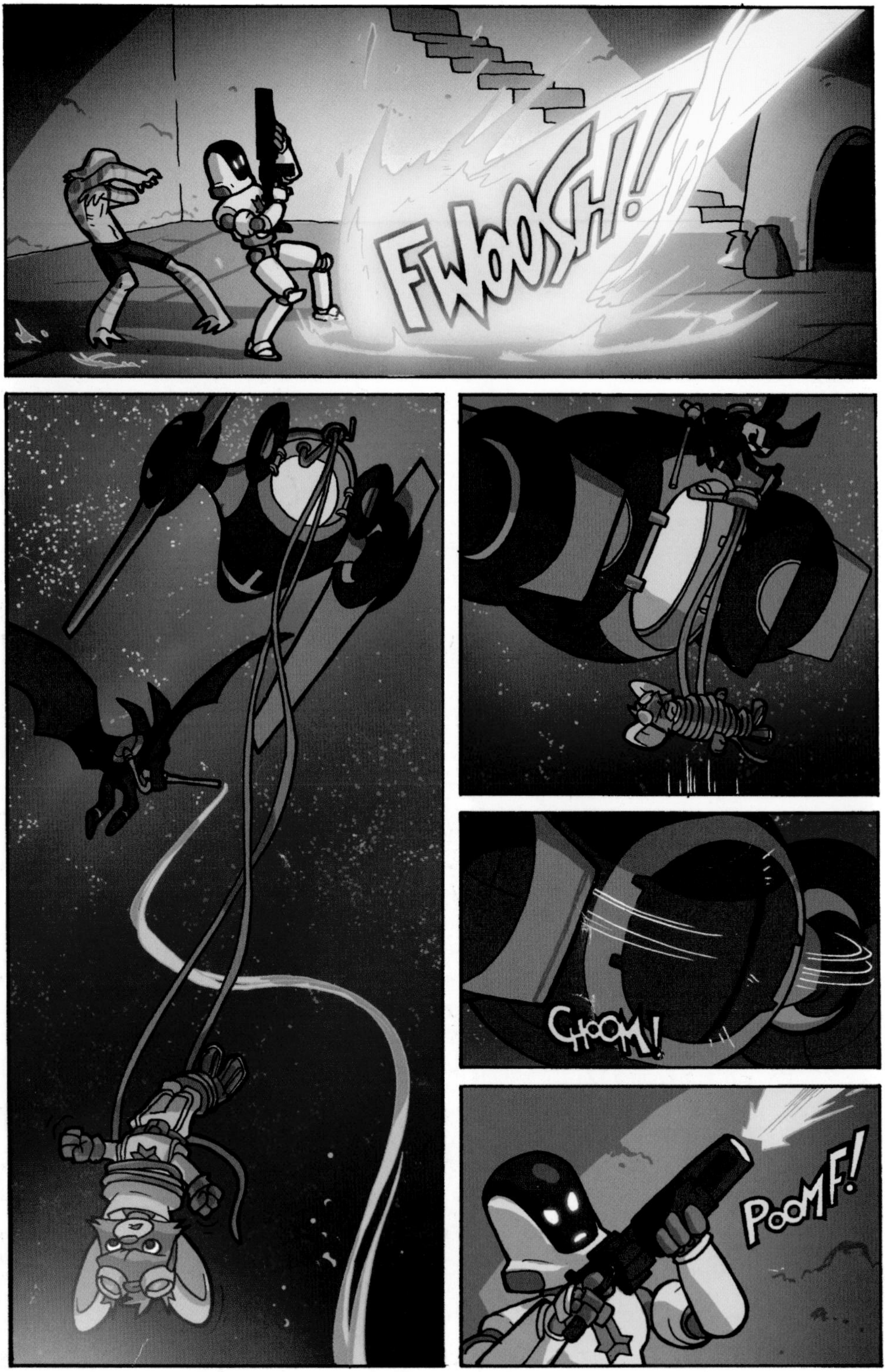
FWOOSH!!
CHOOM!
POOMF!

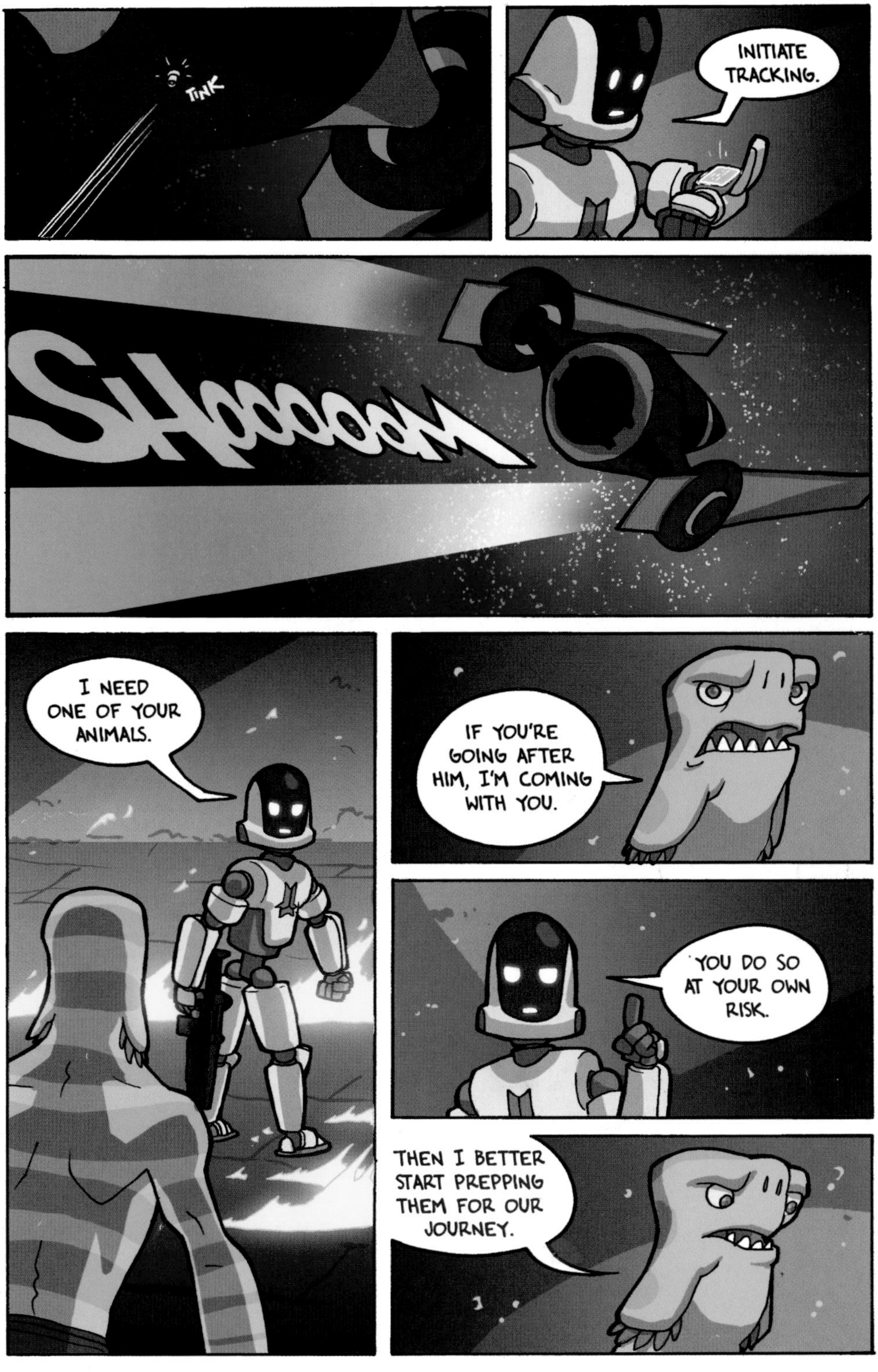
TINK
INITIATE TRACKING.
SHOOOOOM
I NEED ONE OF YOUR ANIMALS.
IF YOU'RE GOING AFTER HIM, I'M COMING WITH YOU.
YOU DO SO AT YOUR OWN RISK.
THEN I BETTER START PREPPING THEM FOR OUR JOURNEY.

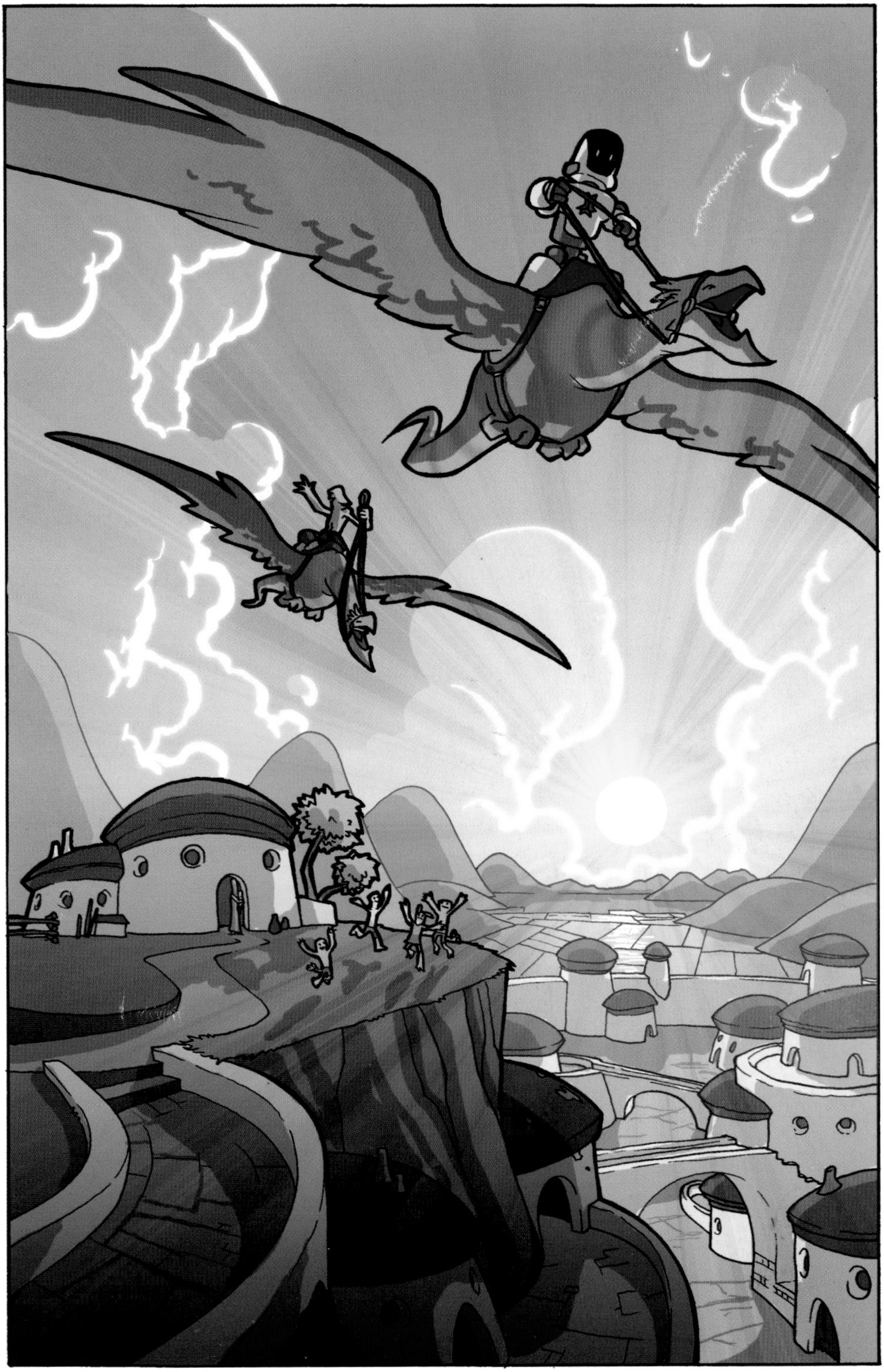

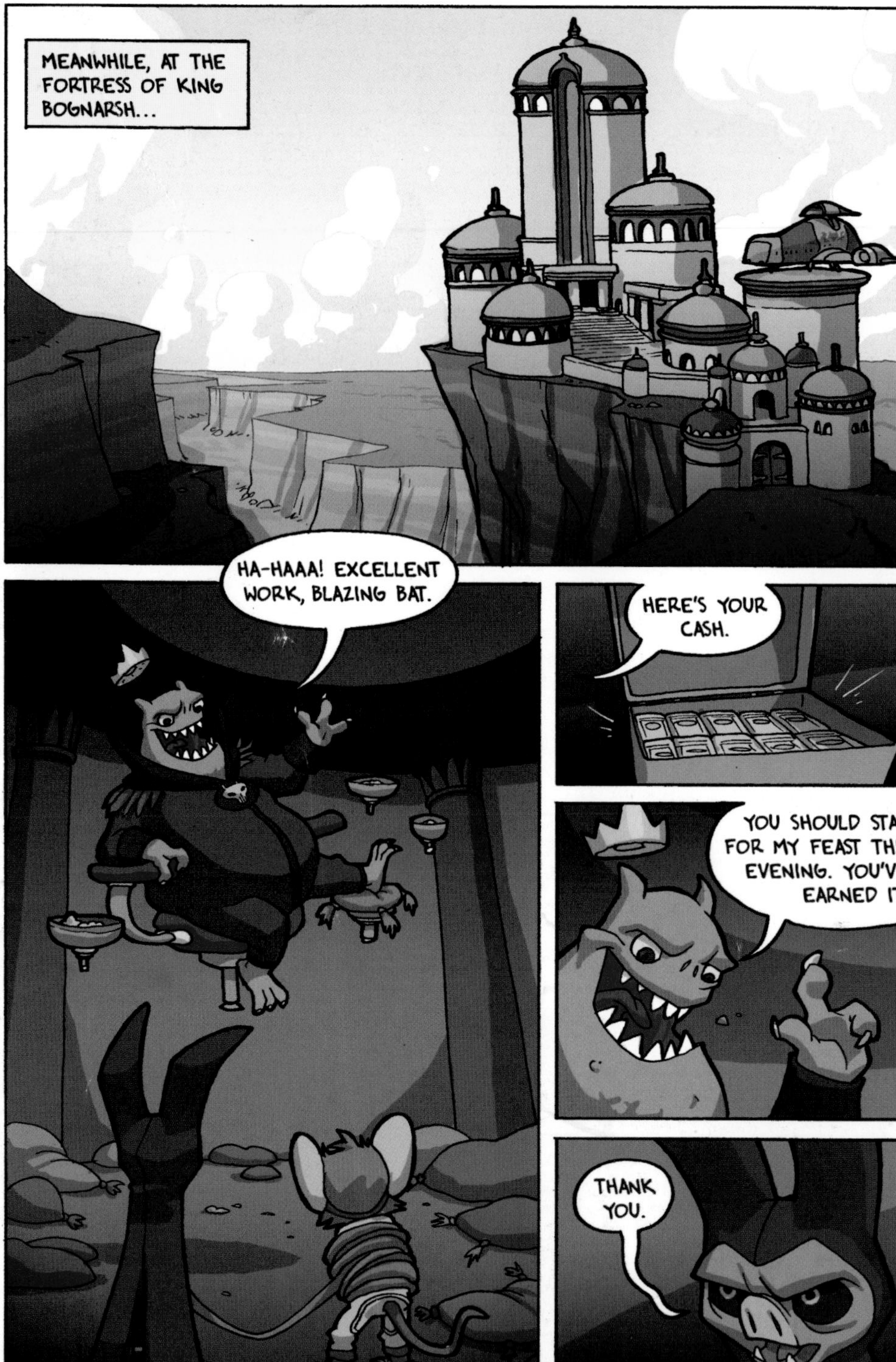
MEANWHILE, AT THE FORTRESS OF KING BOGNARSH...
HA-HAAA! EXCELLENT WORK, BLAZING BAT.
HERE'S YOUR CASH.
YOU SHOULD STAY FOR MY FEAST THIS EVENING. YOU'VE EARNED IT.
THANK YOU.

SO, MISSILE MOUSE, I'VE HEARD A LOT ABOUT YOU.

FUNNY, NEVER HEARD OF *YOU* BEFORE.

HA! THAT'S HOW I LIKE IT.

NAME'S BOGNARSH... KING BOGNARSH. I RULE THIS PLANET.

CAME HERE A FEW YEARS AGO AND DECIDED I HAD TO HAVE IT.

BUT I KEEP A LOW PROFILE.

DON'T WANT THE GSA FIDDLING AROUND IN MY BUSINESS.

AND WHAT BUSINESS WOULD THAT BE?

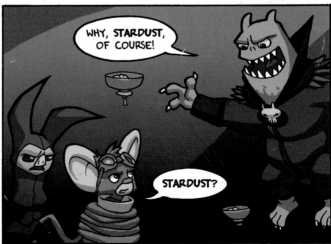

WHY, STARDUST, OF COURSE!

STARDUST?

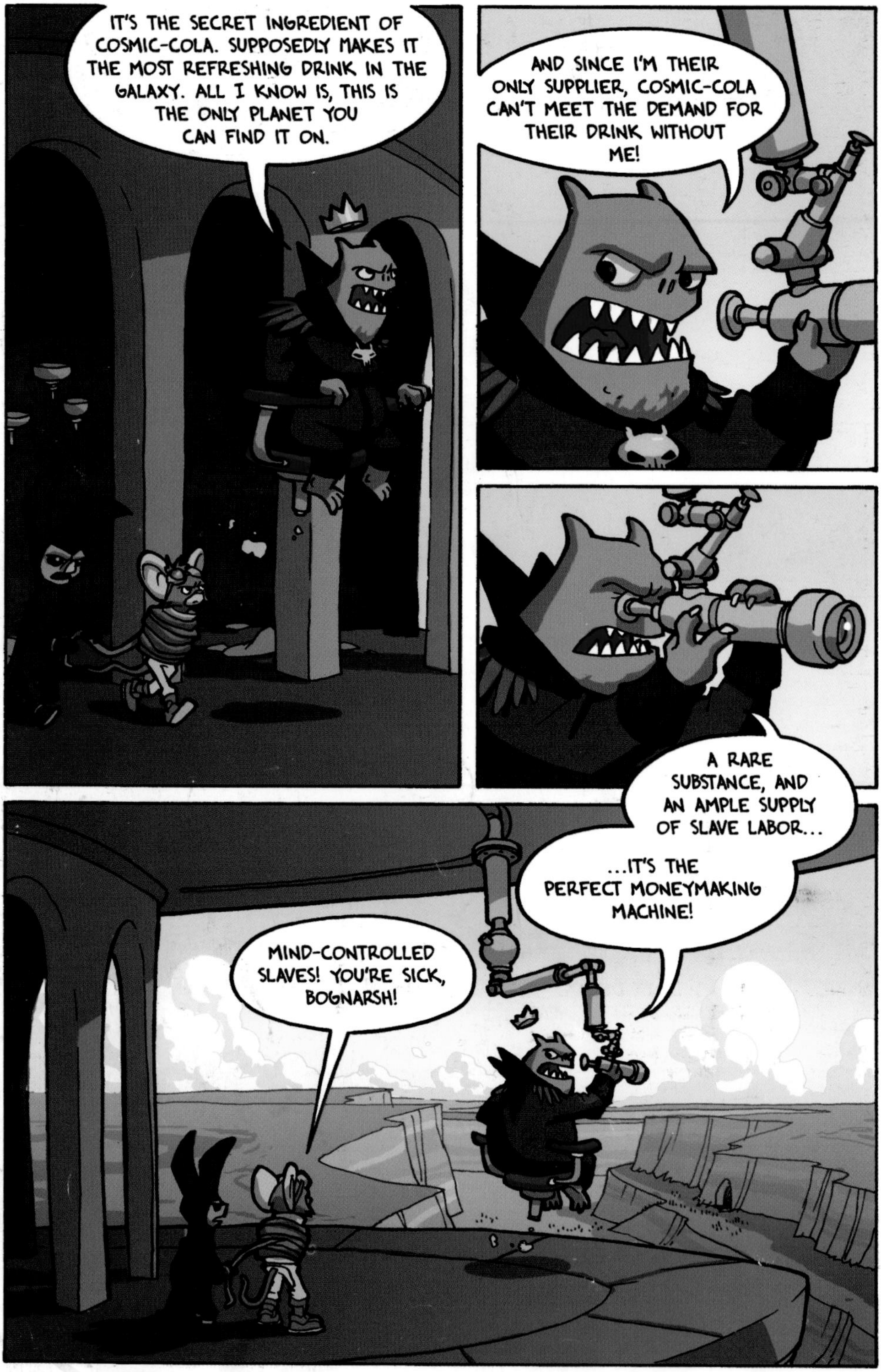
IT'S THE SECRET INGREDIENT OF COSMIC-COLA. SUPPOSEDLY MAKES IT THE MOST REFRESHING DRINK IN THE GALAXY. ALL I KNOW IS, THIS IS THE ONLY PLANET YOU CAN FIND IT ON.
AND SINCE I'M THEIR ONLY SUPPLIER, COSMIC-COLA CAN'T MEET THE DEMAND FOR THEIR DRINK WITHOUT ME!
A RARE SUBSTANCE, AND AN AMPLE SUPPLY OF SLAVE LABOR...
...IT'S THE PERFECT MONEYMAKING MACHINE!
MIND-CONTROLLED SLAVES! YOU'RE SICK, BOGNARSH!

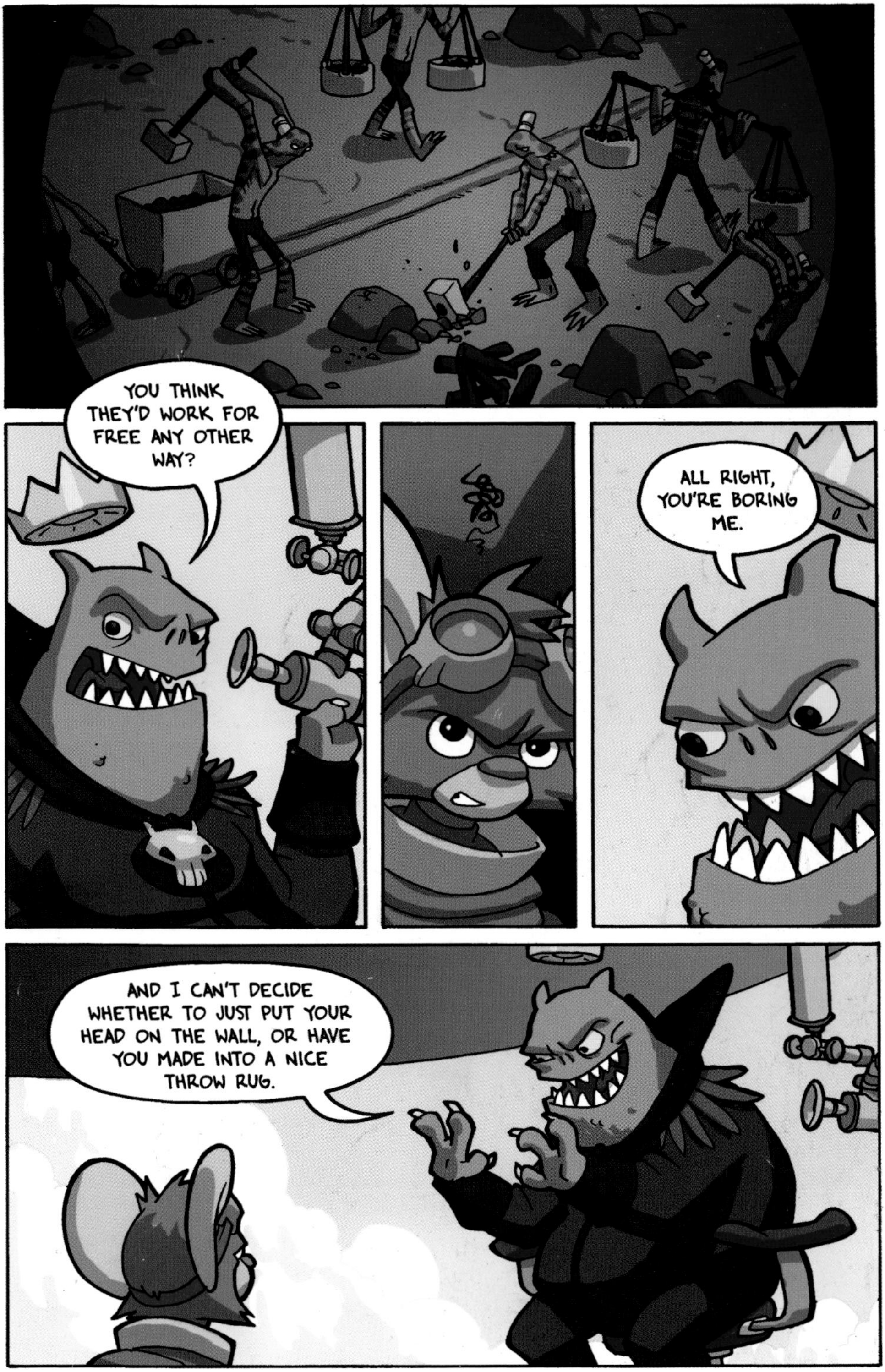
YOU THINK THEY'D WORK FOR FREE ANY OTHER WAY?
ALL RIGHT, YOU'RE BORING ME.
AND I CAN'T DECIDE WHETHER TO JUST PUT YOUR HEAD ON THE WALL, OR HAVE YOU MADE INTO A NICE THROW RUG.

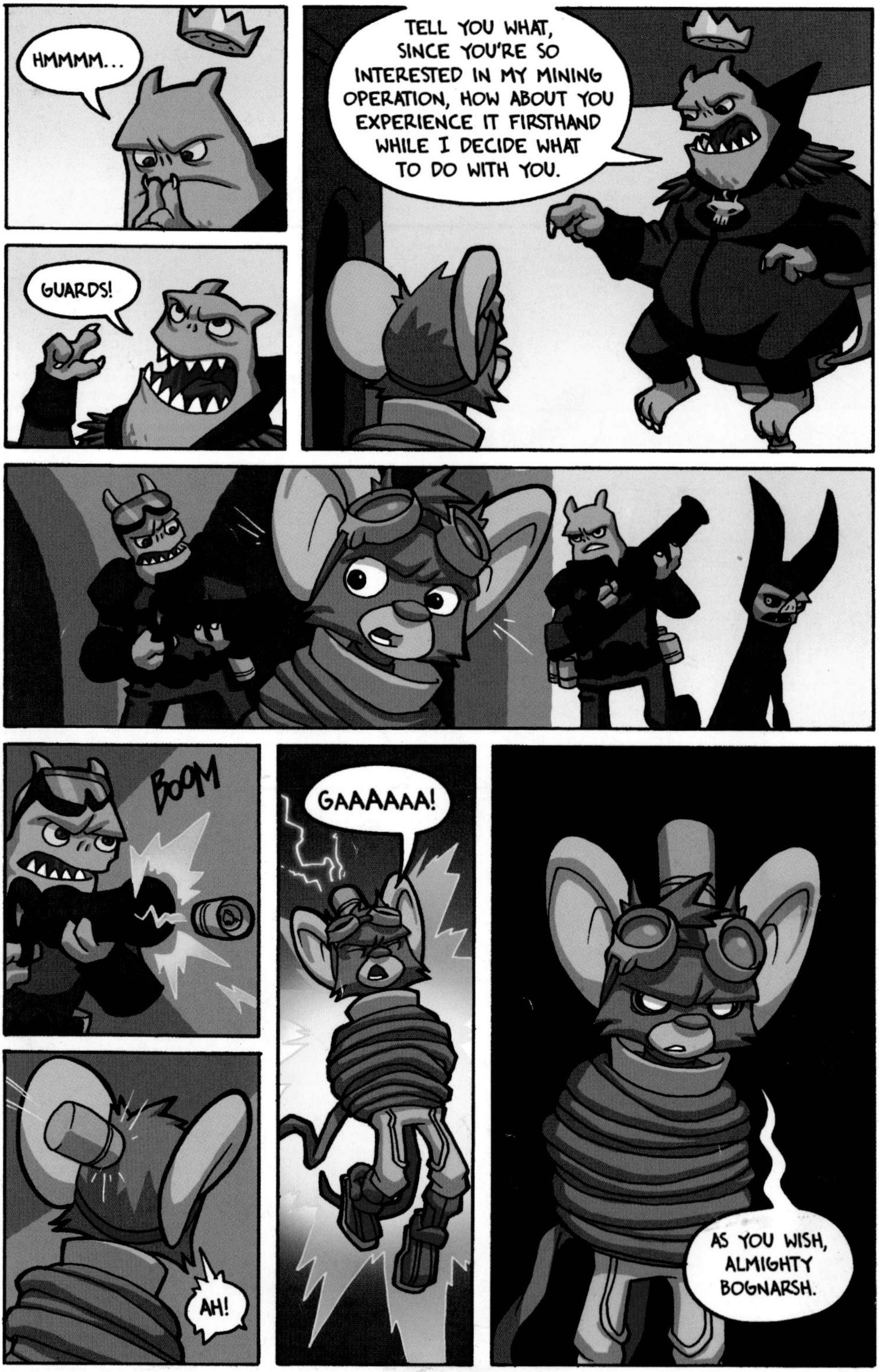
HMMMM...
TELL YOU WHAT, SINCE YOU'RE SO INTERESTED IN MY MINING OPERATION, HOW ABOUT YOU EXPERIENCE IT FIRSTHAND WHILE I DECIDE WHAT TO DO WITH YOU.
GUARDS!
BOOM
GAAAAAA!
AH!
AS YOU WISH, ALMIGHTY BOGNARSH.

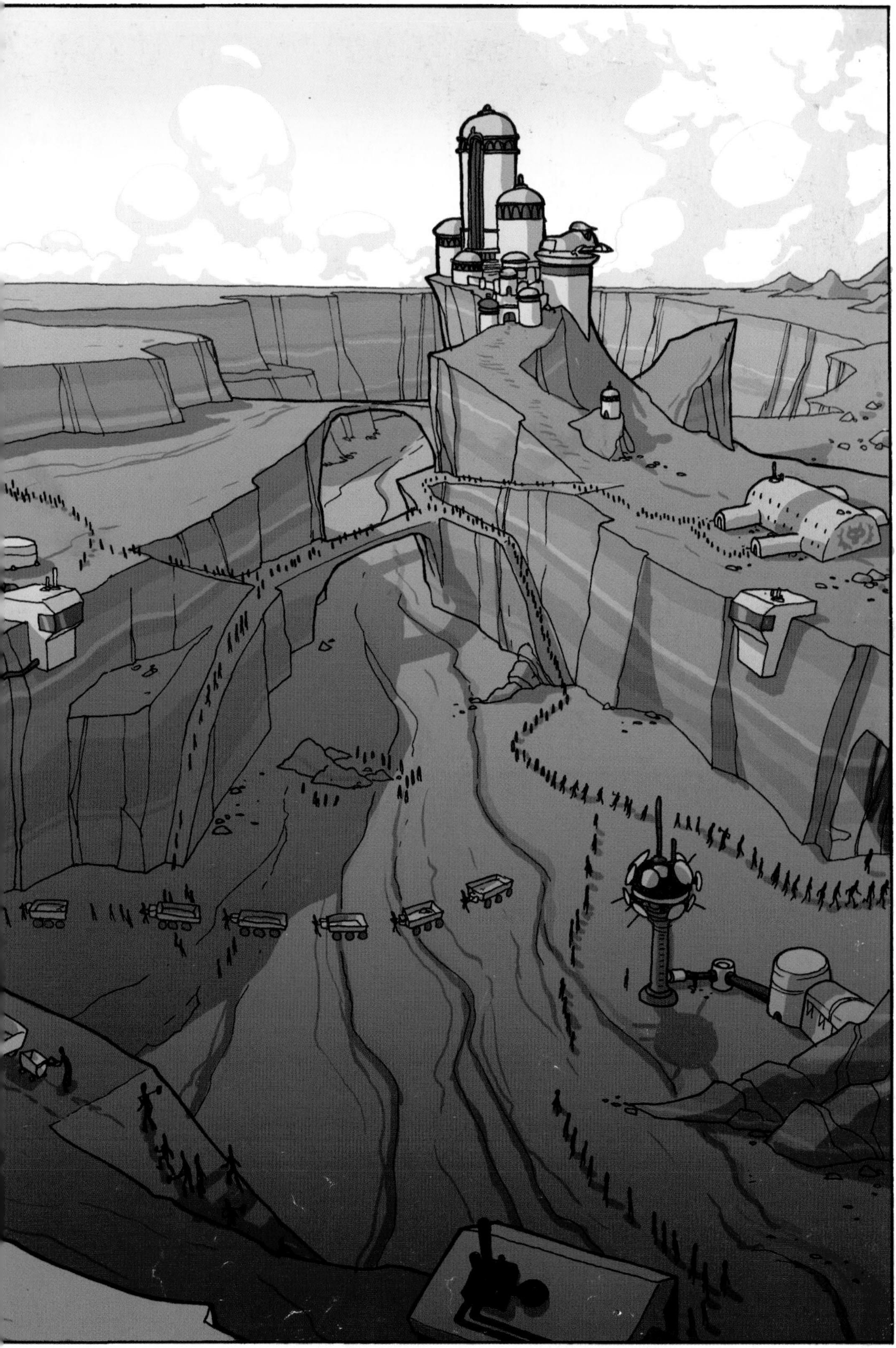

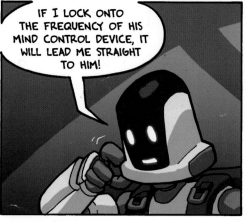

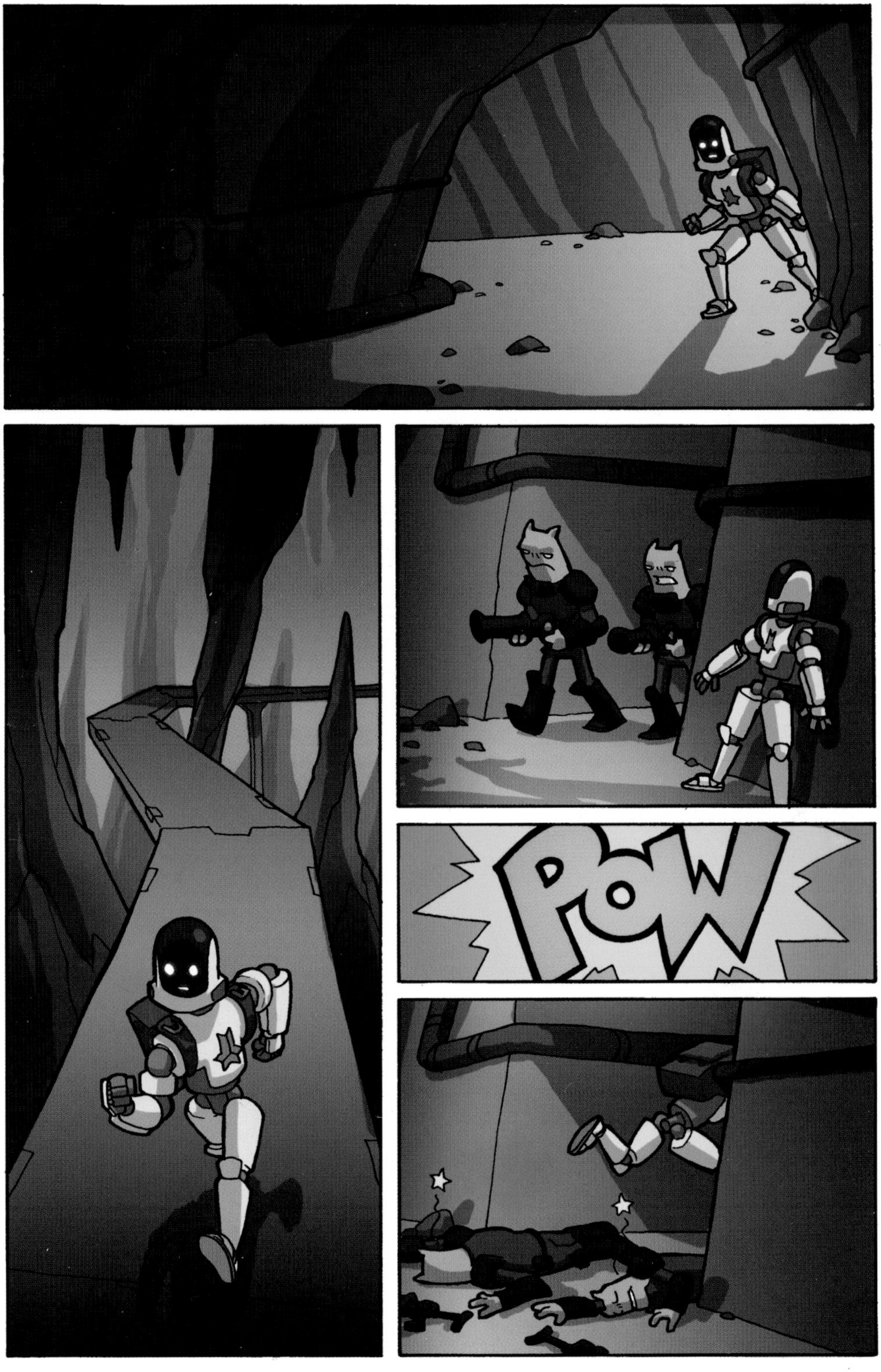
POW

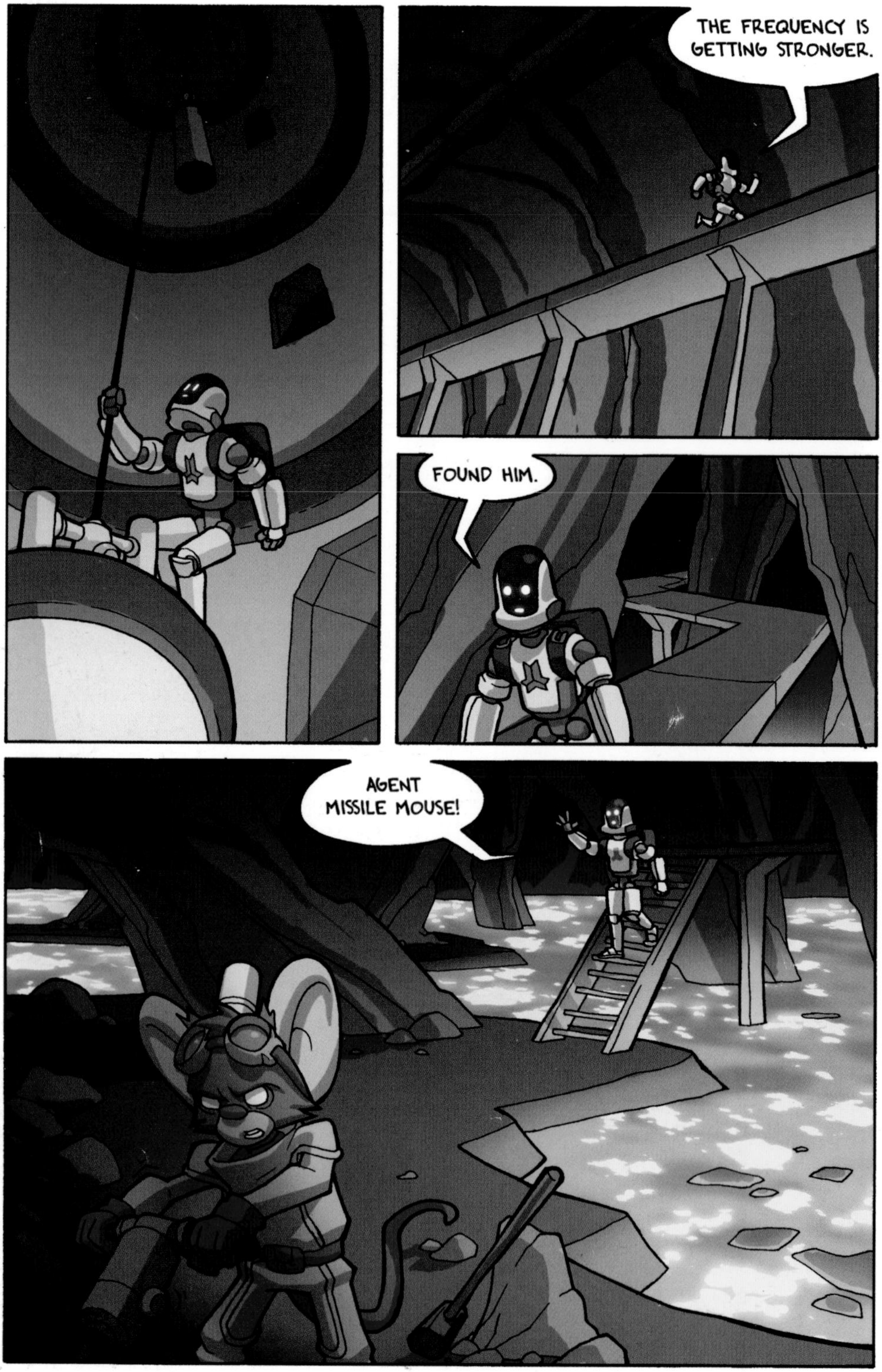
THE FREQUENCY IS GETTING STRONGER.
FOUND HIM.
AGENT MISSILE MOUSE!

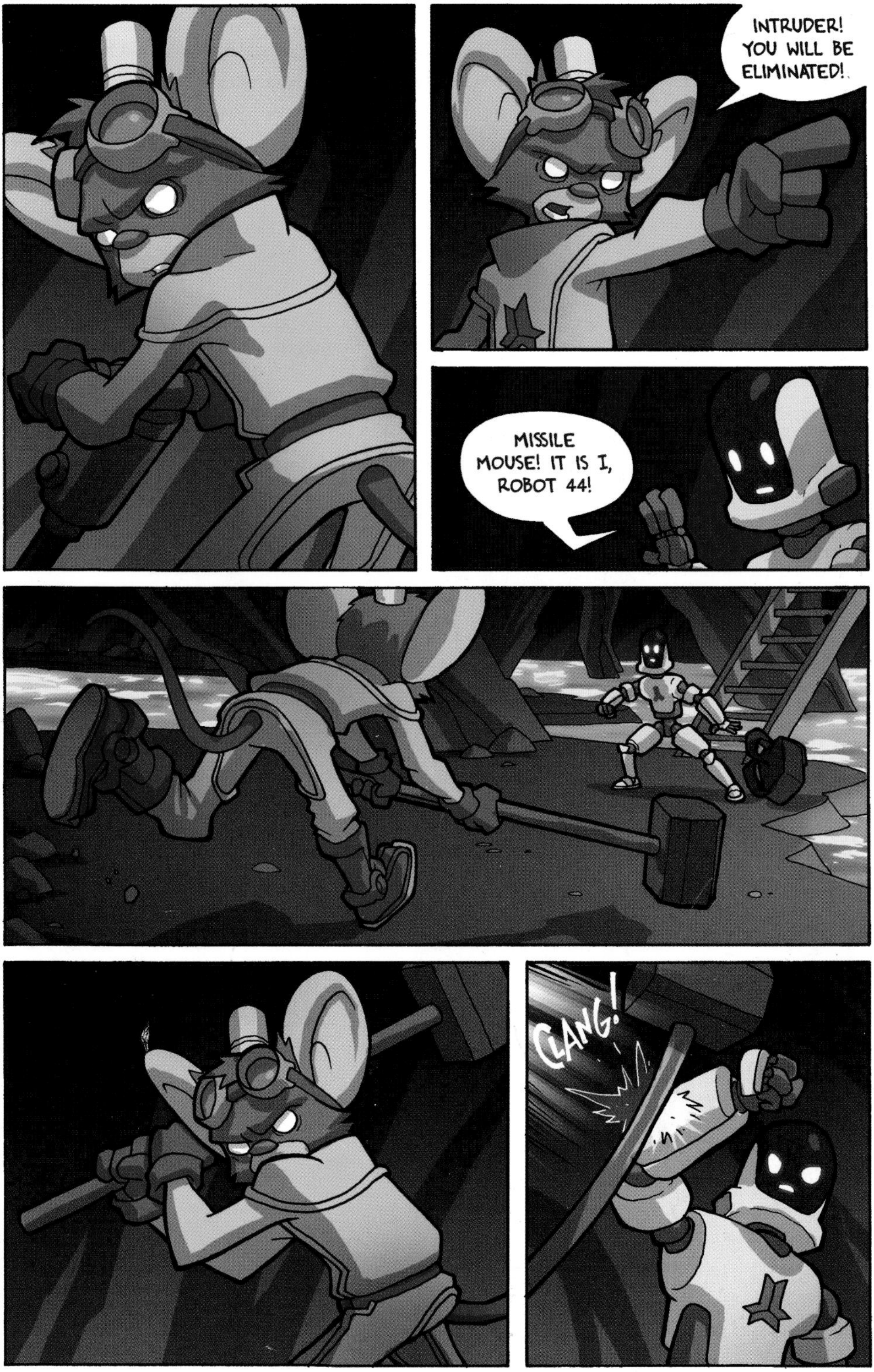
INTRUDER! YOU WILL BE ELIMINATED!
MISSILE MOUSE! IT IS I, ROBOT 44!
CLANG!

WHACK!

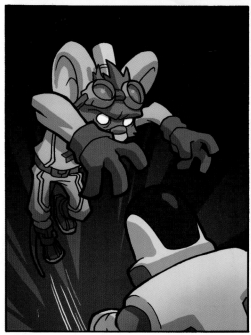

BAM!

WHIP!

CRACK!

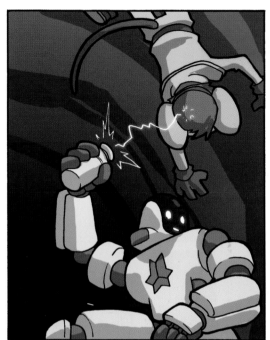

44...WHAT'S GOING ON?

YOU HAD A MIND CONTROL DEVICE ATTACHED TO YOU.

ALL OF THE SLAVES ARE RECEIVING ORDERS FROM A CENTRAL ANTENNA ARRAY, WHICH LASUKUS IS TRYING TO DISABLE.

OOOH, MY HEAD.

WUMP!

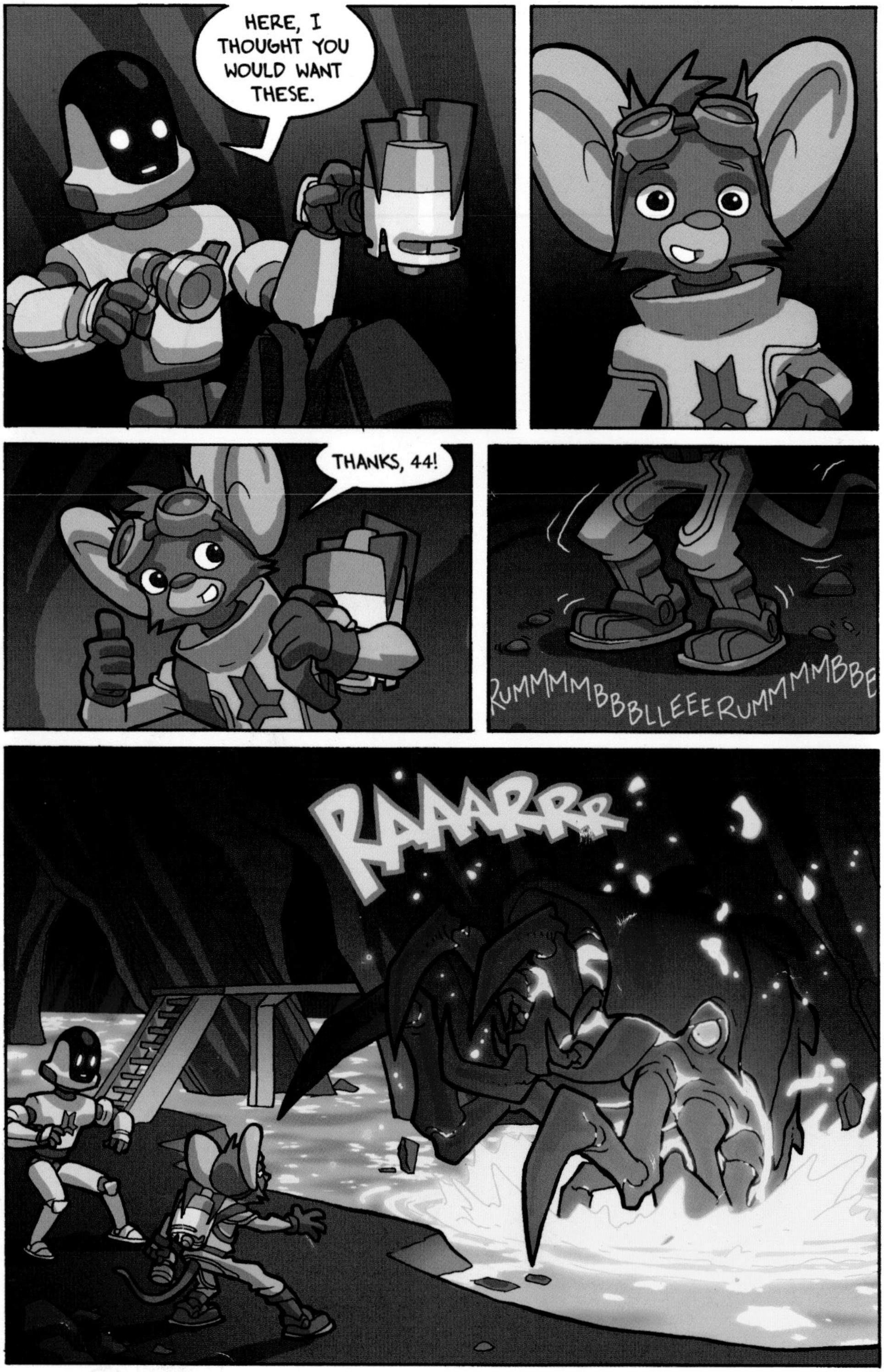
HERE, I THOUGHT YOU WOULD WANT THESE.
THANKS, 44!
RUMMMMBBBLLEEERUMMMMBBE
RAAARRR

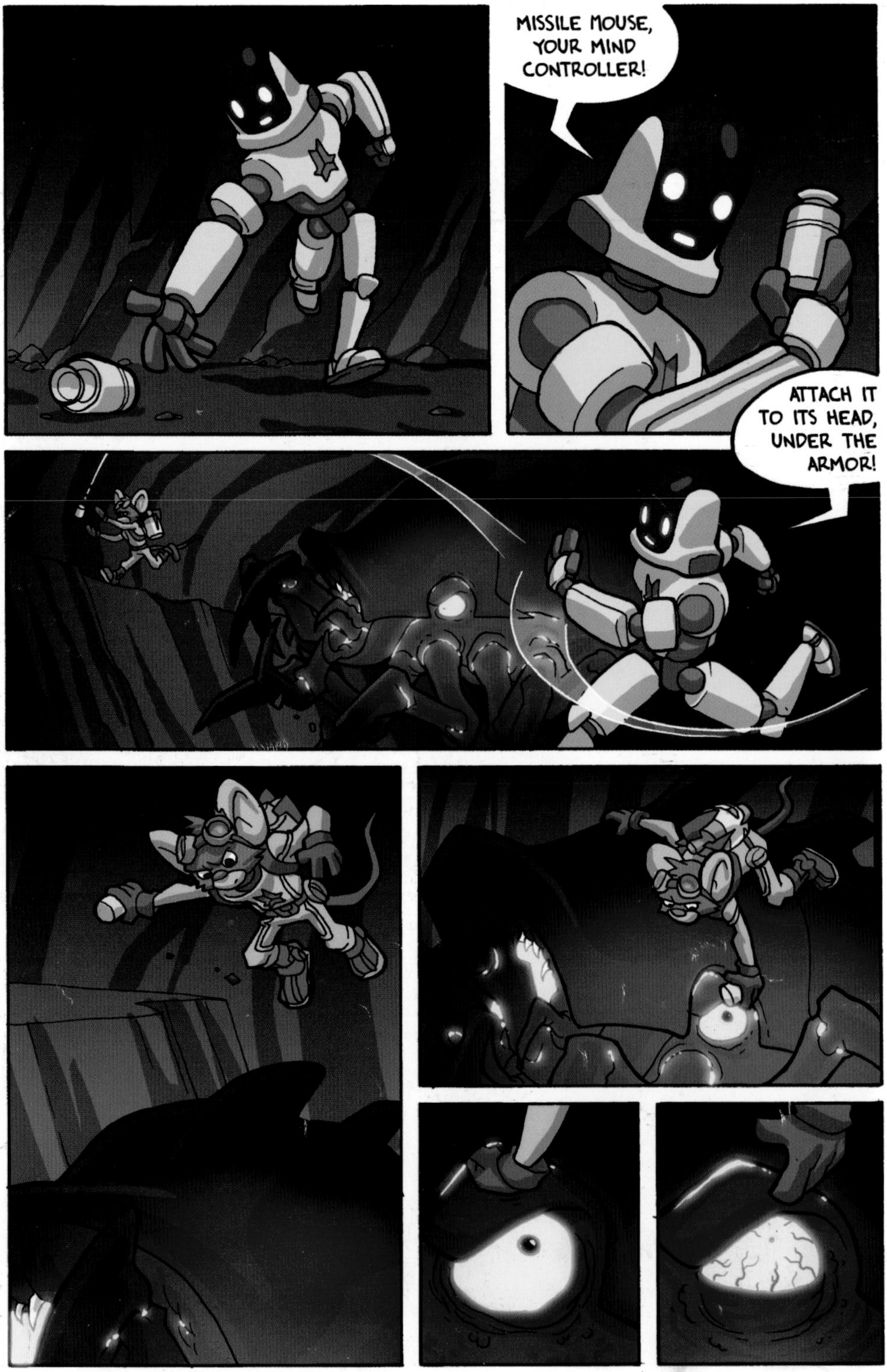
MISSILE MOUSE, YOUR MIND CONTROLLER!
ATTACH IT TO ITS HEAD, UNDER THE ARMOR!

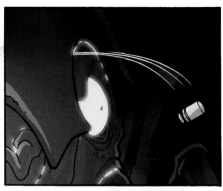

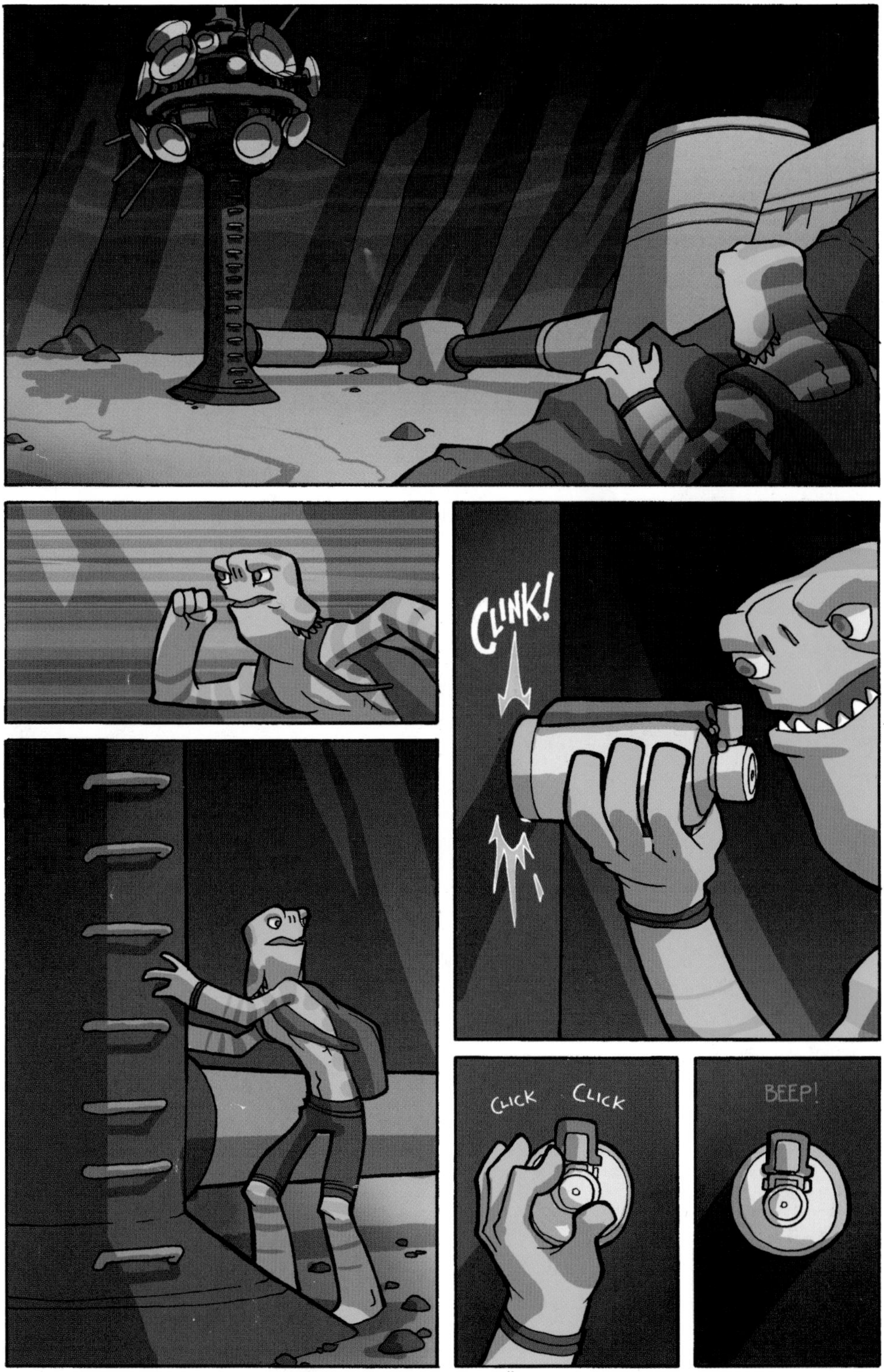
CLINK!
CLICK CLICK
BEEP!

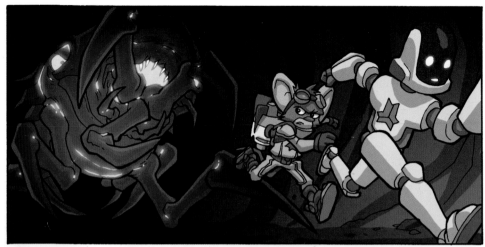

LOOK!

THAT PIPE CARRIES A COOLANT FOR THE UNDER-GROUND COOLING SYSTEM.

ARE YOU THINKING WHAT I'M THINKING?

AFFIRMATIVE. I'LL CREATE THE DIVERSION.

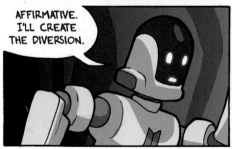

HALT, BEAST!

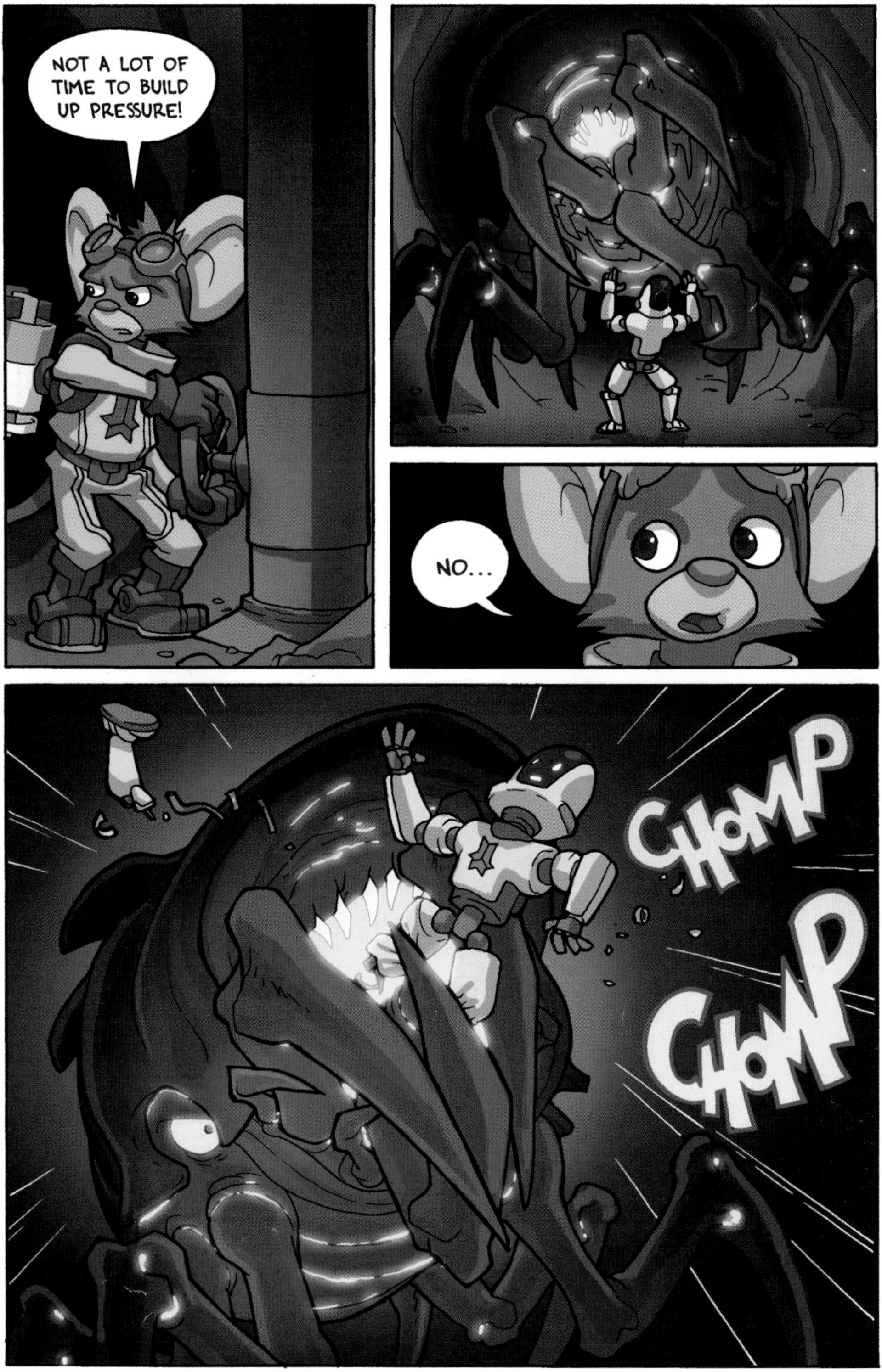
NOT A LOT OF TIME TO BUILD UP PRESSURE!
NO...
CHOMP
CHOMP

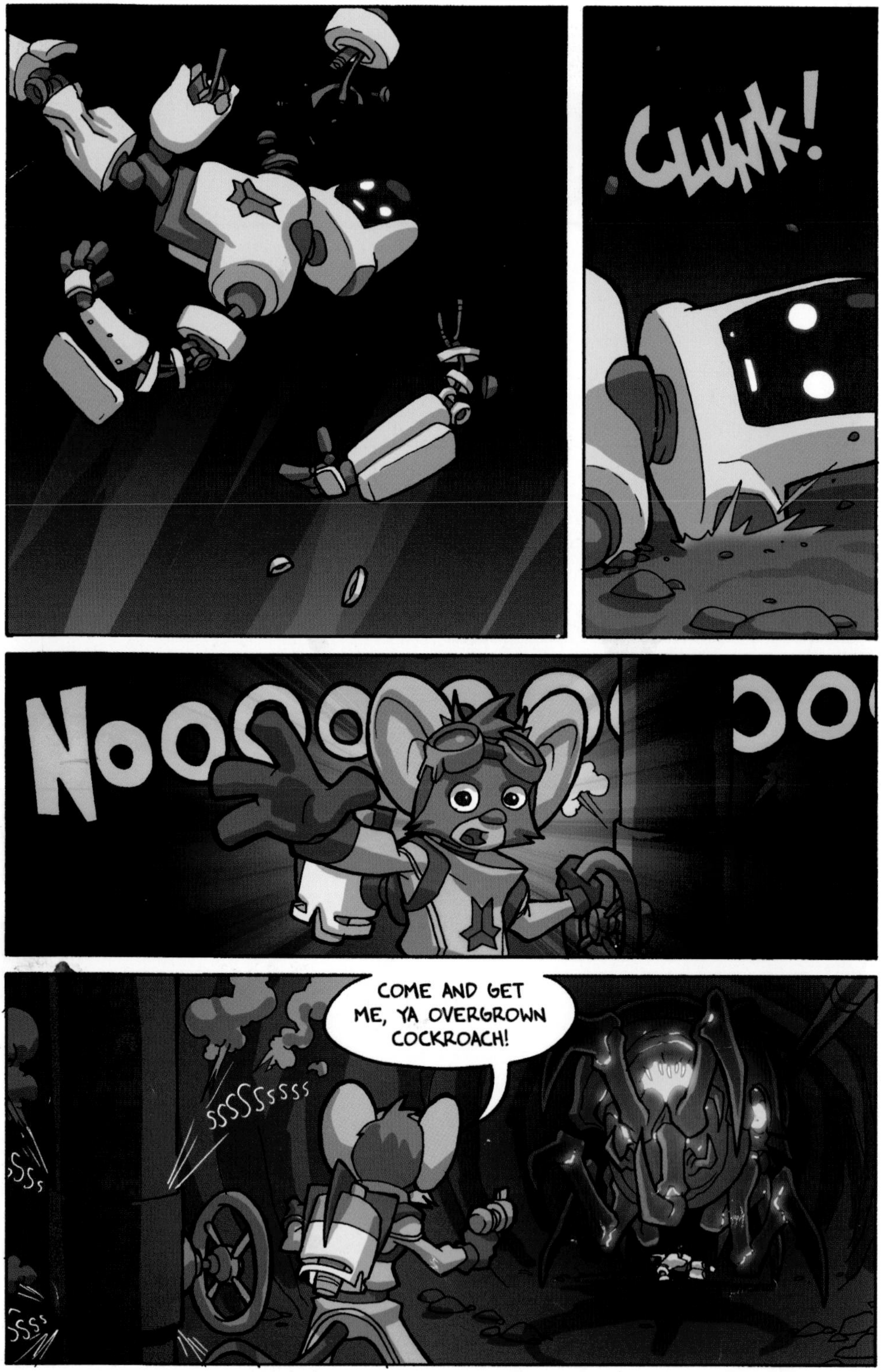
CLUNK!
NOOOOOOOO
COME AND GET ME, YA OVERGROWN COCKROACH!
SSSSSSSSS

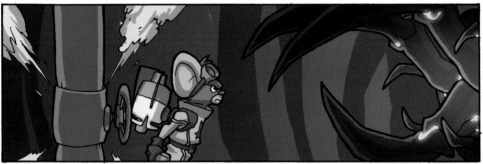

BRANG!

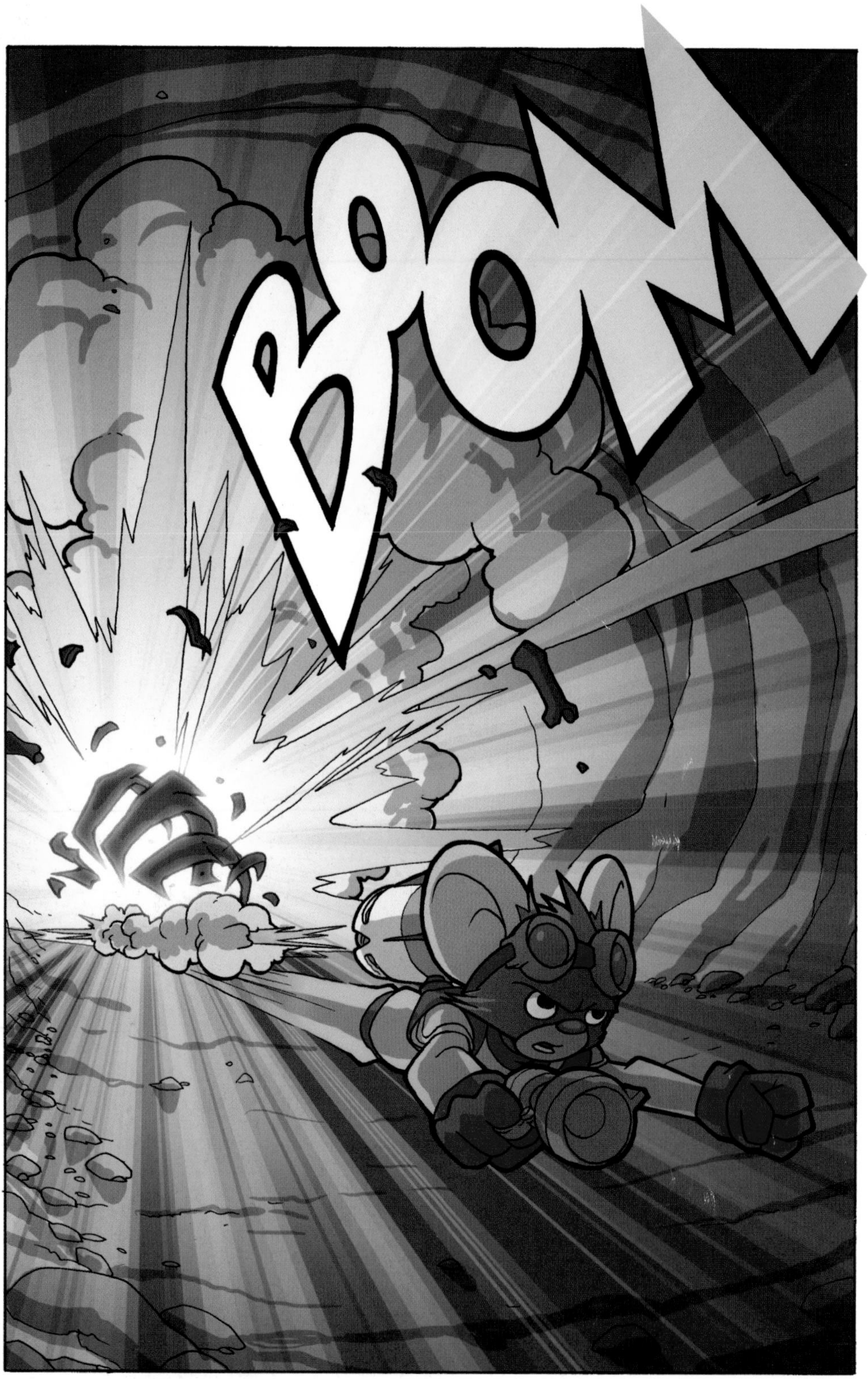
BOOM

44!

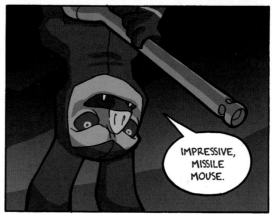

IMPRESSIVE, MISSILE MOUSE.

BWOOSH

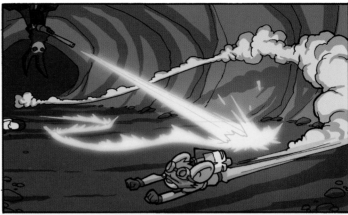

SHOOT, WHERE'S MY BLASTER?!

DANG IT!

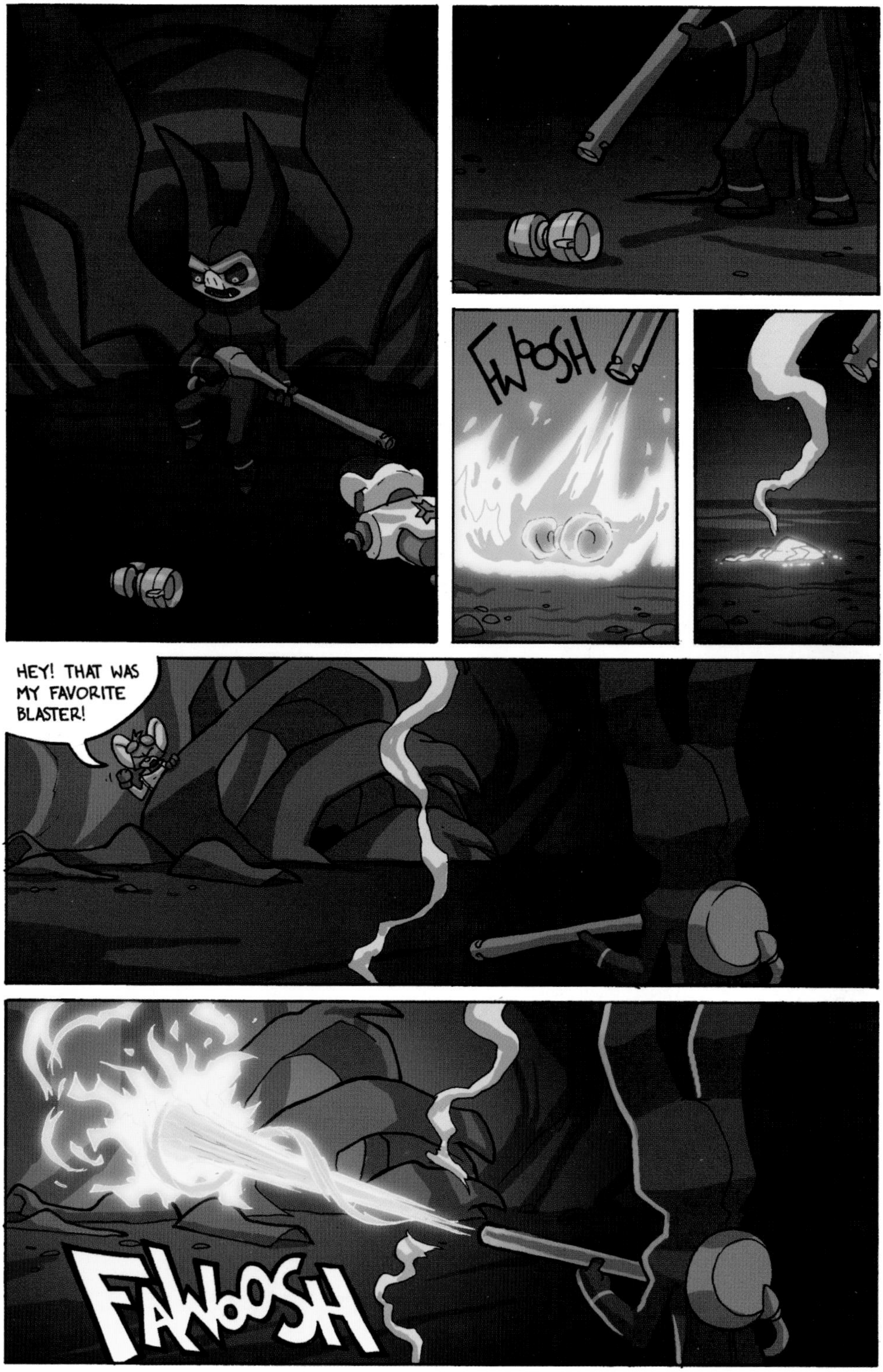
FWOOSH
HEY! THAT WAS MY FAVORITE BLASTER!
FAWOOSH

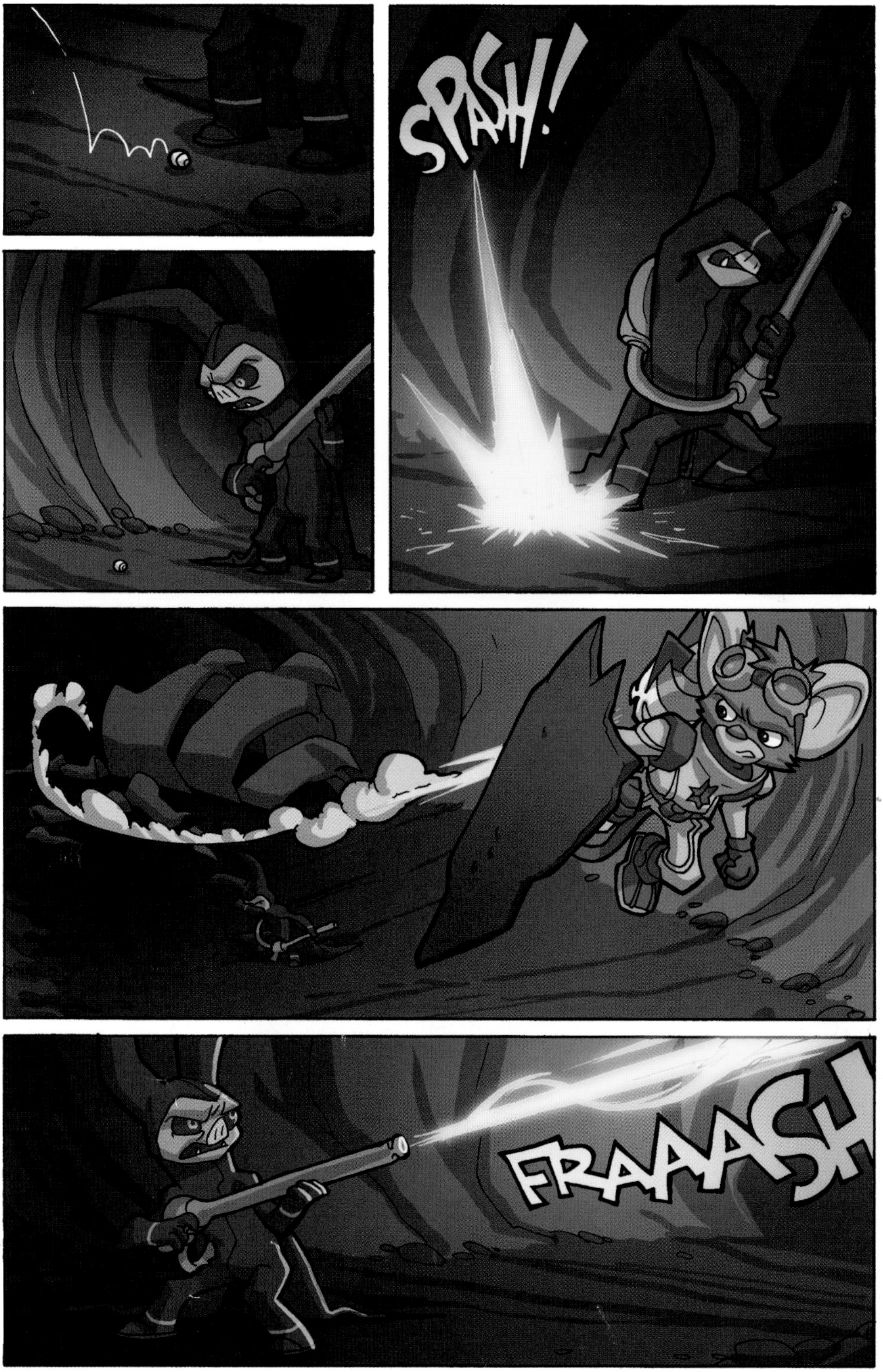
SPASH!
FRAAASH

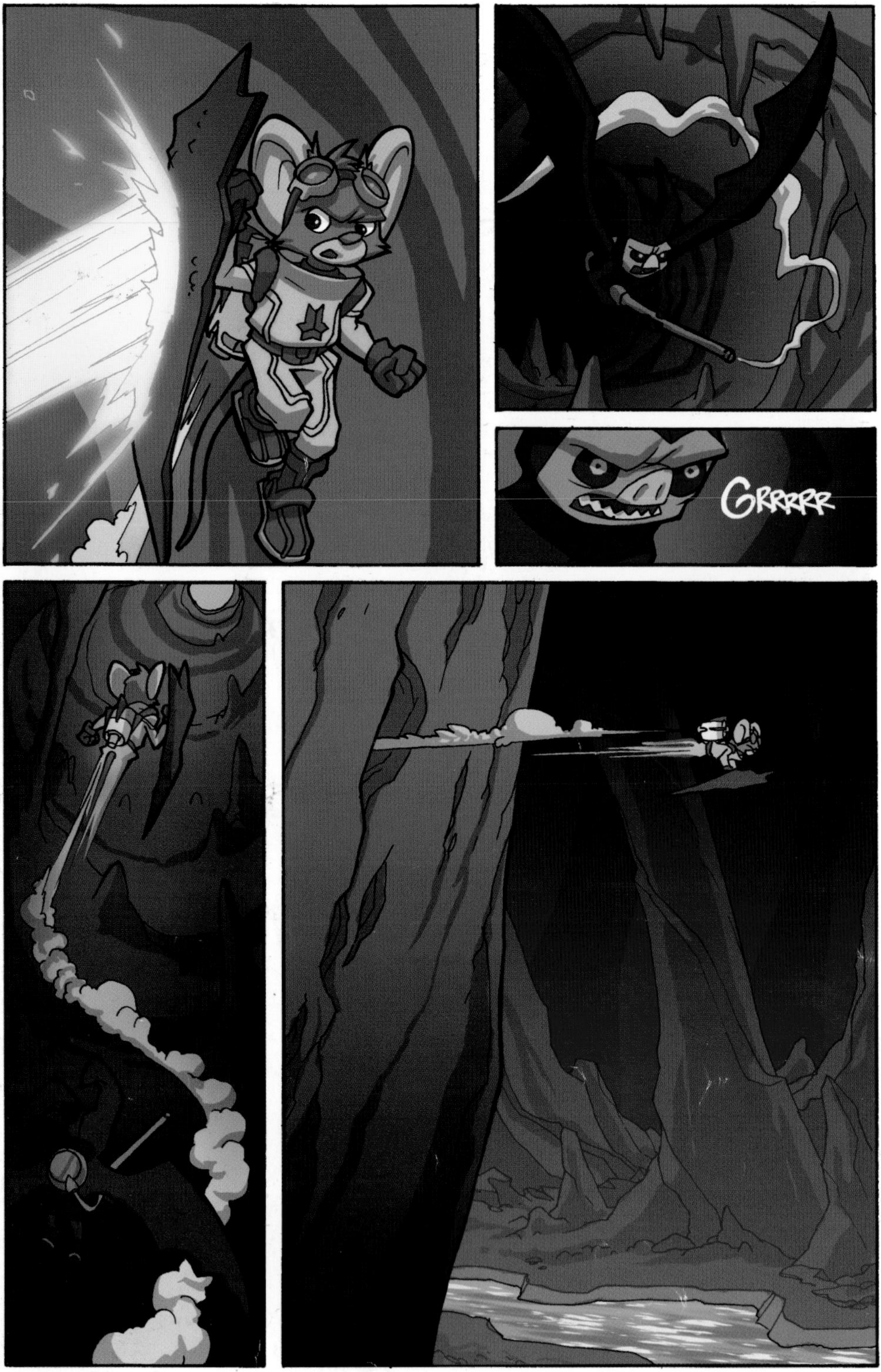
GRRRRR

AH!

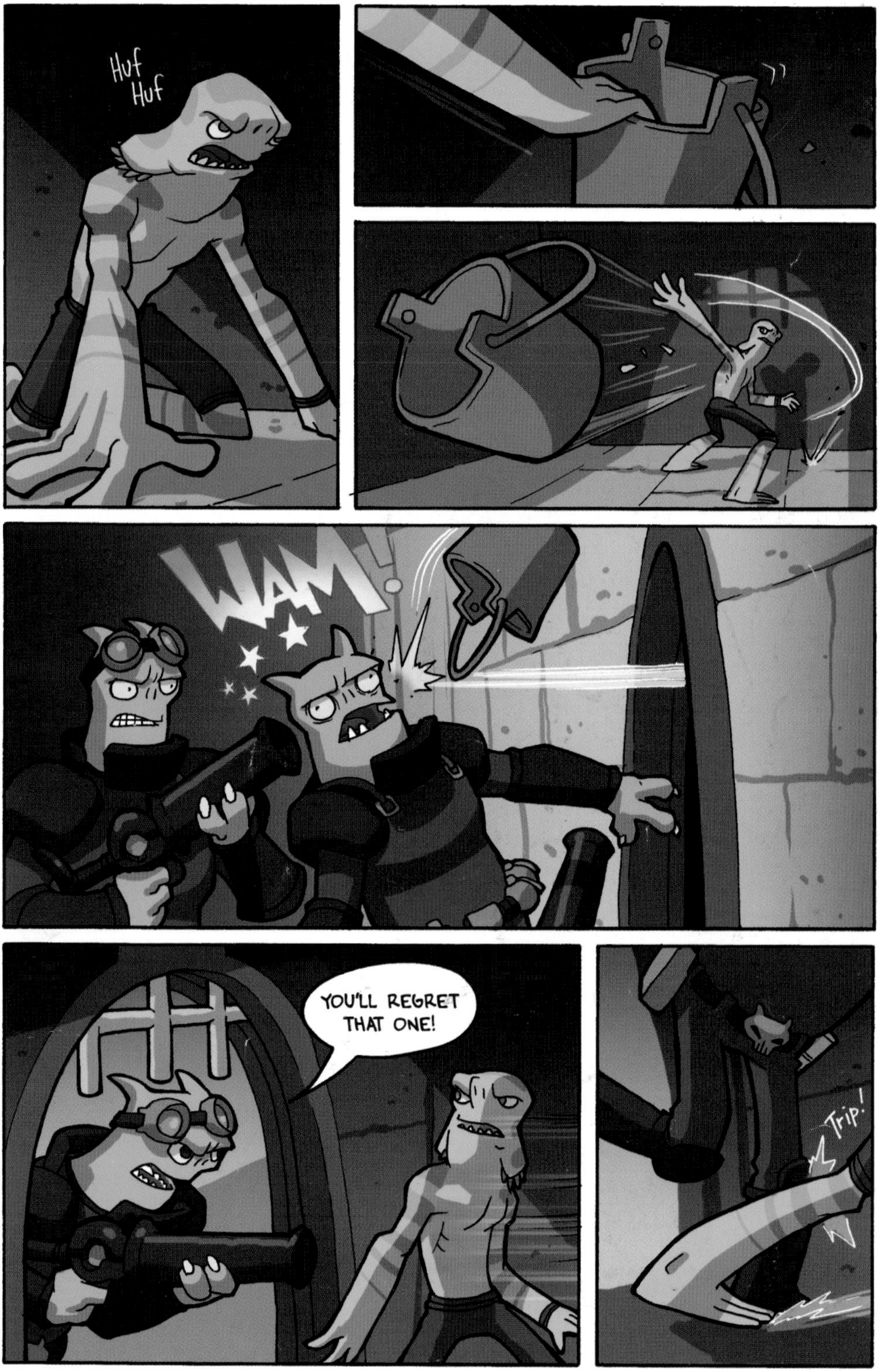
Huf
Huf
WAM!
YOU'LL REGRET THAT ONE!
Trip!

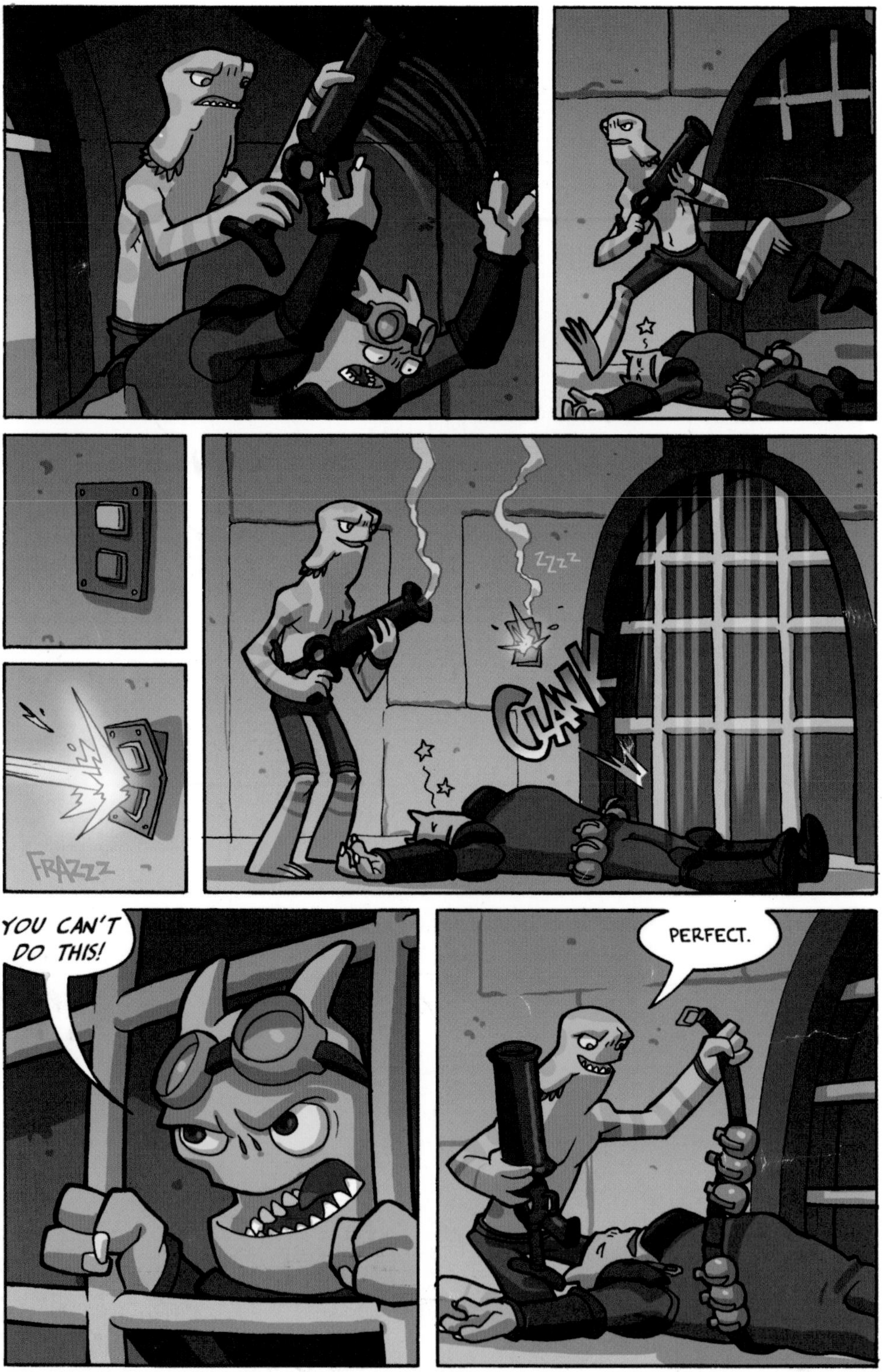
ZZZZ
CLANK
FRAZZZ
YOU CAN'T DO THIS!
PERFECT.

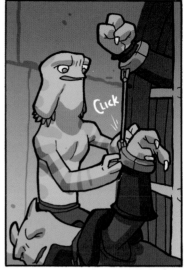

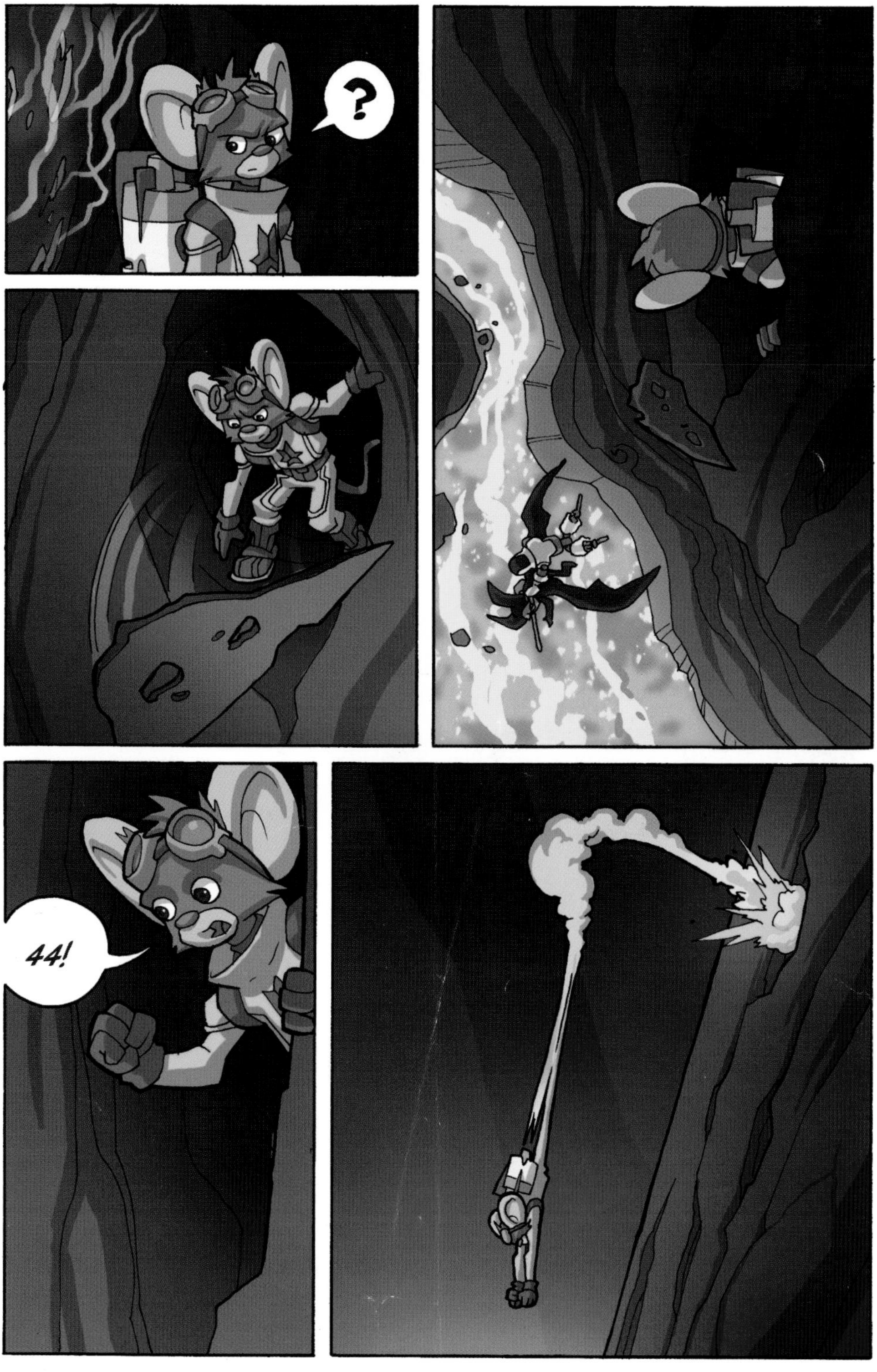
?
44!

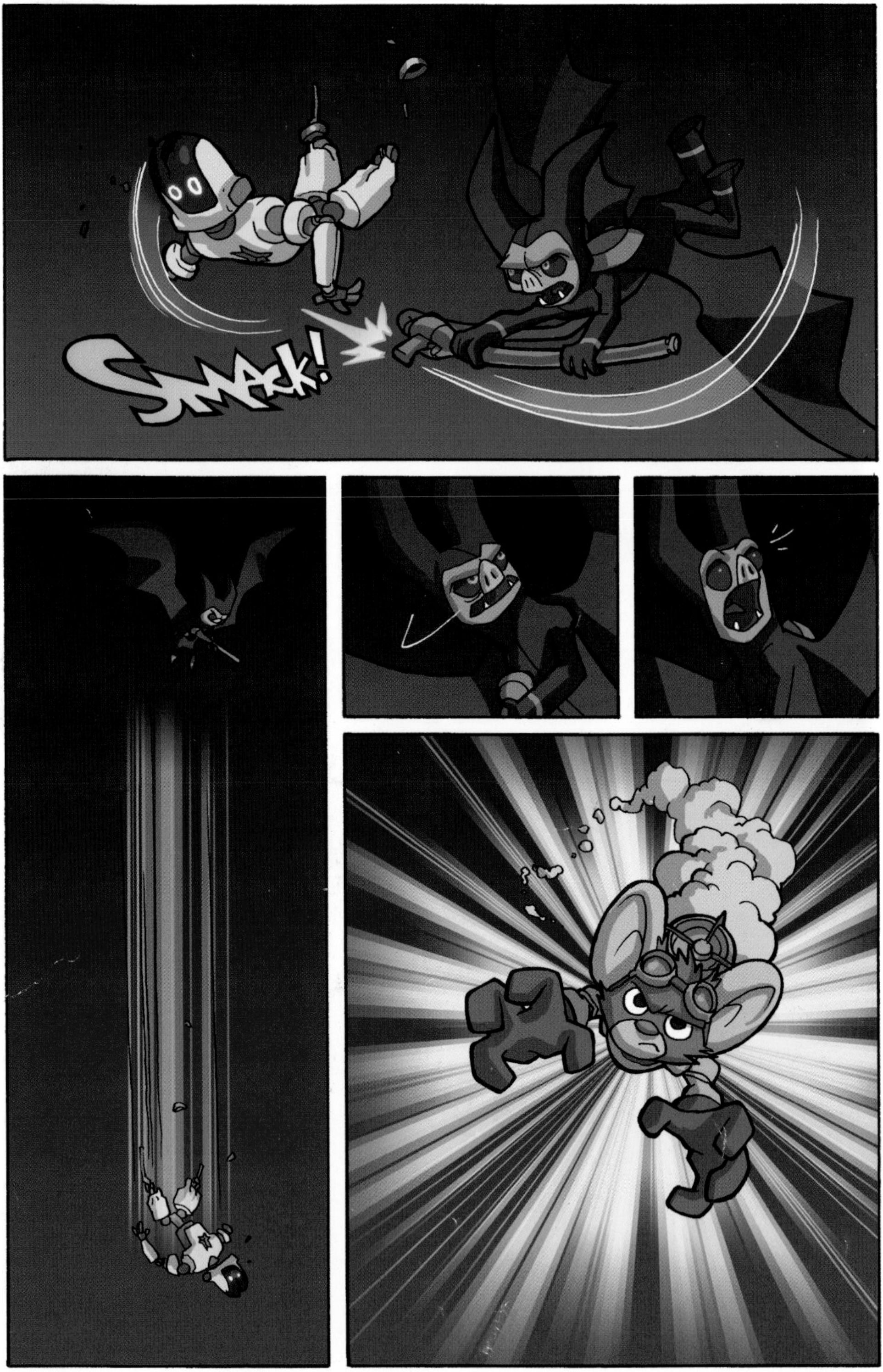
SMACK!

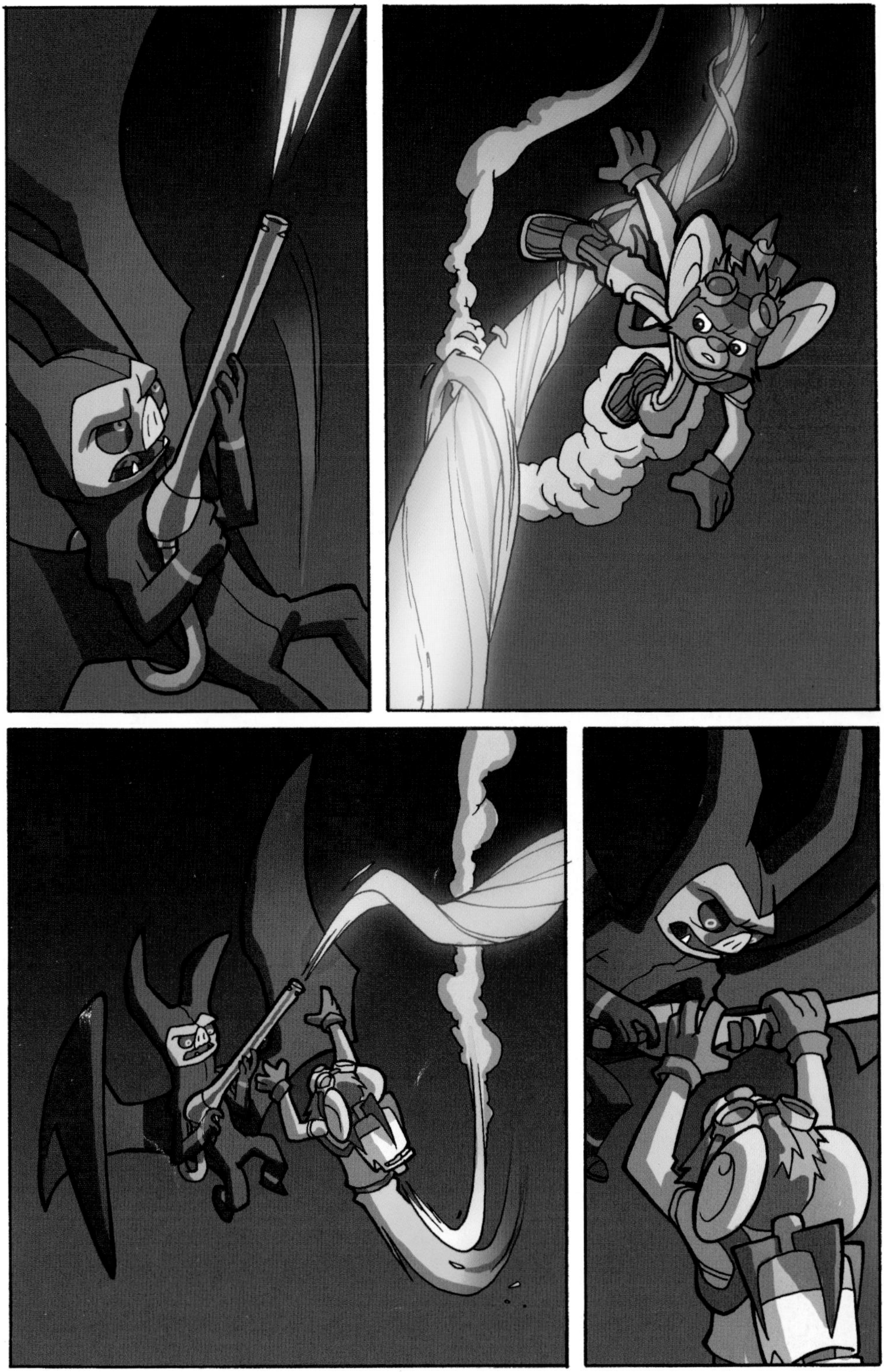

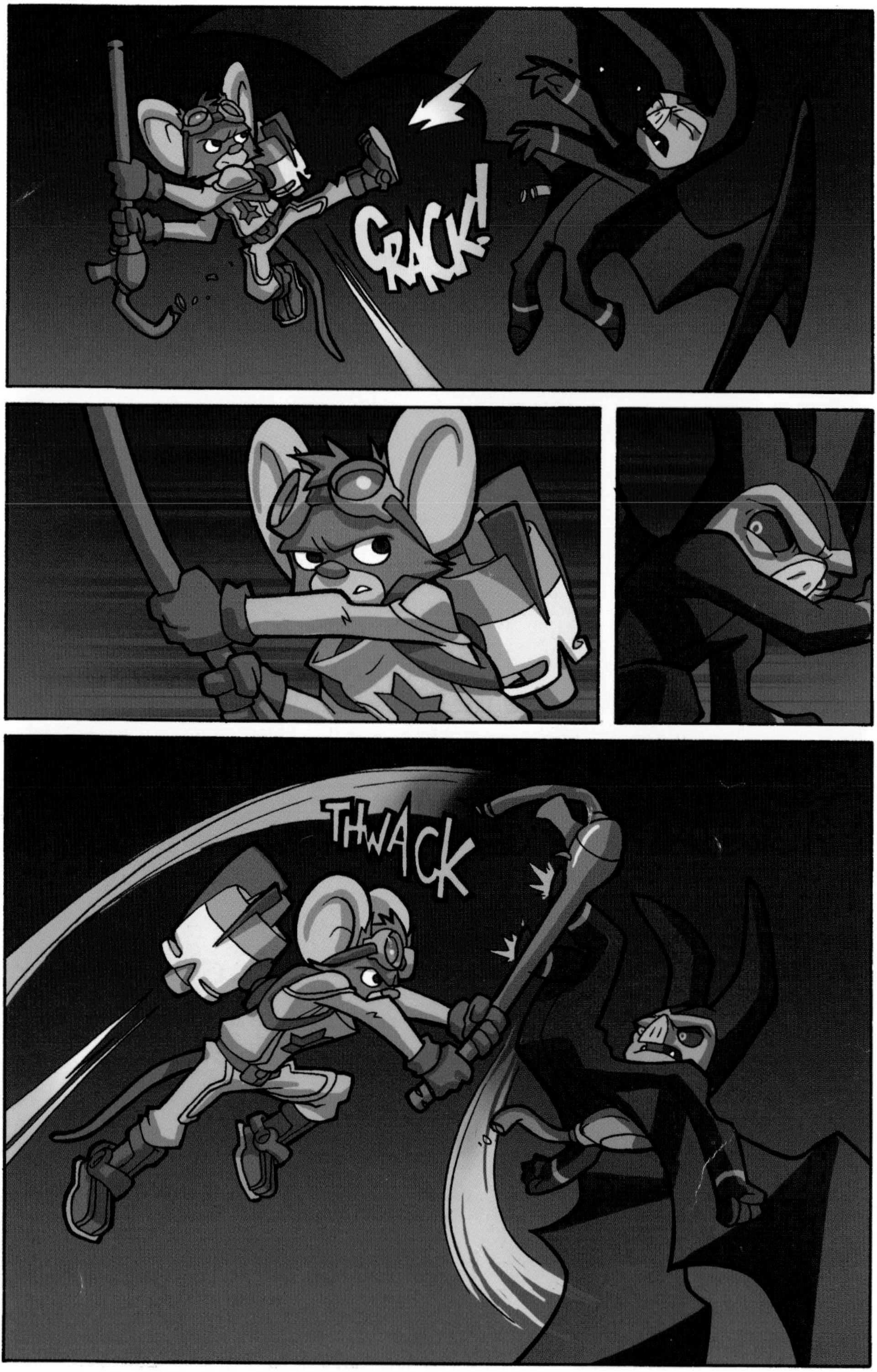
CRACK!
THWACK

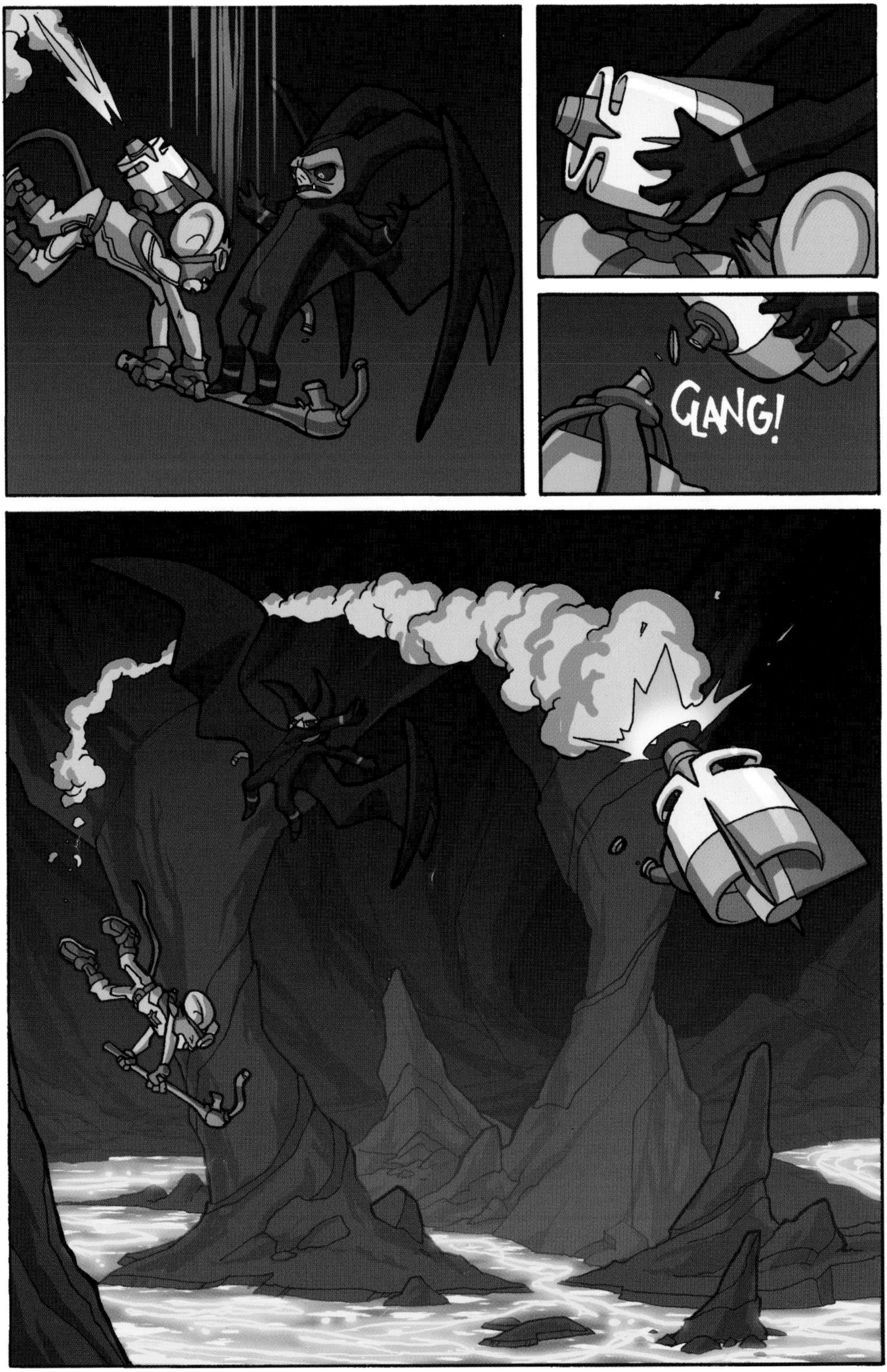
CLANG!

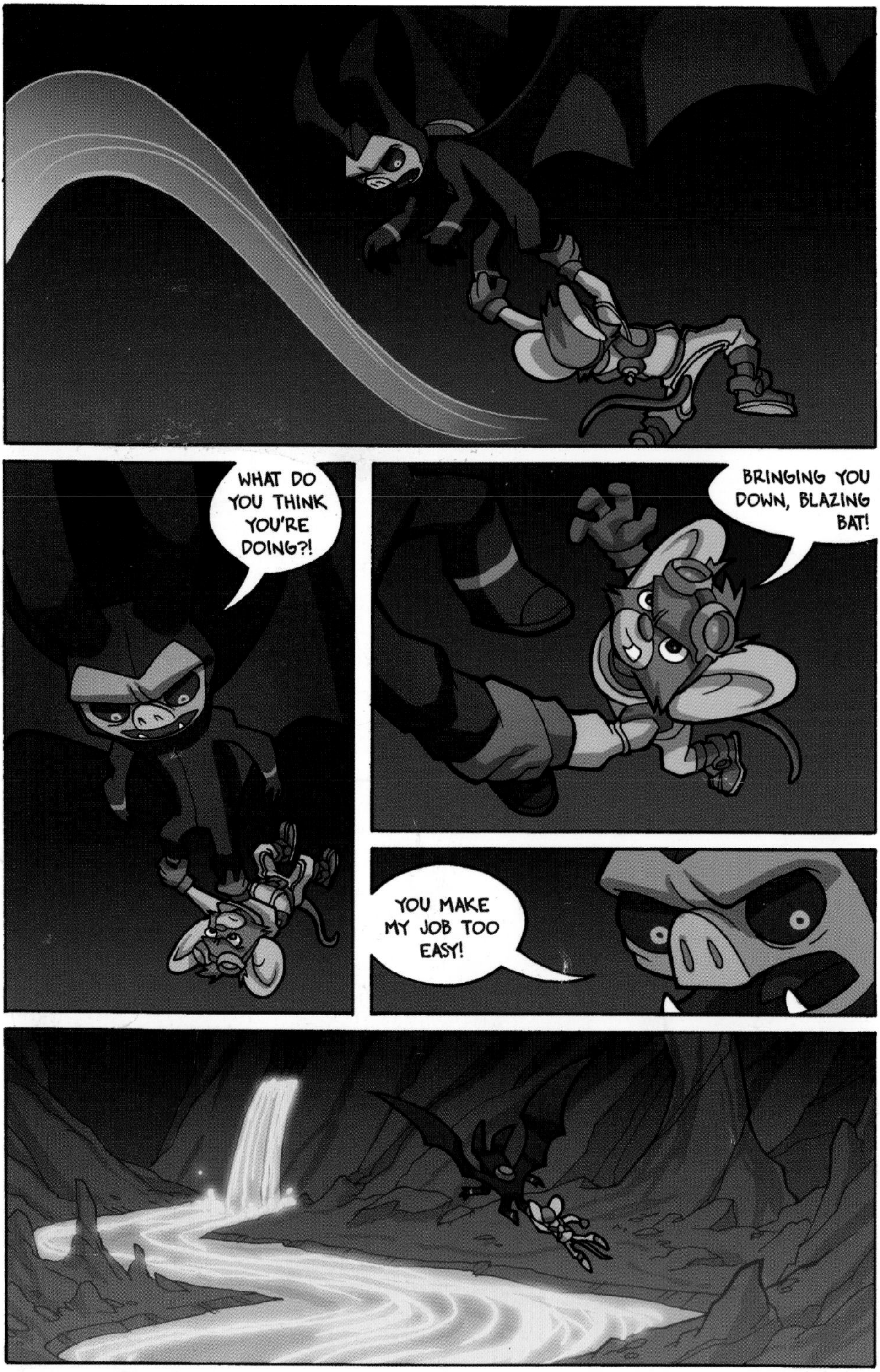
WHAT DO YOU THINK YOU'RE DOING?!
BRINGING YOU DOWN, BLAZING BAT!
YOU MAKE MY JOB TOO EASY!

WAY TOO
EASY.

BLOP

CLICK

WHA-?

WHIP

WHIP

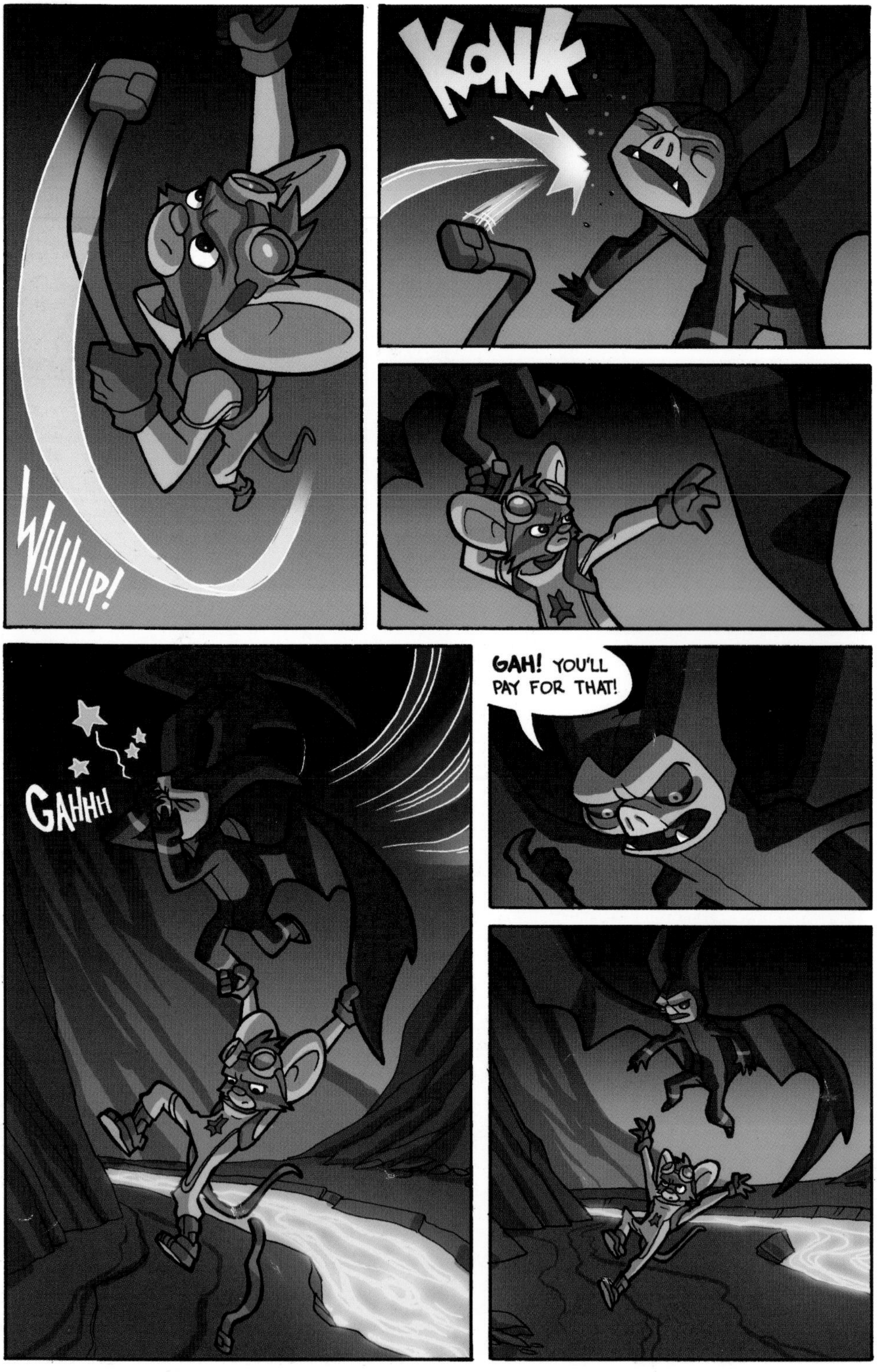
WHIIIIP!
KONK
GAHHH
GAH! YOU'LL PAY FOR THAT!

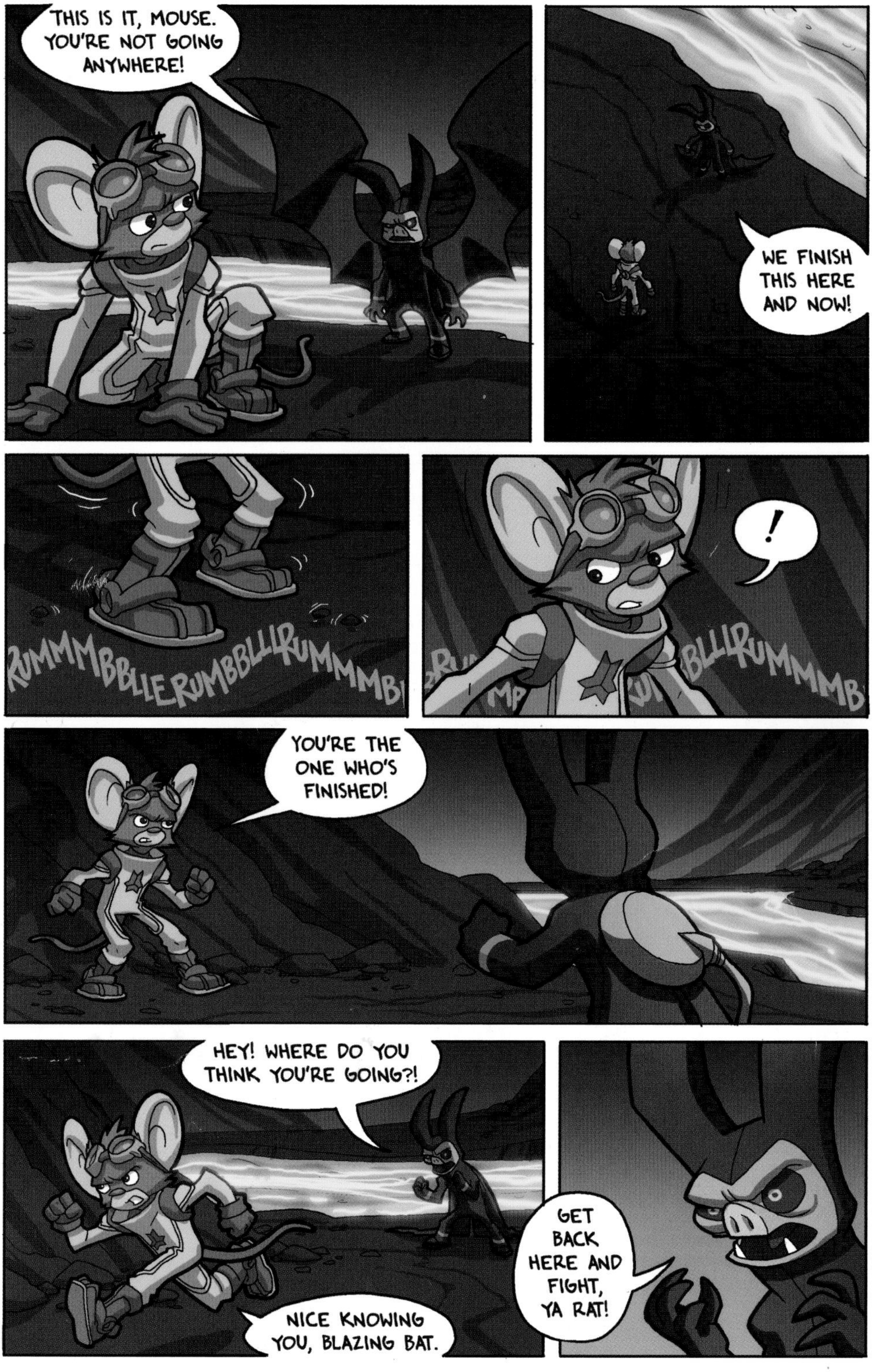
THIS IS IT, MOUSE. YOU'RE NOT GOING ANYWHERE!
WE FINISH THIS HERE AND NOW!
RUMMMBBLLE RUMBBLLLRUMMMB
!
BLLLRUMMMB
YOU'RE THE ONE WHO'S FINISHED!
HEY! WHERE DO YOU THINK YOU'RE GOING?!
NICE KNOWING YOU, BLAZING BAT.
GET BACK HERE AND FIGHT, YA RAT!

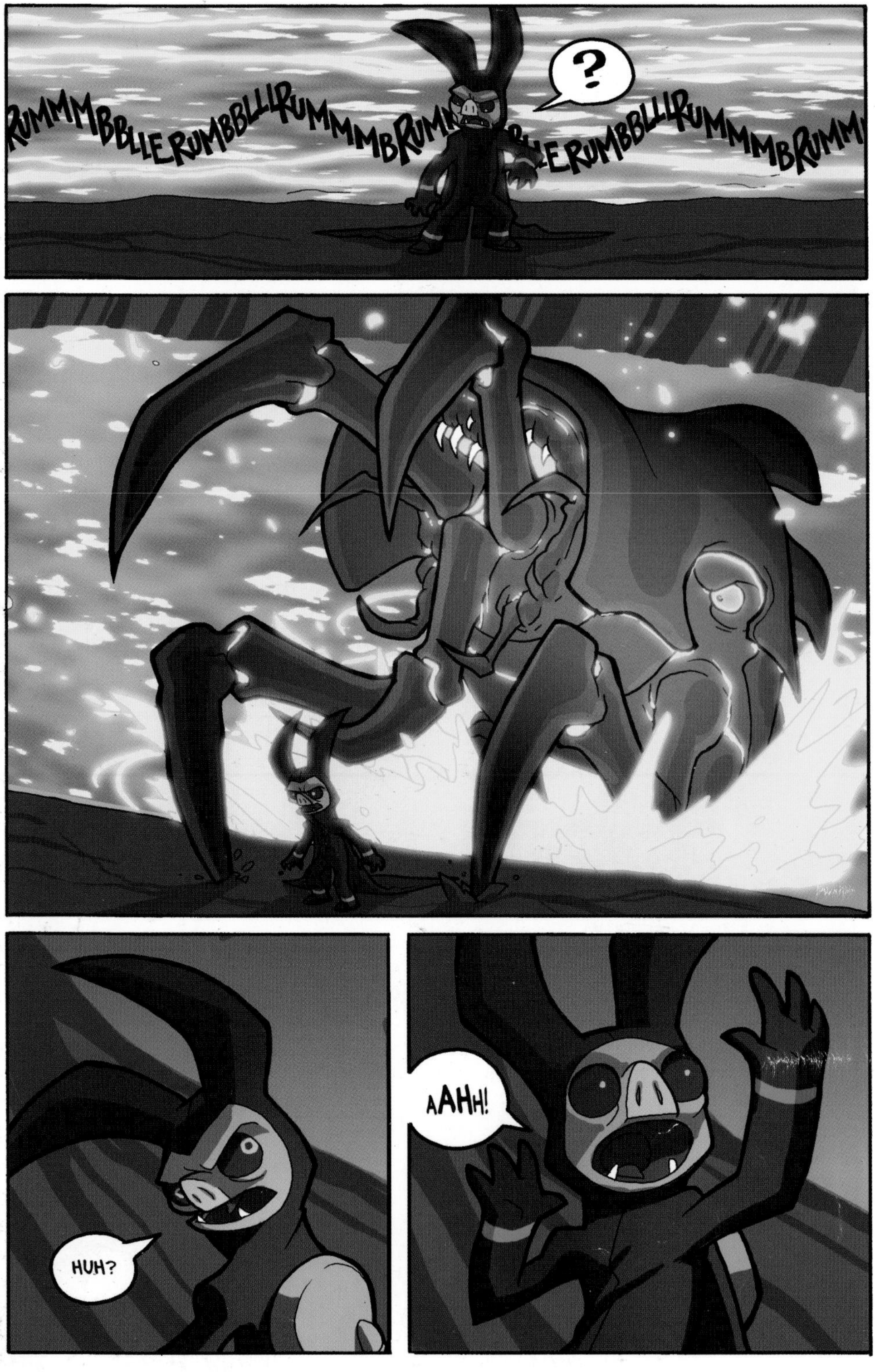
RUMMMBBLLERUMBBLLLRUMMMBRUMM
?
LLERUMBBLLLRUMMMBRUMM
HUH?
AAHH!

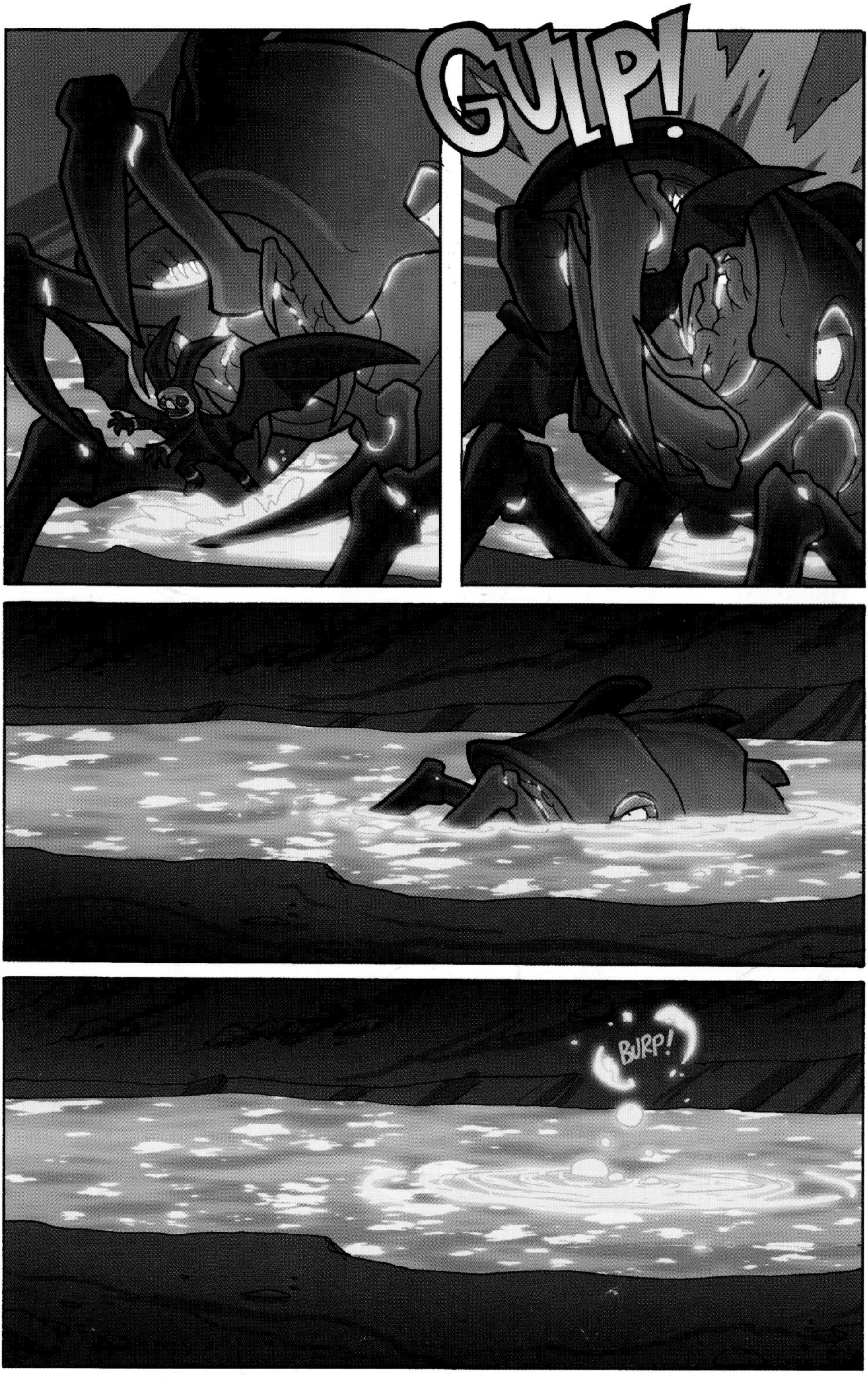
GULP!
BURP!

KING BOGNARSH.

SNORT

AHEM, BOGNARSH!

I AM *SO* SORRY TO INTERRUPT.

IT'S MY TURN TO RIDE THE PONY!

HUH...WHAT? WHAT IS IT?

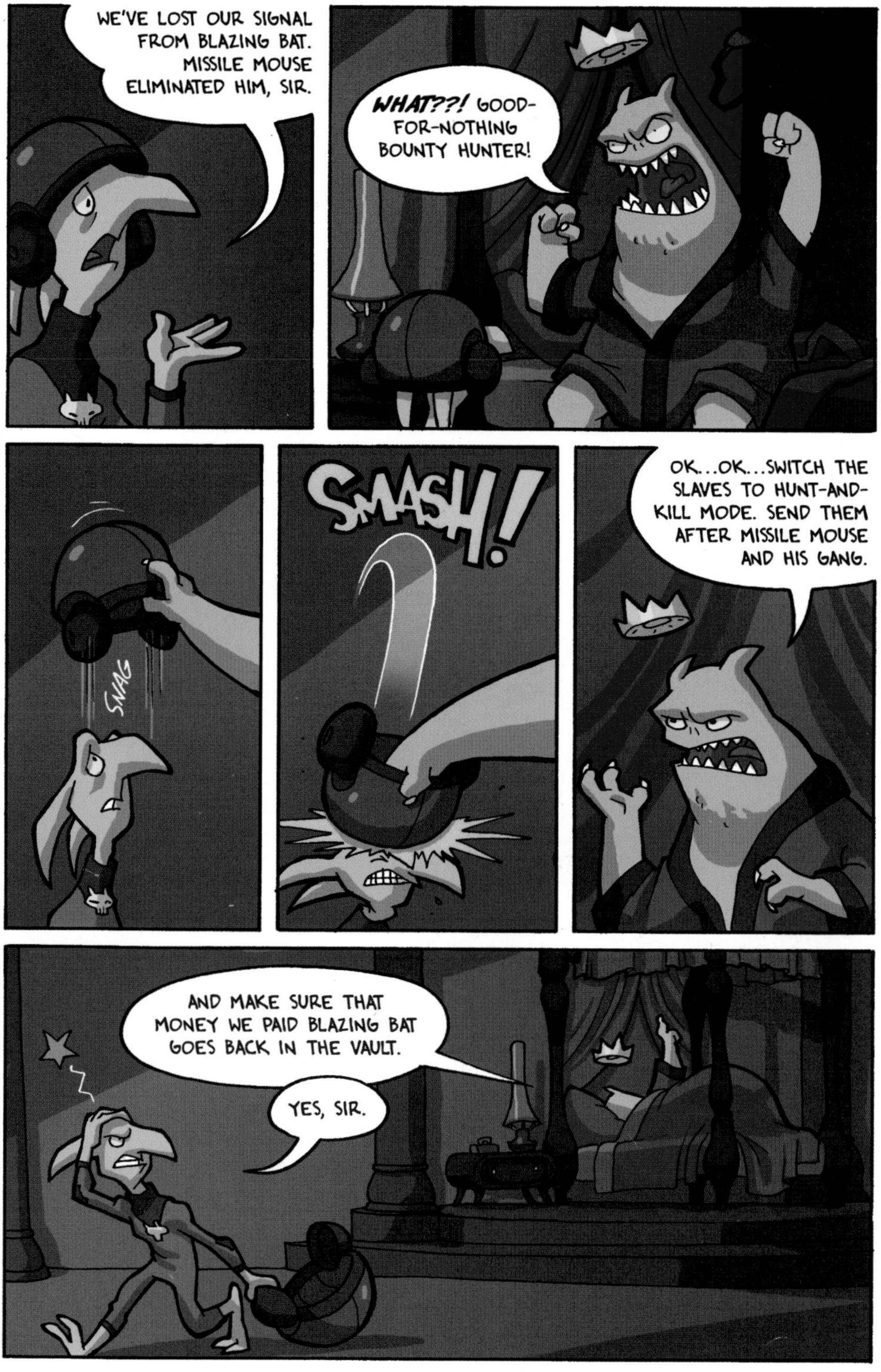
WE'VE LOST OUR SIGNAL FROM BLAZING BAT. MISSILE MOUSE ELIMINATED HIM, SIR.
WHAT??! GOOD-FOR-NOTHING BOUNTY HUNTER!
SNAG
SMASH!
OK...OK...SWITCH THE SLAVES TO HUNT-AND-KILL MODE. SEND THEM AFTER MISSILE MOUSE AND HIS GANG.
AND MAKE SURE THAT MONEY WE PAID BLAZING BAT GOES BACK IN THE VAULT.
YES, SIR.

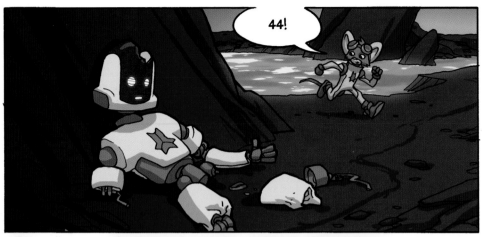

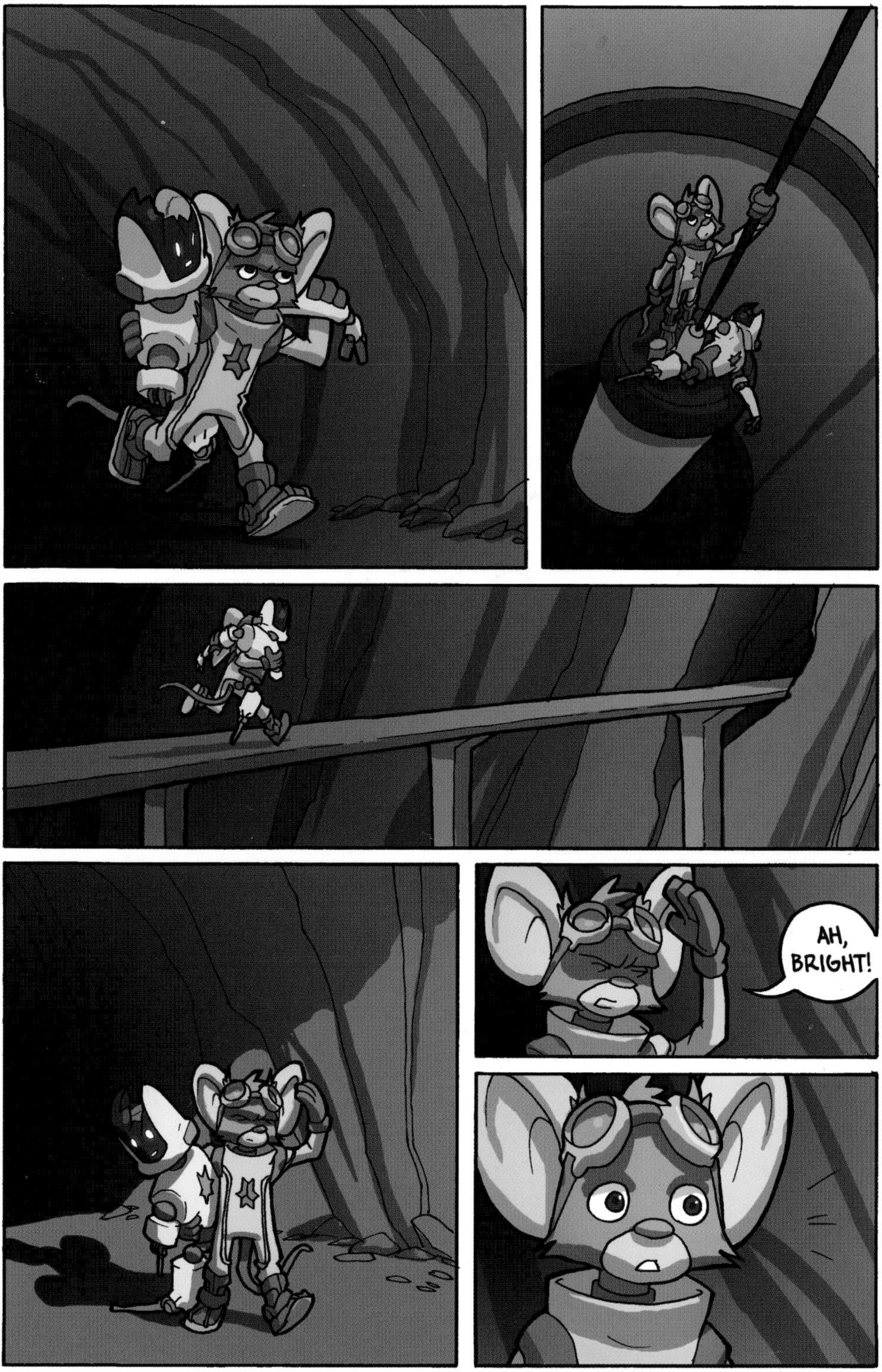
AH,
BRIGHT!

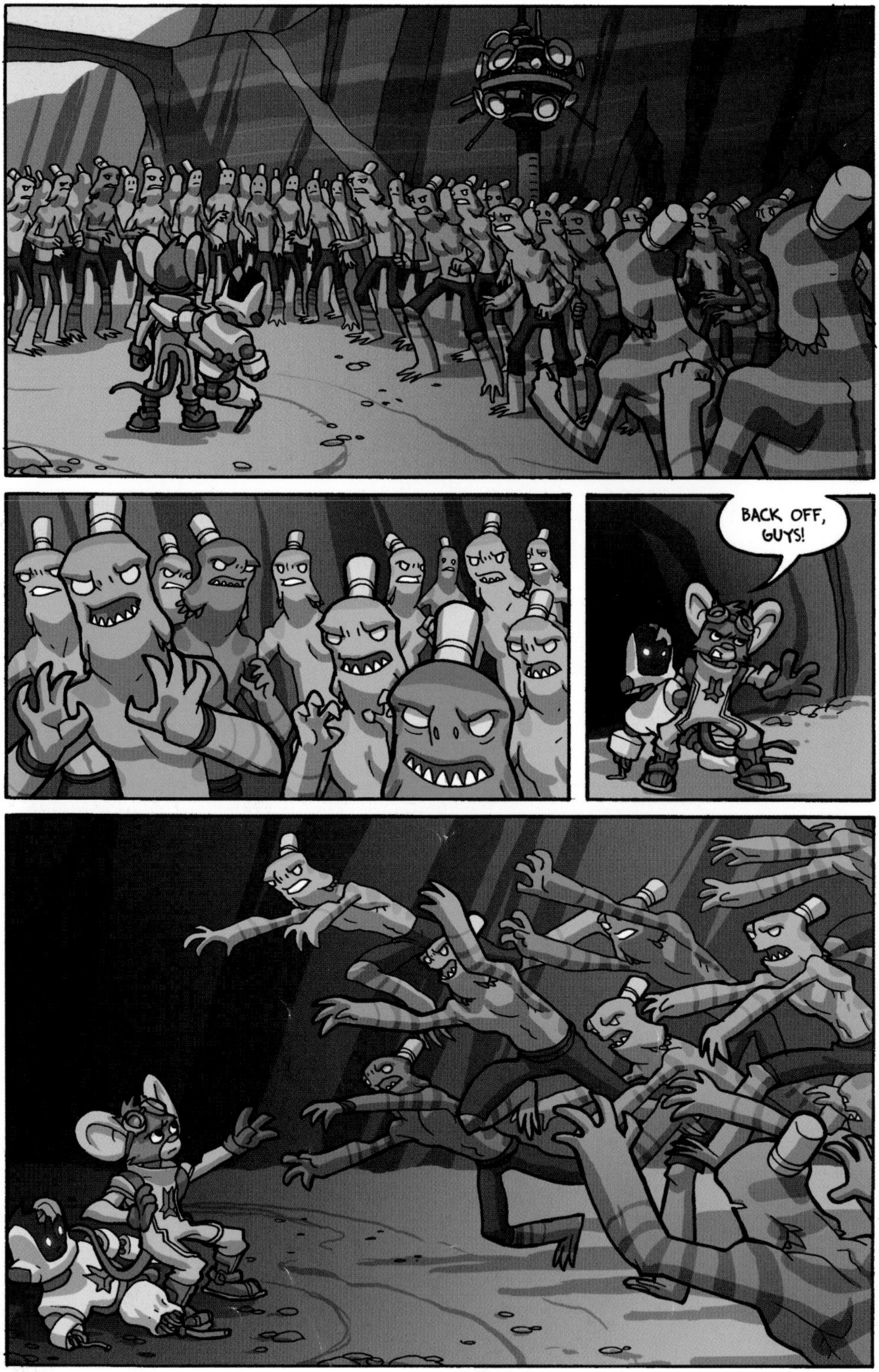
BACK OFF, GUYS!

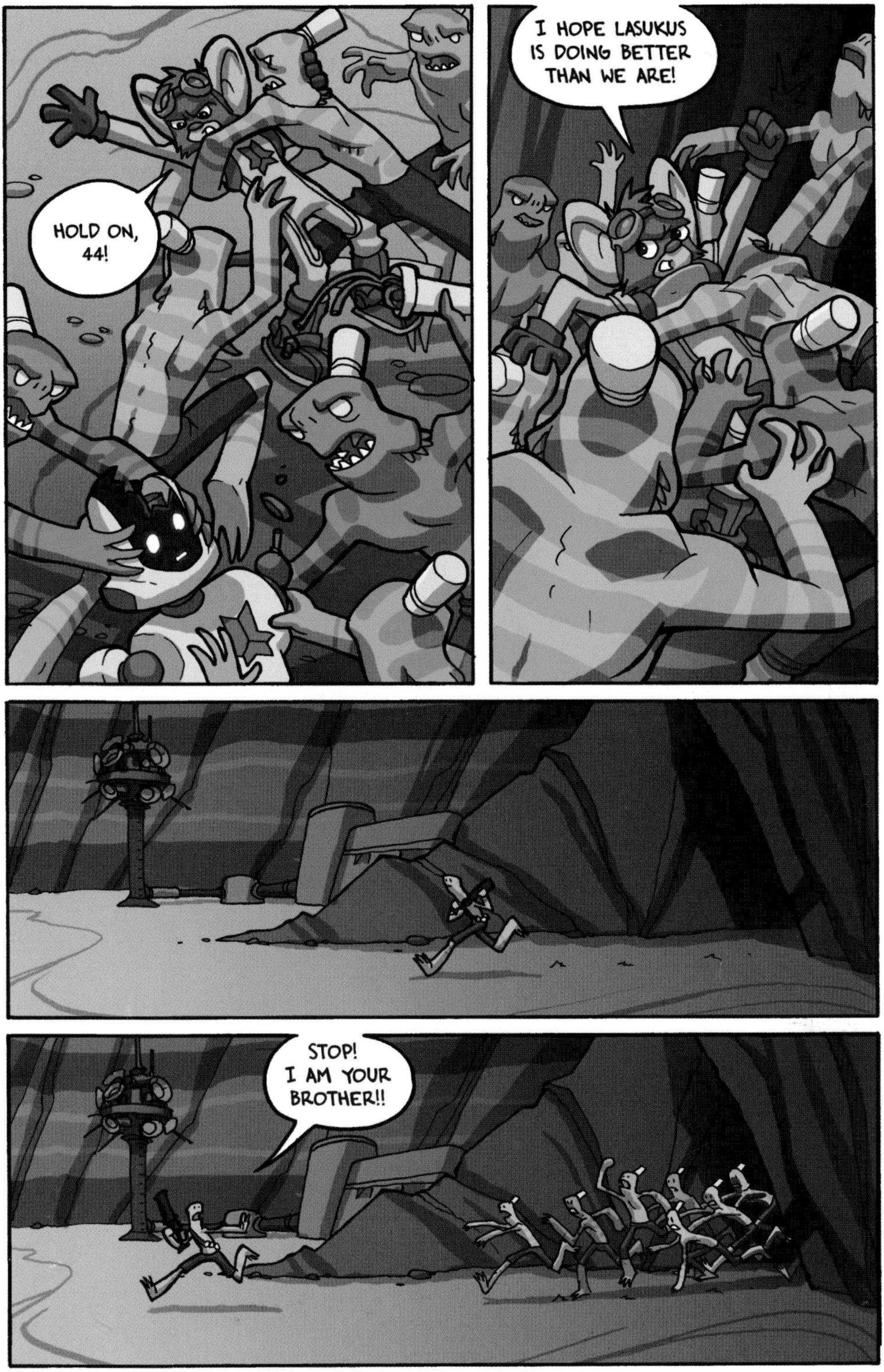
HOLD ON, 44!
I HOPE LASUKUS IS DOING BETTER THAN WE ARE!
STOP! I AM YOUR BROTHER!!

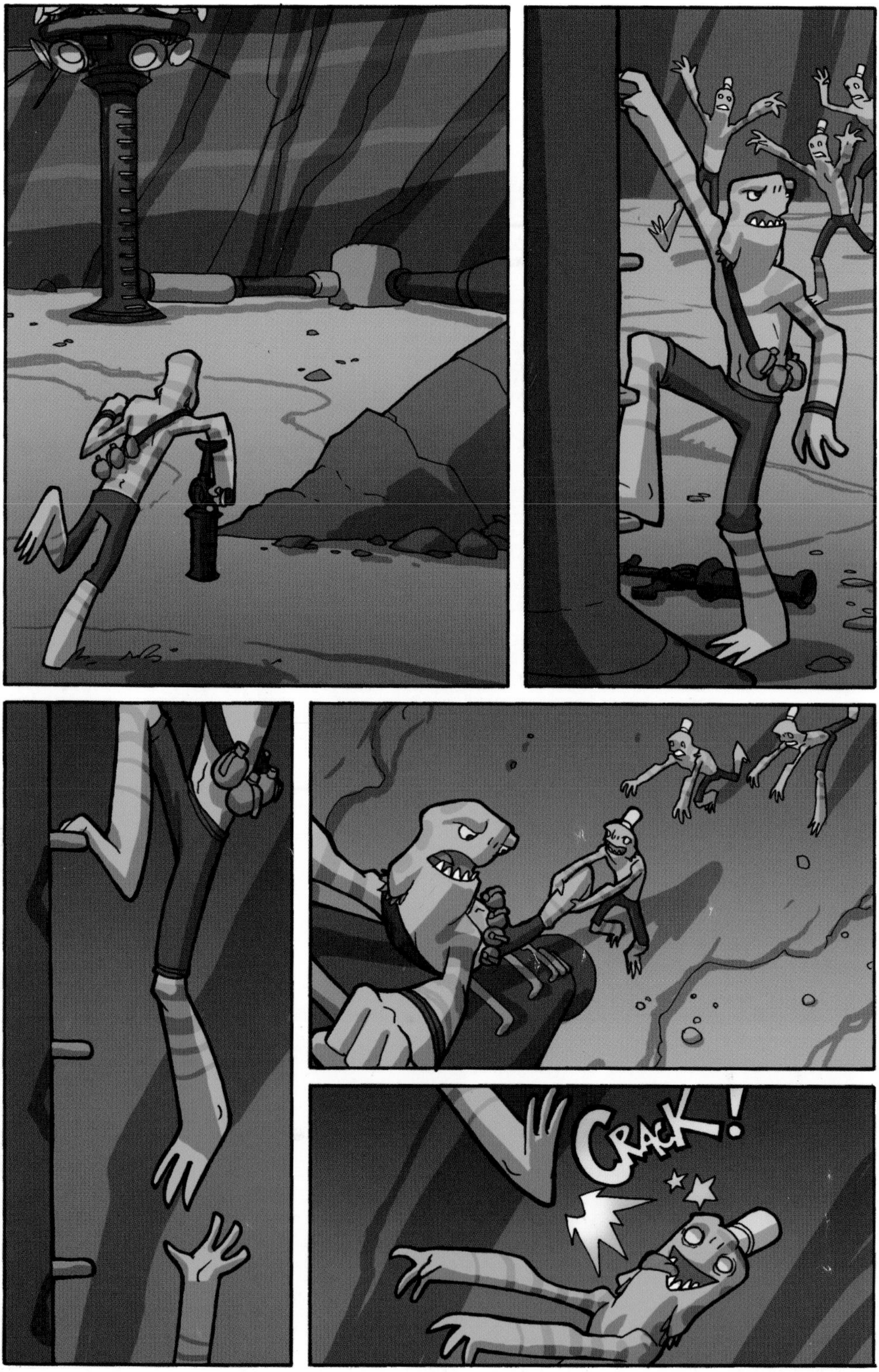
CRACK!

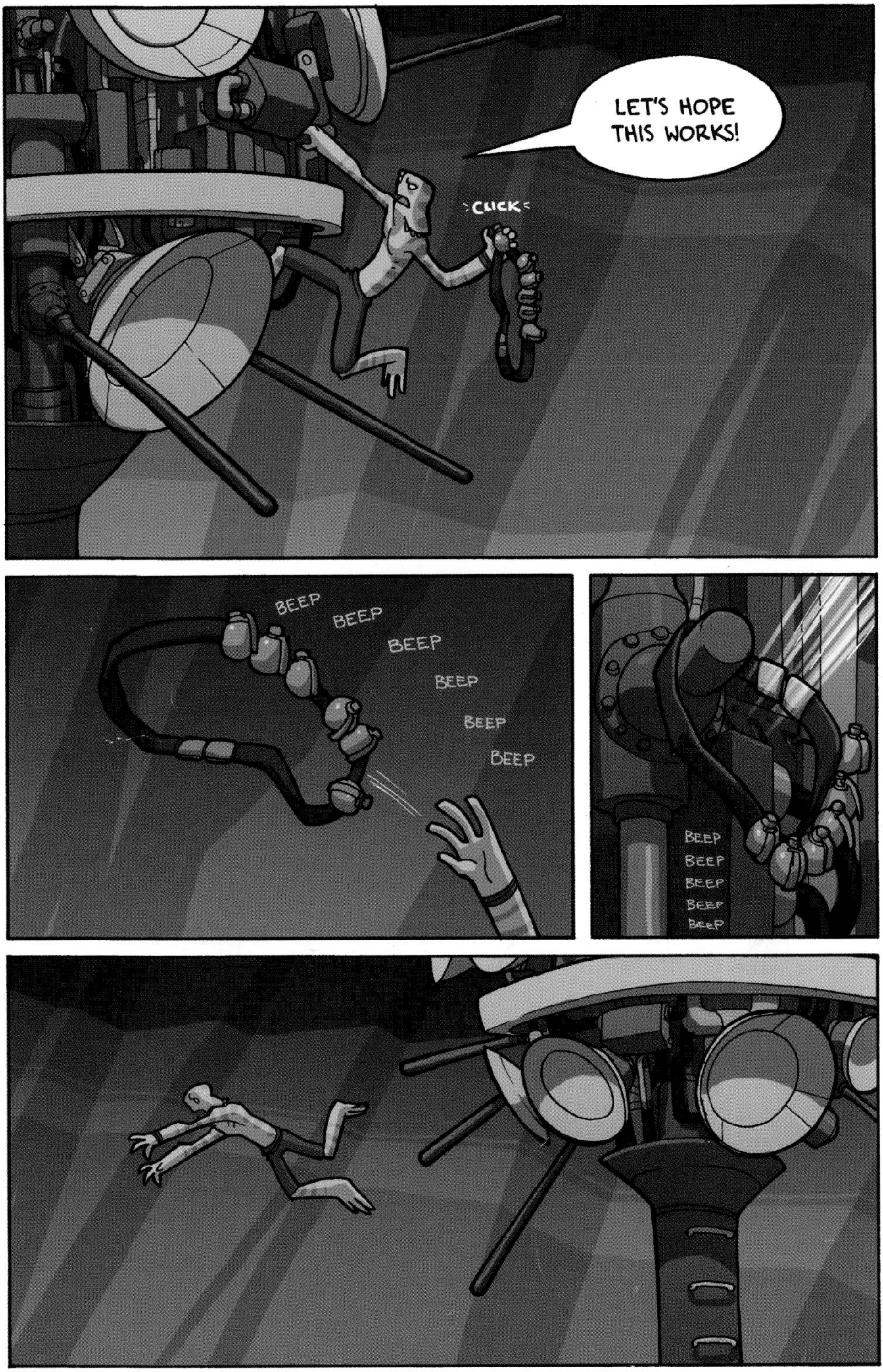
LET'S HOPE THIS WORKS!
CLICK
BEEP
BEEP
BEEP
BEEP
BEEP
BEEP
BEEP
BEEP
BEEP
BEEP
BEEP

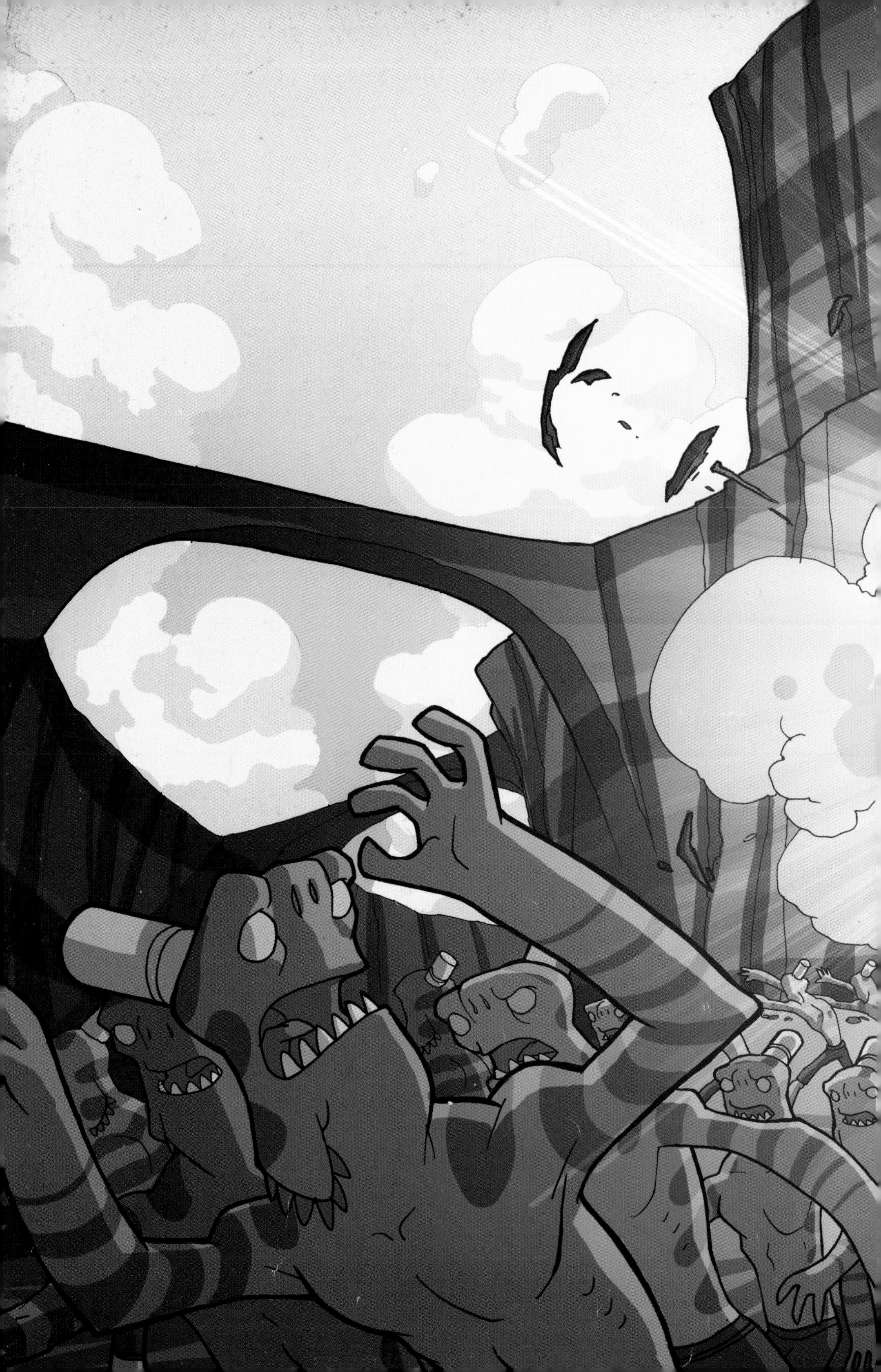

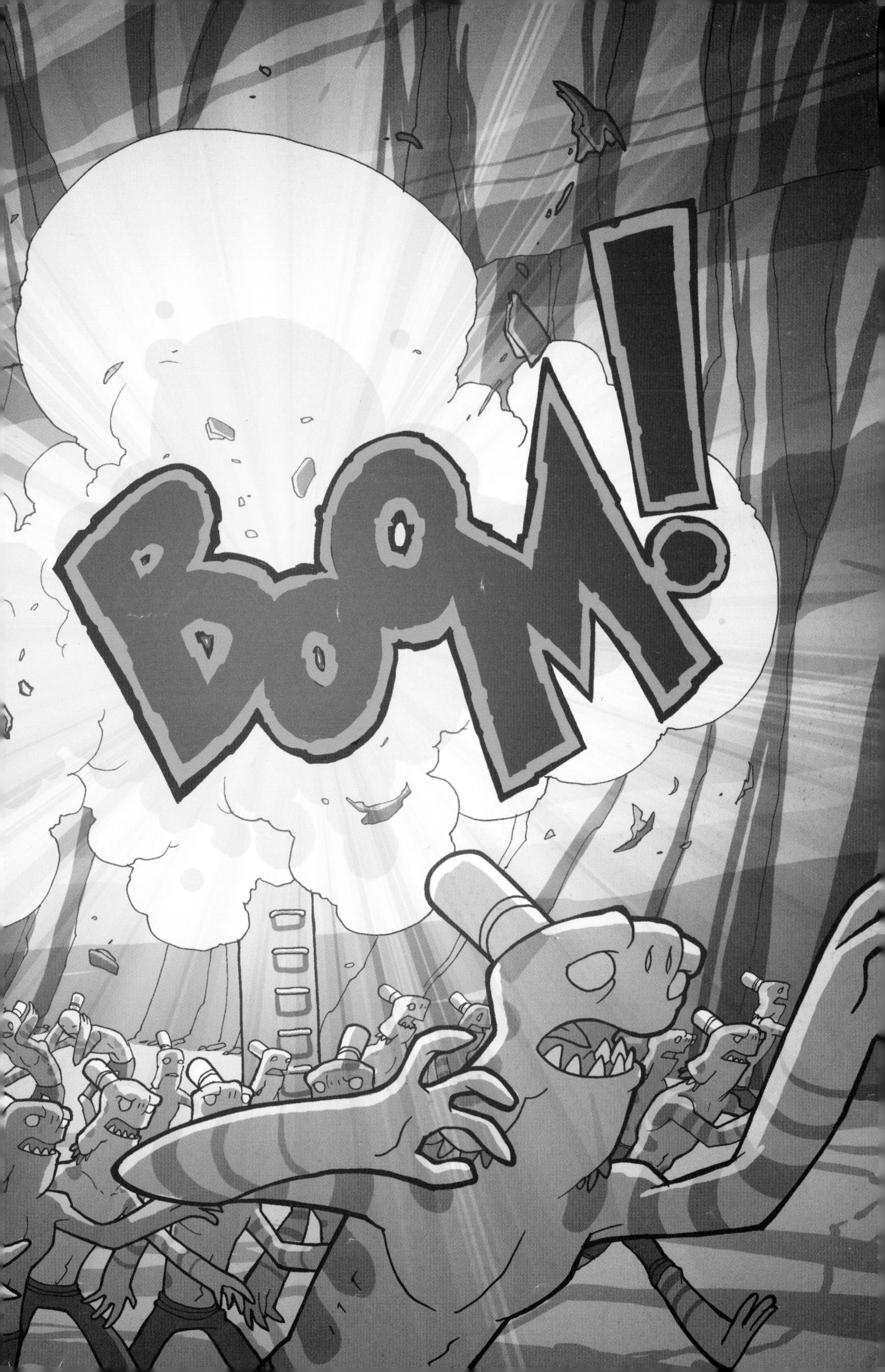
BOOM!

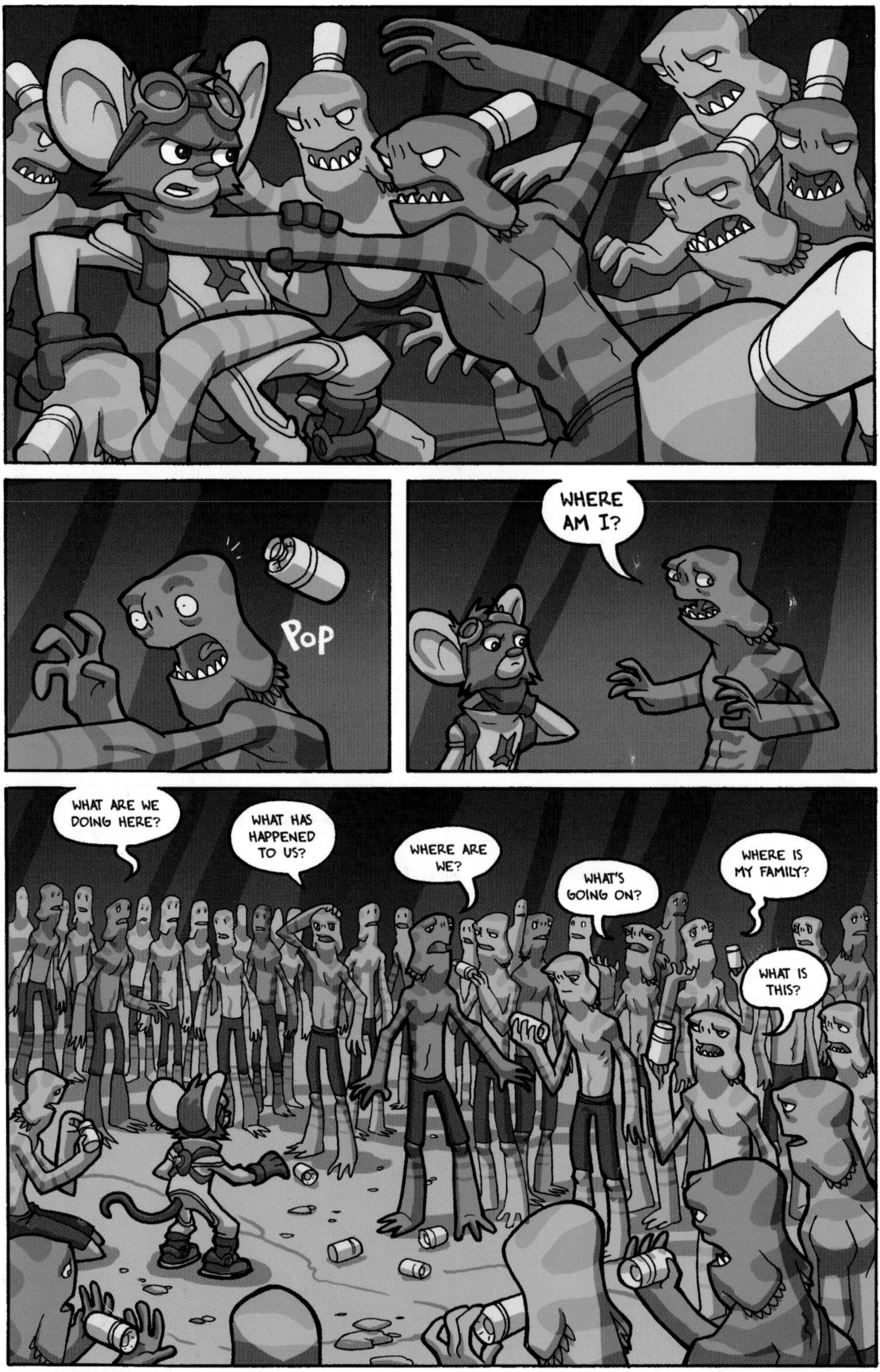
POP
WHERE AM I?
WHAT ARE WE DOING HERE?
WHAT HAS HAPPENED TO US?
WHERE ARE WE?
WHAT'S GOING ON?
WHERE IS MY FAMILY?
WHAT IS THIS?

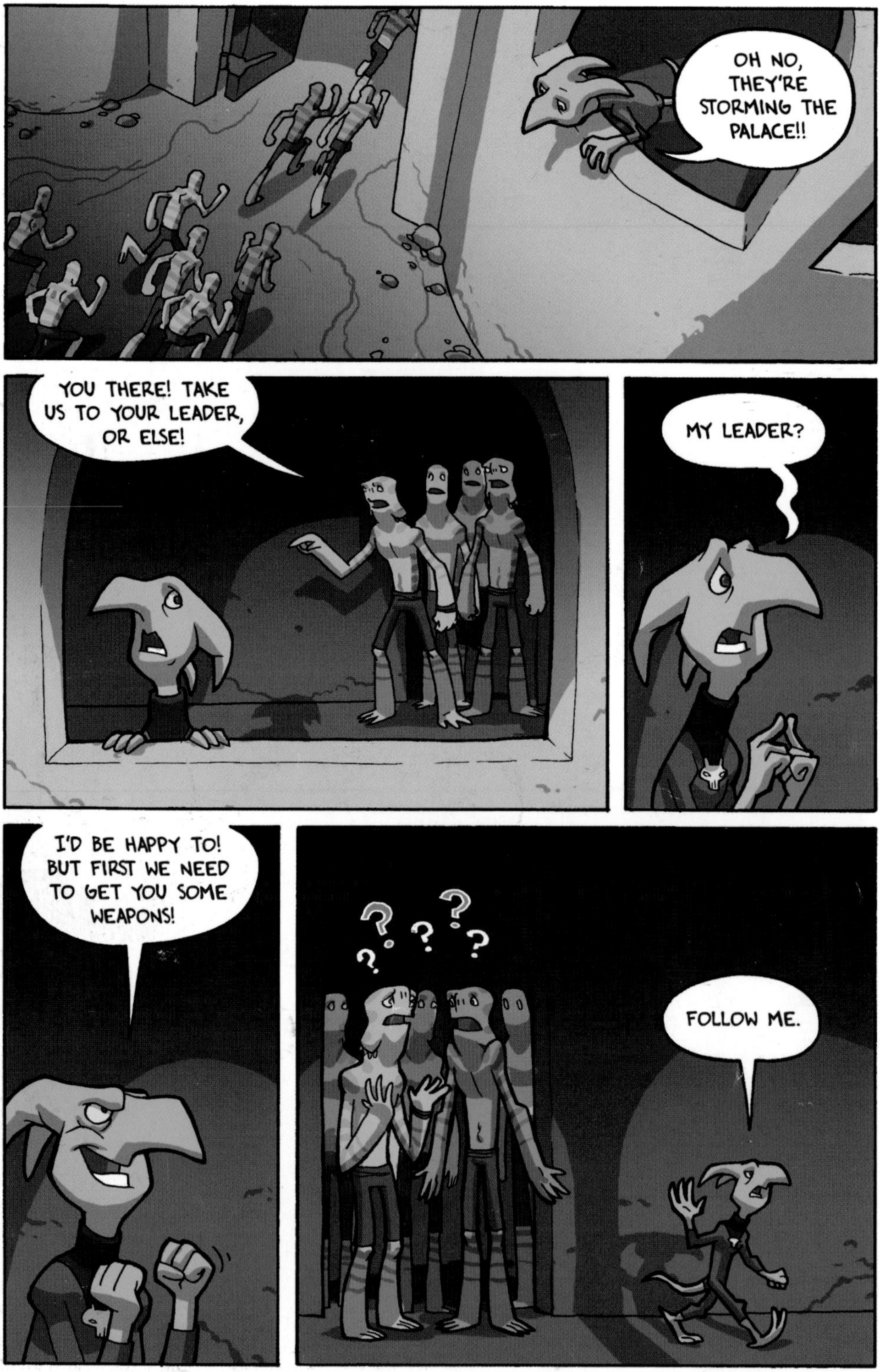
OH NO, THEY'RE STORMING THE PALACE!!
YOU THERE! TAKE US TO YOUR LEADER, OR ELSE!
MY LEADER?
I'D BE HAPPY TO! BUT FIRST WE NEED TO GET YOU SOME WEAPONS!
?
?
?
?
?
FOLLOW ME.

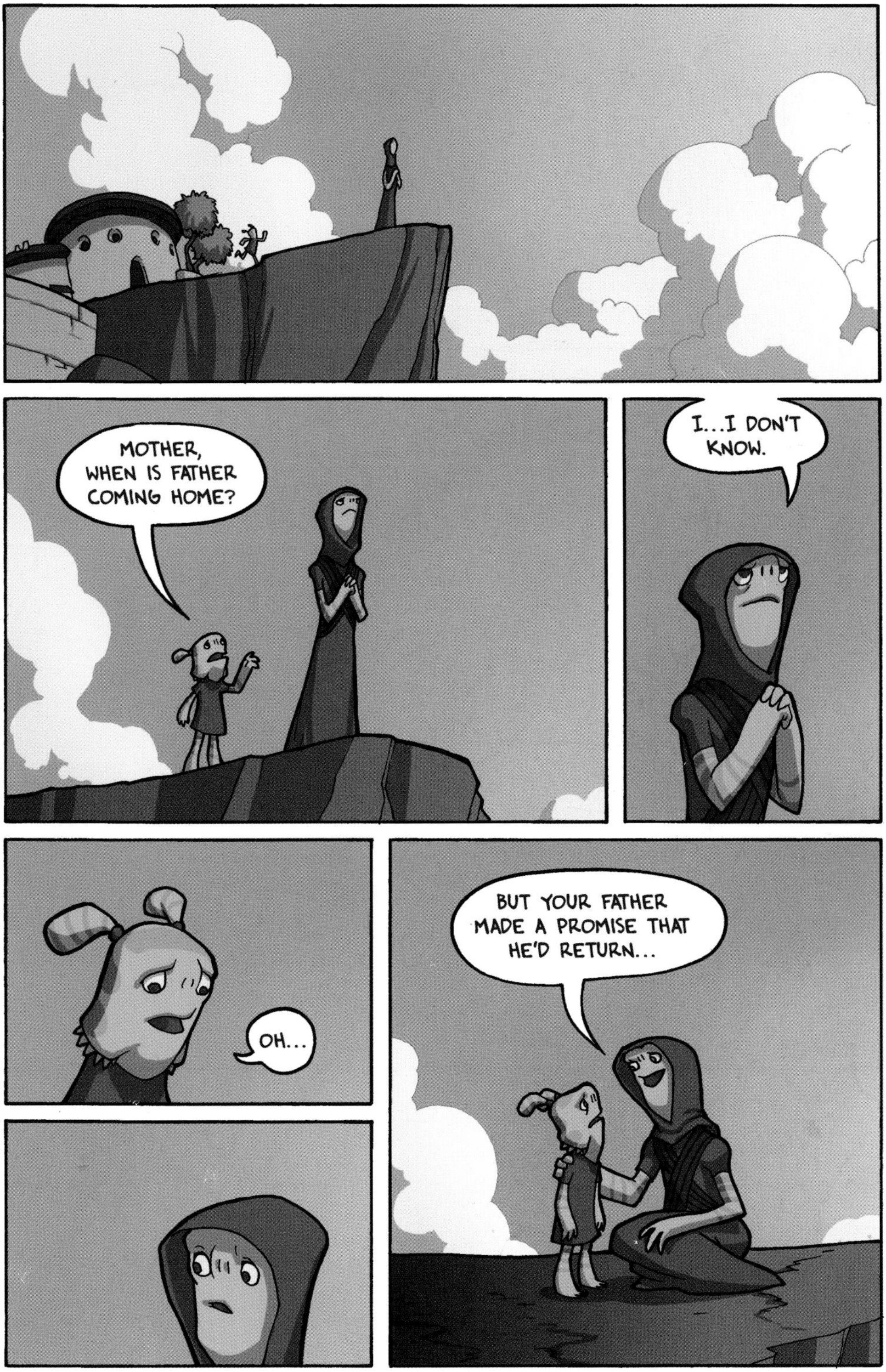
MOTHER, WHEN IS FATHER COMING HOME?
I...I DON'T KNOW.
OH...
BUT YOUR FATHER MADE A PROMISE THAT HE'D RETURN...

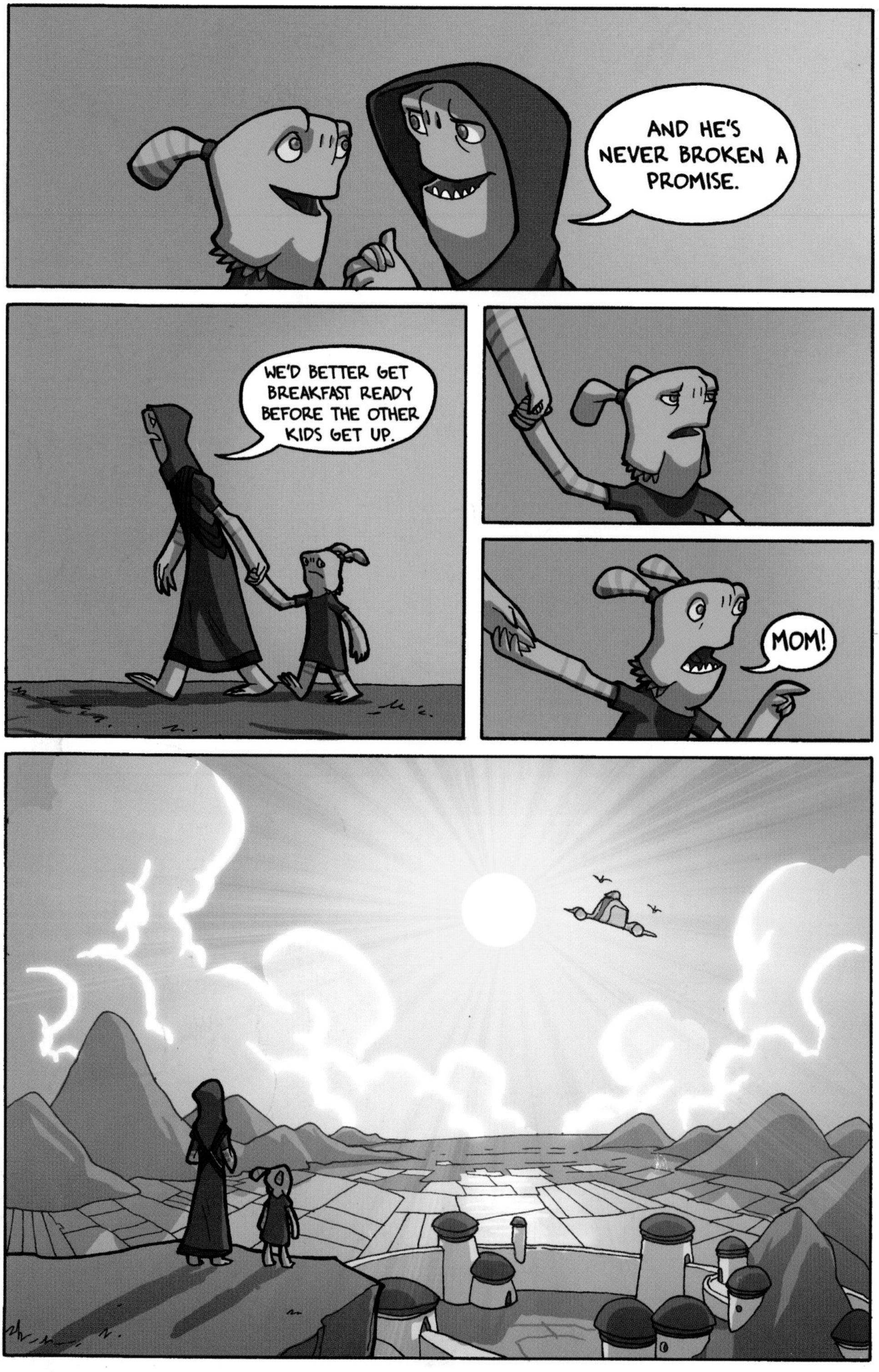
AND HE'S NEVER BROKEN A PROMISE.
WE'D BETTER GET BREAKFAST READY BEFORE THE OTHER KIDS GET UP.
MOM!

I TOLD YOU
I'D RETURN.

HUG!

KISS!

HUG!

I MUST GO REPORT TO
THE ELDERS NOW.

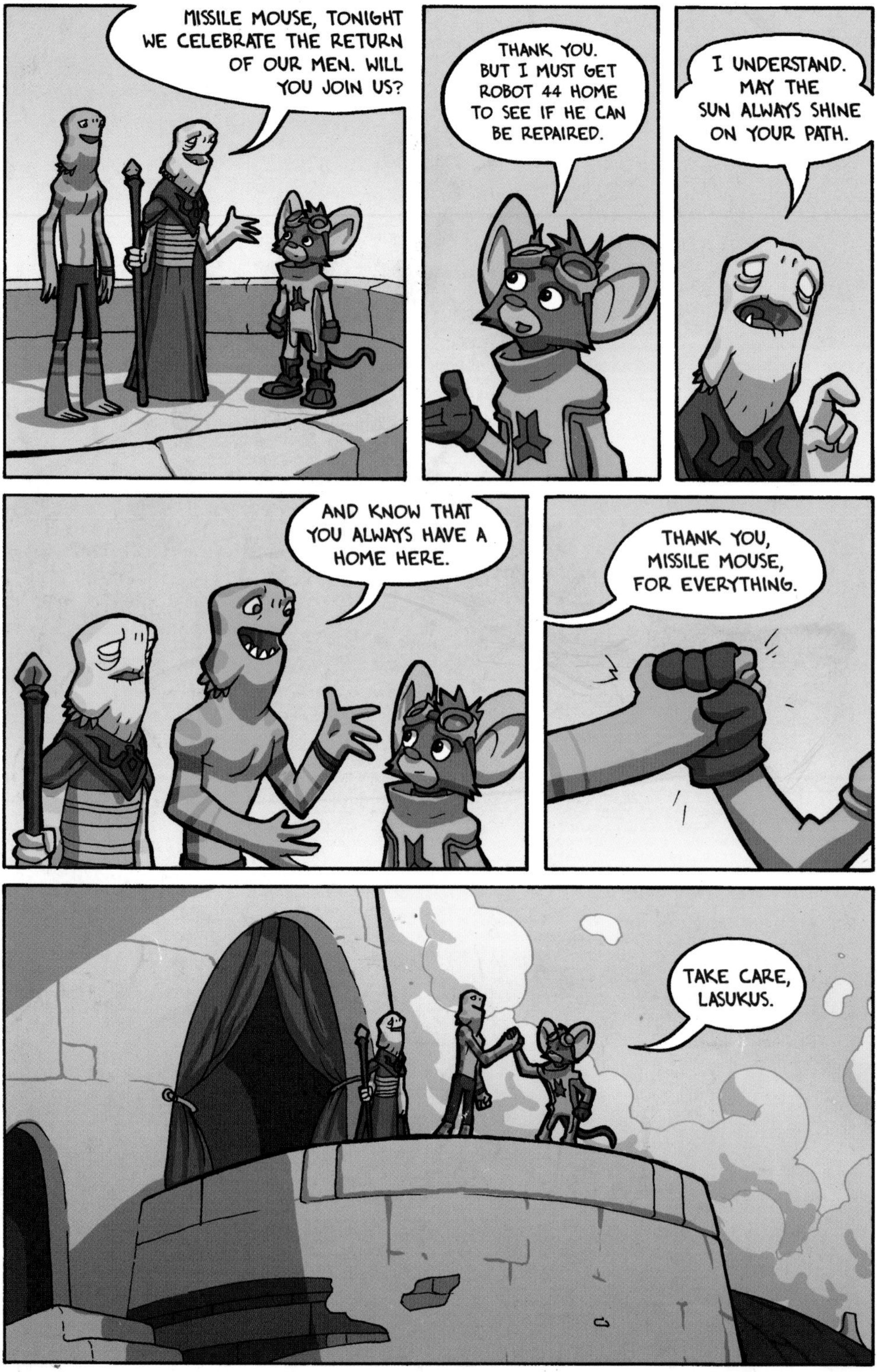
MISSILE MOUSE, TONIGHT WE CELEBRATE THE RETURN OF OUR MEN. WILL YOU JOIN US?
THANK YOU. BUT I MUST GET ROBOT 44 HOME TO SEE IF HE CAN BE REPAIRED.
I UNDERSTAND. MAY THE SUN ALWAYS SHINE ON YOUR PATH.
AND KNOW THAT YOU ALWAYS HAVE A HOME HERE.
THANK YOU, MISSILE MOUSE, FOR EVERYTHING.
TAKE CARE, LASUKUS.

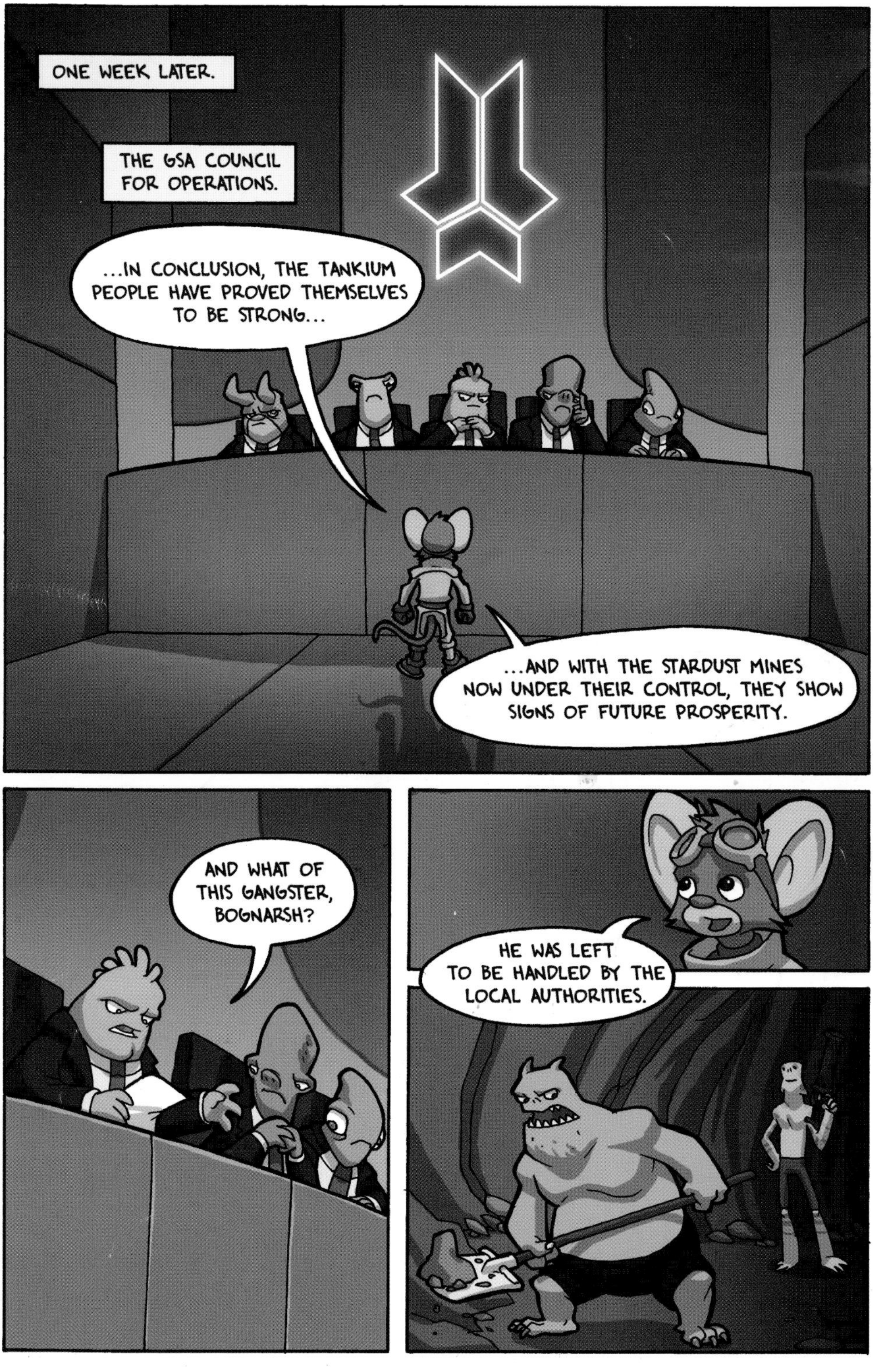
ONE WEEK LATER.
THE GSA COUNCIL FOR OPERATIONS.
...IN CONCLUSION, THE TANKIUM PEOPLE HAVE PROVED THEMSELVES TO BE STRONG...
...AND WITH THE STARDUST MINES NOW UNDER THEIR CONTROL, THEY SHOW SIGNS OF FUTURE PROSPERITY.
AND WHAT OF THIS GANGSTER, BOGNARSH?
HE WAS LEFT TO BE HANDLED BY THE LOCAL AUTHORITIES.

DESPITE LOSING AN ENTIRE SQUAD OF GSA ROBOTS, GOOD WORK, AGENT MISSILE MOUSE. MISSION ACCOMPLISHED.

I HAVE ONE LAST THING TO SAY ABOUT ROBOT 44.

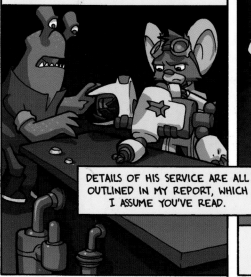

I'VE SERVED WITH A LOT OF AGENTS ON A LOT OF MISSIONS, AND ROBOT 44 WAS NO LESS HEROIC, LOYAL, OR CAPABLE THAN ANY OF THOSE AGENTS.

DETAILS OF HIS SERVICE ARE ALL OUTLINED IN MY REPORT, WHICH I ASSUME YOU'VE READ.

BITNER REPORTS THAT, DESPITE HIS BEST EFFORTS, ROBOT 44 CANNOT BE REVIVED AND HAS BEEN DECOMMISSIONED.

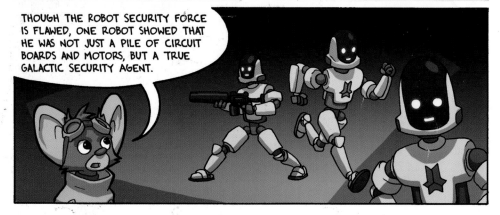

THOUGH THE ROBOT SECURITY FORCE IS FLAWED, ONE ROBOT SHOWED THAT HE WAS NOT JUST A PILE OF CIRCUIT BOARDS AND MOTORS, BUT A TRUE GALACTIC SECURITY AGENT.

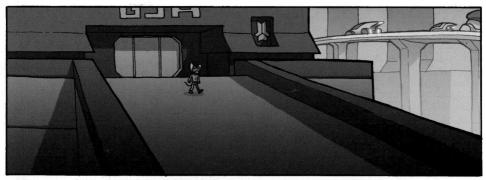

AGENT MISSILE MOUSE!

WHAT'S GOING ON??

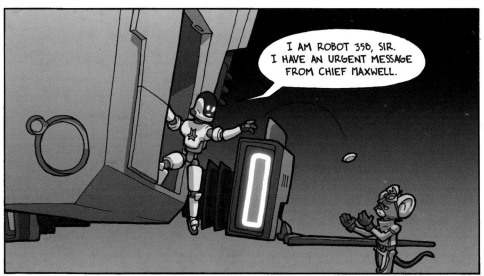

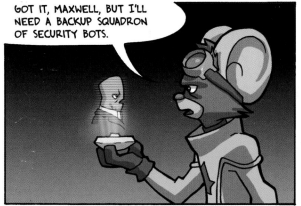

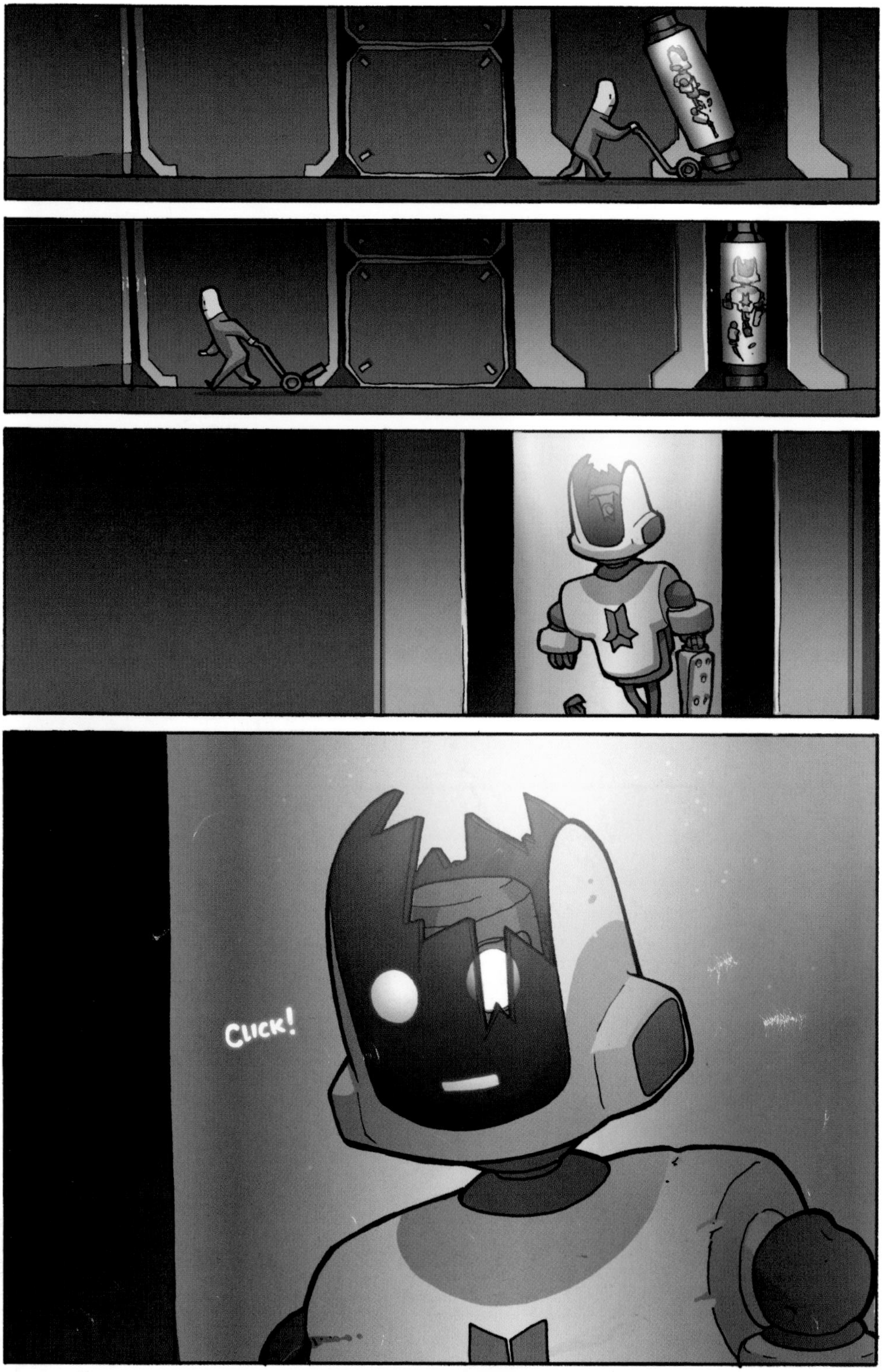
CLICK!

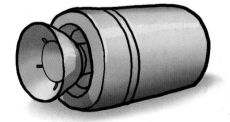

MISSILE MOUSE

MOUSE

GUIDE TO THE UNIVERSE

TO EXPLORE AND TO DRAW

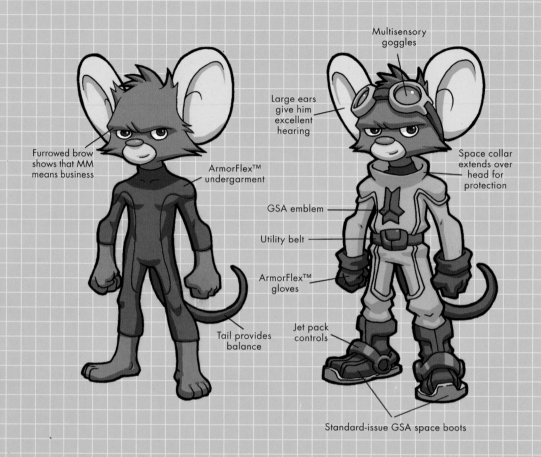

Multisensory goggles

Large ears give him excellent hearing

Space collar extends over head for protection

GSA emblem

Utility belt

Furrowed brow shows that MM means business

ArmorFlex™ undergarment

ArmorFlex™ gloves

Jet pack controls

Tail provides balance

Standard-issue GSA space boots

MISSILE MOUSE is an agent for the Galactic Security Agency. He is an expert pilot and a crack shot. What he lacks in finesse he makes up for in dogged determination. Just when the GSA thinks he's too much of a liability, he proves them wrong and becomes an asset they can't function without.

He is a native Rodentian, but he does not remember his home world. Dire circumstances forced his father to escape the planet in secret with baby M and relocate to an asteroid belt in a nearby system. When tragedy struck and his father was killed, M joined the GSA and became known as Missile Mouse.

MM wears a standard GSA flight suit. His ArmorFlex™ undergarment is blaster and blade resistant, waterproof, and chemical proof. The outer suit provides thermal insulation, shielding from solar radiation, and protection from micrometeoroids and other space debris. MM sports the GSA elite rank colors of gold and red, indicating that he is a solo agent.

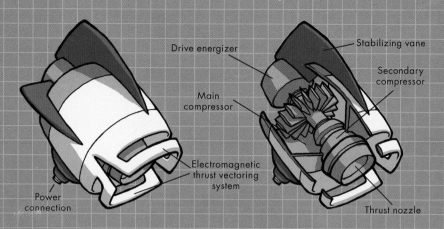

Drive energizer

Stabilizing vane

Secondary compressor

Main compressor

Electromagnetic thrust vectoring system

Power connection

Thrust nozzle

JET PACK

One of the few agents with enough coordination to pilot a jet pack, Missile Mouse prefers the UberTech™ RS600. Its compact size and extremely quiet operation perfectly fit his needs. He pilots the jet pack using control devices worn around each ankle.

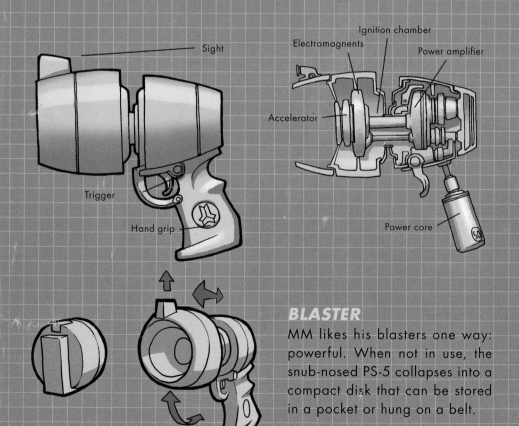

Sight

Ignition chamber

Electromagnets

Power amplifier

Accelerator

Trigger

Hand grip

Power core

BLASTER

MM likes his blasters one way: powerful. When not in use, the snub-nosed PS-5 collapses into a compact disk that can be stored in a pocket or hung on a belt.

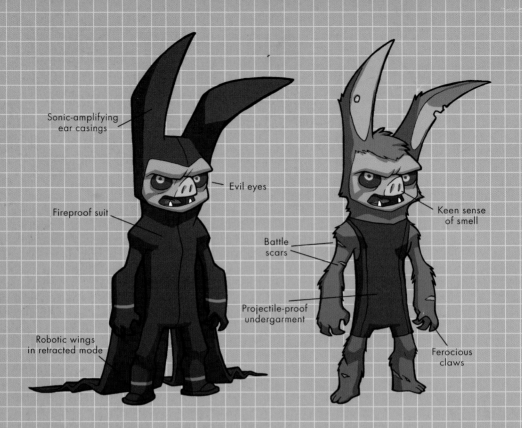

Sonic-amplifying
ear casings

Evil eyes

Fireproof suit

Keen sense
of smell

Battle
scars

Projectile-proof
undergarment

Robotic wings
in retracted mode

Ferocious
claws

BLAZING BAT is an intergalactic bounty hunter. His origins are clouded in mystery, but his reputation as a calculating and efficient hunter is known throughout the galactic underground. With his custom-made flamethrower, he is a lethal force not to be trifled with. Blazing Bat has taken on assignments that have pushed the limits of his unique capabilities, as his many scars can attest. One job early in his career ended badly and caused him to lose his wings. Undeterred, the tenacious bounty hunter developed a pair of robotic wings faster and more powerful than his original wings, making him even more formidable.

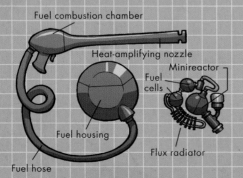

Fuel combustion chamber

Heat-amplifying nozzle

Minireactor

Fuel
cells

Fuel housing

Flux radiator

Fuel hose

FLAMETHROWER

Blazing Bat's custom weapon utilizes advanced hyperfuels – allowing it to cut through any material with ease. Its primary purpose is less known and more sinister: intimidating his prey.

ROBO-WING TECHNOLOGY

Blazing Bat prefers maneuverability over flat-out speed. He had this function in mind when he lost his own wings and replaced them with powerful custom-made robo-wings rather than with a common jet pack. The skeleton wings retract and compact themselves into a tight cluster on the wing harness when not in use.

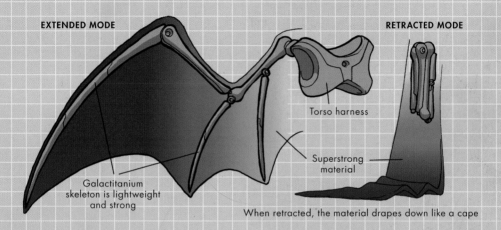

EXTENDED MODE

RETRACTED MODE

Torso harness

Superstrong material

Galactitanium skeleton is lightweight and strong

When retracted, the material drapes down like a cape

BLAZING BAT'S SHIP

Blazing Bat flies a retrofitted Gorgonian Space Fleet fighter. The unique cockpit allows for impressive 360° visibility, a crucial advantage in dangerous situations. Blazing Bat replaced a rear gunner cockpit with cargo space and installed powerful Snake-Cords for detaining his targets.

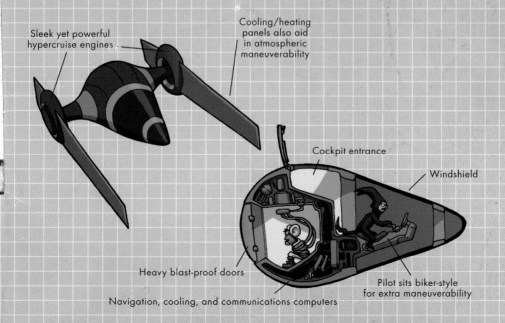

Sleek yet powerful hypercruise engines

Cooling/heating panels also aid in atmospheric maneuverability

Cockpit entrance

Windshield

Heavy blast-proof doors

Navigation, cooling, and communications computers

Pilot sits biker-style for extra maneuverability

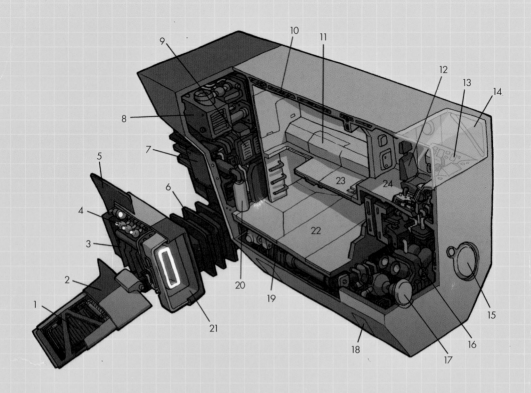

YA-33 FOXRUNNER is a formidable ship, despite its boxy
appearance. It is a twin-ion-engine intergalactic utility vessel designed to perform
an array of missions, including tactical transport of galactic agents, evacuations,
and intergalactic transport. It can be customized depending on the needs of the
mission and is a valuable asset to the GSA. One variation includes a much larger front-
loading version capable of carrying an entire team of security bots.

1. Radiator panel

2. Durable astrotanium plating

3. Retrothruster accelerators

4. Ionic capacitors

5. Electromagnetic vector vane

6. Cooling vanes

7. External flux drive

8. Internal energy router

9. Main-stage reactor

10. Internal wiring

11. Personnel cargo space

12. Pilot's seat

13. Main controls

14. Transparent astrotanium windshield

15. Active scanner module

16. Communcations processor

17. Long-wave sensor array

18. Landing pad

19. Internal landing gear components

20. Fuel cell

21. Thruster intake

22. Main cargo space

23. Personnel space

24. Cockpit

ROBOT 44, *GALACTIC SECURITY SUPPORT BOT*

When the Galactic Security Agency found itself short on security agents, they turned to robotics. An elite team of scientists, field agents, engineers, and programmers developed the Galactic Security Support Bot to alleviate some of the pressure on the security agents. Robot 44 is considered one of the successes of this program. Where other bots faltered, 44 rose to the occasion and proved capable of handling anything assigned to him.

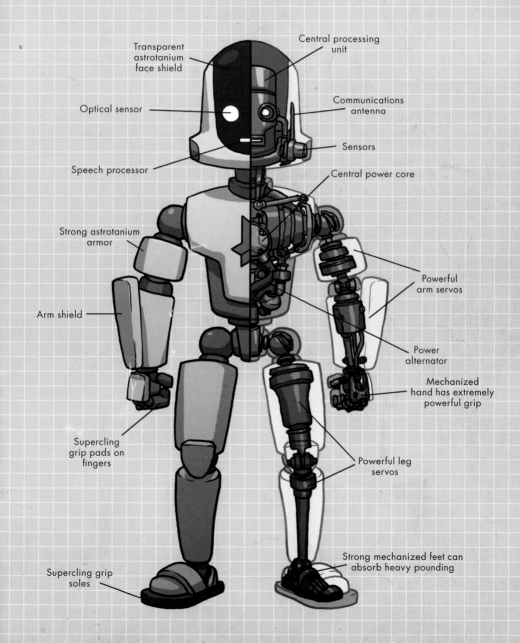

Transparent astrotanium face shield

Central processing unit

Optical sensor

Communications antenna

Speech processor

Sensors

Central power core

Strong astrotanium armor

Powerful arm servos

Arm shield

Power alternator

Mechanized hand has extremely powerful grip

Supercling grip pads on fingers

Powerful leg servos

Supercling grip soles

Strong mechanized feet can absorb heavy pounding

LASUKUS, TANKIAN FLIGHTKEEPER

Lasukus is a member of the predominant sapient species on the planet Tankium3. Never far from water, the Tankians built a mighty fortress city surrounded by flooded grain fields. These fields are harvested twice a year and the grain is stored in silos around the city. Every Tankian has a specific job to do for the community. Lasukus is the latest in a long line of Flightkeepers. Flights are flying reptiles that the Tankians use for scouting missions. Lasukus learned to keep flights from his father and will pass this skill on to his children when they are old enough to fly.

TANKIAN GROWTH CYCLE

1. The first year of a Tankian's life is spent under water as a small fertilized egg.

2. The egg hatches and a tadpole emerges.

3. Soon legs have grown and the gills are fully functioning.

4. With all limbs fully developed and gills suited for both water and air, the Tankian can now survive on land.

5. After about 3 years, the tail begins to shrink. The Tankian becomes bipedal and learns to speak.

6. By the time the Tankian is 12, the tail is completely gone.

7. Roughly five feet tall with slender yet powerful muscles, the Tankian is now matured.

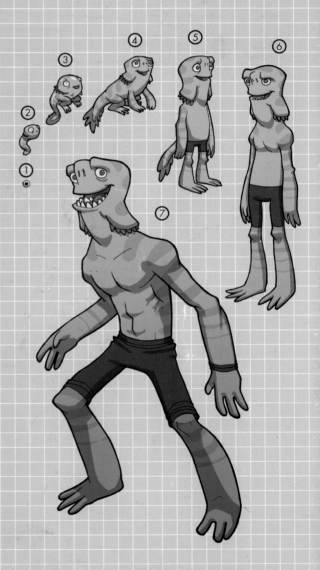

A TANKIUM HOME

Tankian family units are very important to the society's strength. More than just a shelter from the elements, the home is a central hub for the family, a refuge in case of emergencies, and a symbol of unity. Each home is self-sustaining, utilizing large water reservoirs in the basement to grow food for the family. Tankian homes are usually multiple stories tall, to save space in the walled city.

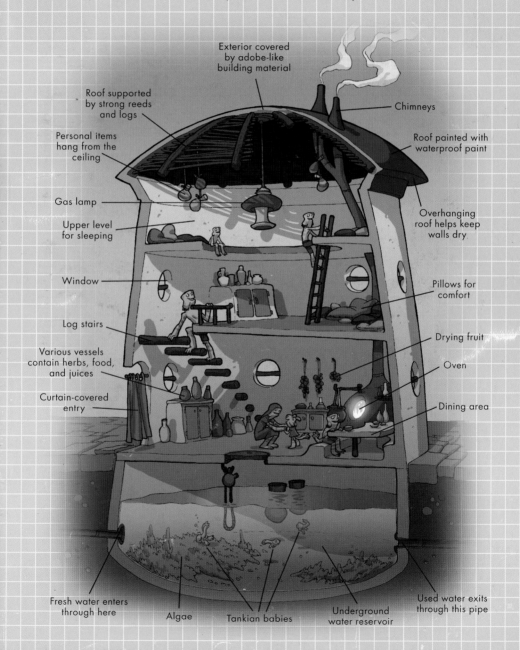

Exterior covered by adobe-like building material

Roof supported by strong reeds and logs

Chimneys

Personal items hang from the ceiling

Roof painted with waterproof paint

Gas lamp

Overhanging roof helps keep walls dry

Upper level for sleeping

Window

Pillows for comfort

Log stairs

Drying fruit

Various vessels contain herbs, food, and juices

Oven

Curtain-covered entry

Dining area

Fresh water enters through here

Used water exits through this pipe

Algae

Tankian babies

Underground water reservoir

Jake Parker was born in Mesa, Arizona, and raised on a healthy diet of cereal, comic books, and Saturday morning cartoons. Now he draws comic books, works on animated films, and still eats lots of cereal. He's also done artwork for commercials, video games, kids' TV shows, and even a dinosaur exhibit for a museum. He currently lives in Provo, Utah, with his wife and five children.

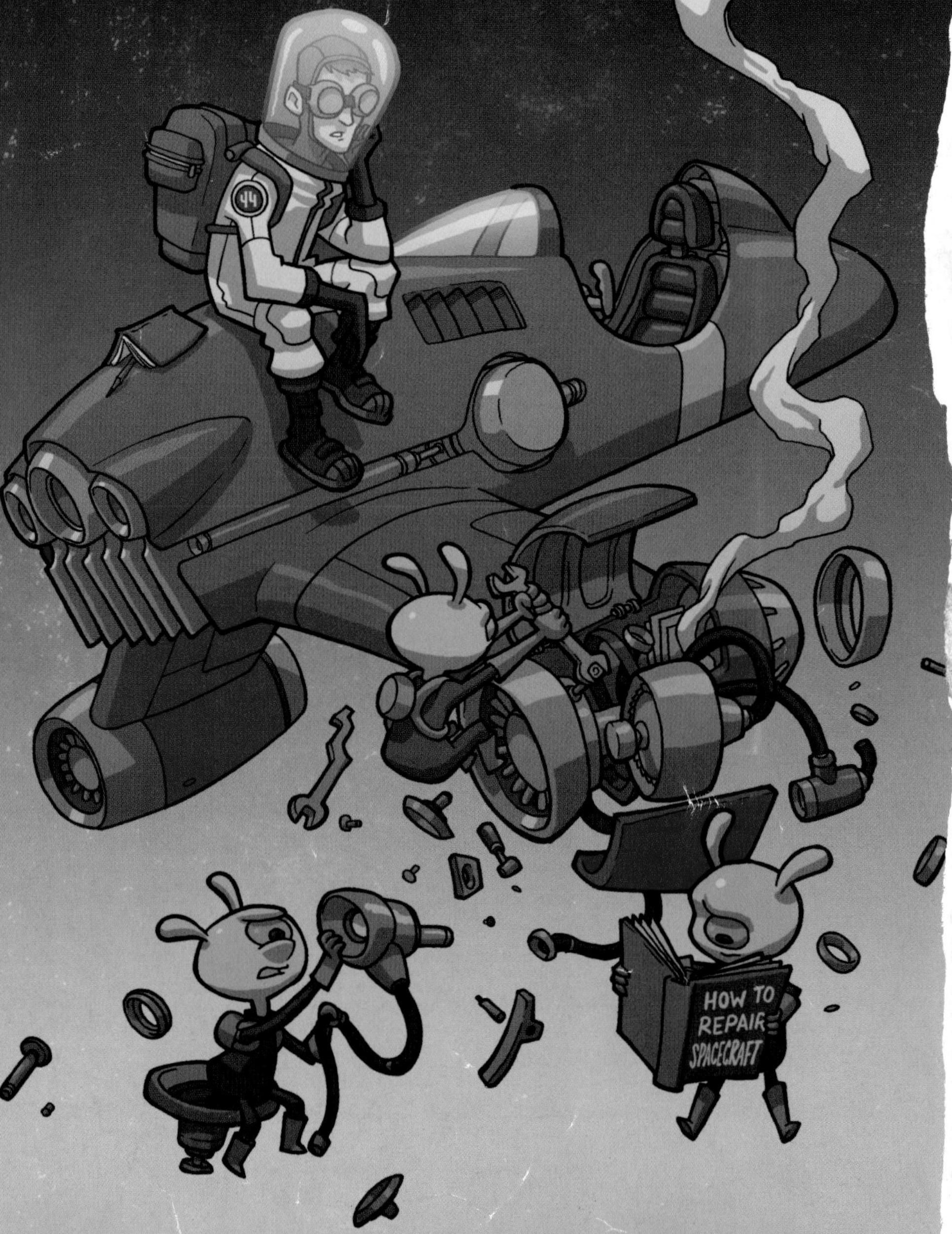
HOW TO REPAIR SPACECRAFT